Queen of Shadow

Chronicles of Aurderia

The Balance

River of Souls

Queen of Shadow

Chronicles of Aurderia
Queen of Shadow

J. Steven Young

To my Mother and my Πεθερά:
Your strength and love guides me to strive for greatness.
You both are an inspiration of perseverance that reminds me that I can
always do more.
Love It You

<u>**Chapter One**</u>

𒀭

Salmetu's form stood against the darkening sky outside the Western shield entrance to Britengate. Her body was not corporeal; it was gathered Shadow taking the form of Salmetu. Traces of wispy tendrils undulated around her frame, as she stood silent, waiting. She was Ereshkigal, and darkness was rising all around her.

Hundreds of Shadow Walkers emerged from the thickening blackness that rose from the ground surrounding Ereshkigal. Chaos came to life in the form of the Shadow and began to creep forward from the hordes of darkness-imbued wielders and transformed citizens of Aurderia. Slow at first, the murky cloud of Shadow billowed toward the shield boundary and spread out along its parameter. The boundary sparked and flashed with resistance to the touch of Chaos.

Salmetu's shadowy form turned toward the figure now standing just inside the shield. She floated forward, advancing on the familiar presence until she hovered inches away from the protesting energy separating her from the subject of her visit. "You should come outside to parlay young asipu. It is rude to speak to a guest from behind your door." Ereshkigal was speaking with restrained rage.

Shuran gazed at his sister's likeness unblinking, as he spoke. "You are no guest of mine or any among those seeking refuge behind this shield, Gizzu'Su!" Shuran could see the rage building behind Ereshkigal's eyes.

"You think you know who you are dealing with do you? I assure you young fool, you have not begun to know the power that you face!" The fury was building as the form of Salmetu began to drift apart. "I will have my Gizzu'Su brethren freed from whatever prison you have placed them!" As the vaporous form melted away, the Shadow expanded around the city shield and began to press upon it.

Screams of fear and horror began to fill the minds of the citizens not imbued with Essence abilities. The Shadow could not enter the city, but its influence could. The feelings of dread, despair, and helplessness filled the air so thickly that the people of Britengate appeared to move about as though in slow motion. Crippled by the emotions being spread by the Shadow, most succumbed to the struggle and collapsed where they stood.

Ereshkigal's wicked laugh echoed throughout Britengate. "You see Shuran, you have no grasp on how powerful the Shadow is, and when I find my missing Gizzu'Su comrades, we shall destroy this city and claim every citizen for the Shadow!"

Shuran remained still while he watched the effects of Ereshkigal's mental attack on the less powerful in Essence among the city's population. Something was scratching at the back of his mind. There was a familiarity to the attack that he could not focus upon, but he knew that it was a ploy of some sort. With a flick of his wrist, he sent a bolt of energy into the shield and was rewarded with a moment of silence from the emotional onslaught of the Shadow. Shuran knew what he needed to do in order to stop the attack.

Calling to his Zidu'Si, Shuran moved toward the center of the city and the location of the Altar of Creation. "The Shadow uses the influence of electric impulses to effect the people emotionally. We need to disrupt the assault with bolts of energy." Shuran instructed the Zidu'Si and any wielders with electric Essence abilities to begin periodic blasts of energy into the shield. The results were soon felt as the crippled citizens began to stir and rise to their feet in relief from the disruption in the flow of negative impulses that were previously affecting them.

"How long must we keep this up Shin'Ar?" Dara asked. "It is not currently taxing us much, but eventually we will begin to weaken."

"I believe that the Shadow will eventually give up the futile attempt to gain the shield, and as the attack wanes we can rest and resume only if and when the Shadow recommences its assault." Shuran was not certain how long the Shadow would remain outside the city. There was a reason for what was happening, but he could not yet determine what Ereshkigal hoped to gain.

The Shadow continued to undulate and spread across the city shield, attempting to influence the inhabitants with dark thoughts and intent. With every emotional charge from the murky cloud, bolts of energy flew from the hands of the Zidu'Si and the few elves in the city. The Shadow would disperse from the area and retreat for no more than an hour before renewing its assault.

The attack on the shield had continued throughout the night and well into the second before Shuran began to understand what was happening. "This is a stall tactic," he realized aloud. "Our energy bolts into the shield are not having any lasting effect on the Shadow, only gugtu would, or direct contact with the Essence."

"What do you mean Lugaldur?" Moltar asked.

Shuran explained to his bonded as well as the rest of the Zidu'Si, that Ereshkigal was directing the Shadow attack in an effort to stall while she searched for the Gizzu'Su. She was likely trying to keep the Zidu'Si busily engaged in Britengate while she searched, and doing so also kept Shuran from seeking out the Lil'Du. "We cannot all remain here while the Shadow distracts us."

"Perhaps we can enlist more elves from Entensiama to assist in the defense while you and a few of us travel to the Highlands in search of the Lil'Du?" Orian suggested.

Shuran sent Orian and Moltar to see the Queen of the Elves while he continued to bolster the strength of the energy being sent periodically into the city shield. The Shadow could hinder travel outside the city by gate, but it could not affect the use of the Emmuku'Gu.

***

Orian arrived in the center of the elfin Capital with Moltar close behind. Their abrupt arrival caused quite a stir as the elves were going about their evening gatherings.

Elves keep a different schedule than most other races of man on Ersetu. They are creatures of a more nocturnal nature and prefer the coolness of the night rather than the heat of mid-Utu. Several market-goers fell back in shocked surprise at the sudden electro-charged appearance of not only an elf but also a massive red drakkon on his heel.

Moltar took to the air immediately, leaving Orian to make arrangements for more elves to come aid in the defense of Britengate. He had been stuck within the city shield and unable to spread his wings to fly comfortably within the boundary. All of the other drakkon in the city were small enough to take to flight around the confines of the shield but due to Moltar's increased bulk, he could not follow suit without risk of damaging what had only recently been rebuilt.

Orian went straight to the Queen's tree to seek an audience when he was stopped in the court by a guard. He was unfamiliar to Orian, but he knew from his dress and sash that this elf served the Queen directly.

"Master Orian, you will not find the Queen within the palace tree," the elf said.

Orian turned to face the guard, then bowed slightly in greeting. "I take then that you know where I might find her majesty?" Orian asked.

"She is in conference with the tree nymphs," the guard responded with a hint of sarcasm in his voice.

The Dryads were known only from myths and legends until recently. Stories of the horrid faces frozen in time amongst the petrified trees were the greatest extent of the knowledge of their kind. The truth of the matter was that the Dryads were only one of the races of beings that lived upon Ersetu long before the Sumerians arrived to begin their experiments with the Essence. These races were mostly unknown or seldom encountered.

Orian did not appreciate the comment. "They are Dryads sir, and far older and wiser a people than even the ancients who engineered the races of man. You might be wise to show them the respect they deserve, especially after their magic kept them alive within those stone trees for thousands of years."

The guard opened his mouth to respond but thought better of it. He pointed out the direction that Orian should travel to find the Queen and hastened his exit back to his post guarding the Queen's Tree.

Orian set off in the direction the guard indicated and signaled for Moltar to stay nearby. The distance to the edge of the boundary of Entensiama was normally an hour walk or more, but with the added strength and stamina afforded the Zidu'Si, Orian ran the distance in a quarter of the time without exerting himself. When he arrived at the outer edge of the elven capital, he located Florisia, the Queen, and approached silently as not to intrude upon her conference with the Dryads.

Without turning to address him, Florisia called out to Orian. "You may approach Orian, this discussion will need sharing with the Shin'Ar."

Orian approached the Queen and greeted her with a bow and turned to silently watch the proceedings of what appeared some sort of ritual being performed by the Dryads. As he looked out at what only weeks earlier had been an empty glade, he took in the sprawling copse of new trees that filled the area. At the center, where he and the others now stood, grew a larger and extraordinary tree of a kind he never before set eyes upon.

The base of the tree was thick as houses with large leg-like roots angled up and then back down into the earth. Vast limbs stretched at opposite incline to the sky before draping back down and burrowing into the ground. The bark along the entire surface glistened with hues of green and purple and a pulsing that likened itself to the flow of blood through a man's vein. Flowers adorned the ends of branches with colors so rich and pure that Orian lost himself in the beauty that captured his very being.

Stepping up beside him and placing a hand upon his arm, Florisia drew his attention away from the splendor. "Words are few to fall from the tongue when witnessing such wonders of creation."

"It is as you say my Queen," Orian replied. "Words could not express what I am seeing." He looked once again at the blossoms and pulsing beat of the tree before continuing. "What is this activity that I am gazing upon?"

Stepping forward to answer, the Dryad nearest guided Orian and Florisia away to an area where they could sit and speak. "It is the Gisa'Ti in your ancient tongue, our tree of life as best we can translate."

"You are born from trees?" Orian asked surprised written upon his face.

The dryad barked with laughter. "Not exactly young one, we are birthed of Coosco and it is Ersetu which gives us life." Seeing the confusion upon the elves' faces, the dryad continued. "We are part of the land as a whole being, this is why we did not die in the trees so long ago. We used the power of Coosco, the navel of the world, to contain our being until the time we would be freed by your Shin'Ar.

"Ersetu is our mother and she guides us where we are meant to best serve her and continue the cycle of life. Much of what was has gone and only now is Ersetu beginning to awaken and put things right. Your Shin'Ar is meant to free Coosco from the bonds that restrain Ersetu. It is the promise of your God Nergal."

Orian was more confused than before the dryad spoke. "Should you not be telling this to Shuran?"

"He will remember in time, the promise he made Ersetu. His mistake is his alone to undo." The dryad then turned to Florisia. "We shall do as you ask and protect the borders of your Entensiama. The tainted workings of this Shadow are no match for the true power of Ersetu, but we will not assist beyond these lands, beyond what we promised Shin'Ar in the Frozen North."

"You were in the Frozen North with Shuran?" Orian asked. "And how is it that you now speak our tongue so well compared to our first meeting in the Stone Forest?"

"So many questions," the dryad mused. "We are all of Ersetu." The dryad gestured to its tree-like form, "This form you see is but a shape we take from the trees we tend. Other places we take to different shapes as best suited for our tasks. Once we adjusted to the freedom from the Stone Forest, we rejoined the whole and learned all.

"Before your so-called Gods arrived upon this world from the heavens, Ersetu existed in harmony with the eternal cycle of life. When Nergal and his ilk placed their ring upon Coosco they tainted the true magic of our world. This must be undone for Ersetu to truly heal." The dryad stood and walked away before turning back and appeared to melt into the earth then being replaced by a small fur-covered creature that hopped off into the woods.

<u>Chapter Two</u>

Orian and Florisia sat for several moments before gathering themselves and heading back to the elfin city deep within the forest. As they walked, they spoke about what they learned and the ramifications that information had on what the Zidu'Si was fighting to protect.

Florisia was the first to speak. "Before you arrived, the dryads explained to me that they were rebuilding their forest and creating more of their like to protect their new home. I witnessed new dryads grow from the earth and immediately go about work spreading the glowing seeds that dropped from those blossoms on the Gisa'Ti.

"They agreed to keep out the Shadow and its agents since we extended our home to them. I wonder that they can follow through with the power they claim to have? The Shadow is strong and the trees will bend to the fist of an ogre."

Orian shook his head in wonder and doubt. "I do not pretend understanding of all that we heard this day, but something within me believes what they spoke. I shall share this information with the Shin'Ar upon my return. It is for Shuran to decide how best to interpret these revelations."

"Agreed, now might I ask what has brought you home to us this day?" Florisia asked as they continued a hastened pace back to the capital.

"Shuran has asked for any help available from the elven people to distract the Shadow attacking Britengate."

Surprised, Florisia stopped and turned Orian to face her. "What do you mean the Shadow attacks Britengate? Do you think you might have lead with this news when first you found me?"

"The attack is merely an effort to prevent egress from the city. Shuran believes that Ereshkigal, whose shi lingers with the Shadow and possesses Salmetu, wishes to prevent Shuran completing the Zidu'Si. The Shadow cannot penetrate the city shield, but the effects upon the minds of the citizens can only be thwarted by continued bolts of energy into the areas covered in Shadow."

Florisia resumed the walk toward her home with Orian stepping up beside her. "You shall have the help you require. I image the great shadow looming from above is Moltar and he will transport elves back to Britengate?"

"You are correct as always my Queen."

"When there is time, I wish further explanation on how the false Gods Ereshkigal and Nergal, as well as the others, are involved in all of these happenings." As they entered the outer boundary of Entensiama, Florisia turned away and headed to her tree before ending their conversation. "Wait here and I will send those willing to meet you for transport to Britengate."

Moltar landed beside Orian and sat down. "What has gotten into her royal elf-ness?"

"I believe finding out that the Gods we have followed and put our faith in for the history of our people were nothing more than flesh and blood has taken a deep toll on her philosophies," Orian answered lowering his head.

"Be at ease my friend, my Lugaldur will make all things right again," Moltar said as the first of the volunteer elves began to arrive. "Look we have our first passengers."

Moltar transported the elves as they arrived in small groups. In all, nearly two hundred elves were sent to Britengate to bolster those already sending force out against the Shadow encroaching upon the shield surrounding the city.

Orian set out to find Shuran as soon as he arrived back in the city. When he found him in the barracks, he decided to locate a more private place to share the information given him by the dryads. Without a spoken word, the understanding was shared and Shuran escorted Orian out the back and into a quiet courtyard.

"What is it that has disturbed you my friend?" Shuran asked.

"If I may Shuran, I would first share with you the images and feelings I had while in the midst of the new dryad settlement. Then rather than repeat and sully the retelling, I would replay the conversation as an experience in your mind." Orian was not one to retell a story incorrectly, but in this case he would share with Shuran every detail in the span of a heartbeat. He would also share more than what his consciousness would have processed.

"It is called Hala'Sa, I believe?" Shuran asked.

"Yes Shuran, we would share one mind for a moment, allowing you to fully experience what I did. Perhaps you will see more than I was able," Orian said. "Also there will be no chance of our conversation being overheard."

"You do realize that the thoughts will likely also flow to Moltar in the least if not the entire Zidu'Si," Shuran reminded him.

"I am not concerned with the Zidu'Si, Shin'Ar. I would be guarded about this information until you are better able to interpret the message it contains."

Shuran leaned forward and closed his eyes. "All right then, let us get this over with."

Orian giggled uncharacteristically. "You need not look like a young maiden leaning in for her first kiss. This can be accomplished simply by my mental touch to your mind and you allowing my intrusion."

Shuran smirked back and then allowed the connection of their minds. When it was finished in the blink of an eye, he sat back with a gasp as his mind began processing the information. He closed his eyes and tilted his head back as he rocked slowly on the tree stump he sat upon.

Orian was concerned with Shuran's reaction. Though it was his first time performing the Hala'Sa, Orian was certain that it was done correctly. Shuran's reaction was not normal, even if he was simply human, his mind should have been able to handle the effects. Before Orian could call for help, Shuran lifted his hand to stop him.

"It is well, Orian. My mind struggles between the memories you have shared and those yet to become revealed of what Nergal left behind. I believe the mistake and promise he made are at the focus of this struggle. I will need time to make sense of the mixed memories." Shuran finally gathered himself and stood. "Let us go to the meeting hall and have a meal while our friends from Entensiama afford us a break."

With the added help, the citizens of Britengate were fully relieved of the effects the Shadow inflicted on their emotional and physical well-being. As the elves and Zidu'Si maintained a consistent assault upon the murky darkness enveloping the city shield, the Shadow began to slowly retreat. In the early light of the third day of defense, the Shadow was entirely dispersed and what remained were a small contingent of dark-aligned agents and the shadowy likeness of Salmetu.

Standing behind Ereshkigal's facade of Shuran's sister, was the kashshaptu who refused his healing along with several trolls, dark weavers, and Shadow Walkers. Ereshkigal floated across the ground toward the barrier boundary. She called out with her falsely sweet voice for Shuran to step forward to parley.

"Shuran, it would appear that you are being called to the field to speak with Ereshkigal," Dara said as she entered the meeting hall. "The Shadow has left and only the dark Sumer and her agents remain."

Shuran exhaled and stood, straightening his shirt, before turning for the door. "Thank you Dara. Please accompany me there as I call for the others to join us in meeting the gathered agents of the Shadow."

As the Zidu'Si arrived at the veil of energy protecting the inhabitants of Britengate, Ereshkigal's misty form focused its attention upon Shuran at the lead of his followers. "You could have left them behind Shuran, you are here to speak with one of your own. The Zidu'Si do not have the right to commune with their betters."

"My Zidu'Si are my equals and stand with me in all, Ereshkigal. It is a matter of interpretation, who are the betters in this situation," Shuran spat back at her. Looking past her, Shuran spotted the kashshaptu that fled the swamps after refusing his healing. "I see what motivates you witch! You hope to find power in the Shadow, but you will find only subjugation, death, and destruction. The dark Sumer want nothing but to see the end of all the others created by the Sumer."

Ereshkigal's misty form billowed as she laughed. "You have been listening to the lies of Nergal, Shuran Shin'Ar. All we ever wanted, those who separated from the restrictive edicts of Nergal, was to see what the people of this world could aspire too. It is Nergal who interfered and would keep the races of man from reaching their full potential.

"You were our children, and still are. The Sumer should be guiding you, not floating around within the confines of the Shadow. Nergal overstepped his place as our leader by imprisoning us within this existence. Once we are free you shall see the true nature and righteousness of the Sumerian Gods!"

Shuran held an emotionless expression when he moved closer to Ereshkigal and answered her. "You need not lie to me Ereshkigal. I know the atrocities you and your Gizzu'Su inflicted upon the Telukukal and continued after your unexpected release into the Shadow. I hold the memories of Nergal within me and have also read his journal.

"You have caused uncountable deaths among the people of Aurderia in my lifetime alone. The Shadow inhabits unwilling men, forcing them to do your will. You call forth enemies to renew old wars, and you cause people to turn on their own kind. Voreen from the elves, the kashshaptu, the trolls, and more unknown to us yet I am certain, you create chaos among these so-called children of yours. What parent would do such deeds?

"You and your wicked contemporaries want nothing but power at the expense of those you see as weaker. Do not misunderstand my intentions now when I tell you that I will see you and the Gizzu'Su removed from the Shadow. I will make it the primary goal of the Zidu'Si to see your shi extracted and destroyed. You madam are no God, the Sumerians are nothing more than arrogance and blight upon the face of Ersetu. You should have left this world when the 'Me' called you to heel!" Shuran remained motionless when Ereshkigal reacted.

An ear-splitting scream echoed through the sky and shook the very ground they stood upon. In an instant, Ereshkigal was gone along with her agents of darkness. The swirl of darkness and accompanying clap of thunder reverberated upon the shield, sending a shockwave into the surrounding forest, knocking leaves from the trees and sending birds and woodland creatures fleeing for safety.

Shuran turned with a satisfied smile upon his face and began walking back to the meeting hall. The Zidu'Si quickly fell into step behind him and a lone figure on the outside of the boundary stood behind a tree taking all of the spectacle in before pulling a crystal from his multi-color cloak and disappearing.

Back in the meeting hall, Shuran met with the Zidu'Si and other members of the weavers' council. The people who filled the hall were split between support of Shuran's actions, and infuriated that he would raise the ire of the Goddess of the Netherworld. Shuran let the arguments go on so they all would let off some steam before he would explain his actions.

Moona, on the other hand, was not going to tolerate the shouting and fighting. With the movement of her hands and a silent whisper, the ground shifted beneath the hall bringing with it a sudden drop in the noise level. "Shut yer traps and listen to Shuran!"

Codger smiled at Moona from across the room. "That's my Moony!" he whispered to Avrank.

"Never raise the ire of a dwarf be she full blood or not!" Avrank remarked back and lifted his tankard to Codger's in salute.

"Thank you Moona," Shuran said as he moved to the center of the hall. "I understand the confusion and level of disagreement with what has just transpired. Believe in me when I say that it was necessary to stand up and call out the lies that Ereshkigal spreads to those who would be her children. She is not now, nor ever was a God. None of the Gods you have known are what they have been portrayed.

"The one called Nergal has possessed a portion of my mind from childhood until only recently. Through his teachings and guidance, along with the memories he has left behind, I know the truth of who they are. They are nothing more than the shi of a group of scientists from an advanced world beyond the heavens in the night sky. They came to Ersetu long ago and performed experiments that ultimately led to the creation of the Telukukal and then the races of man.

"They have rules as a people and some of the Sumer scientists decided to make rules of their own. They fought amongst themselves and used the Telukukal and the early races of man as tools in their war of the gods. There is more to those times to speak to, but that is a story for another telling. The important thing to know now is that we must force the Shadow off the surface of Ersetu and back where it belongs until the time we can rid the world of the Sumer."

Moona moved forward to Shuran's side. "Right then, what do you need from us my boy?"

"Spread the word, stay the course, and prepare to face the darkness!"
Though Ereshkigal and her agents left the area, the Shadow returned to begin coating the city shield and continue attempting an assault upon the inhabitants.

Chapter Three

"Now that the Shadow has left us for the time being, it is time we prepare to leave for the Highlands," Shuran said as he broke his fast with the Zidu'Si. "From what Nagutan has told me, we can find them beyond the Drakkian settlements somewhere near something called the Pillars of Wind."

Gregoran swallowed hard and coughed at the mention of the Pillars. "Madness!"

Shuran looked to his friend. "You have heard of this place?"

"The Drakkian people fear it, and the drakkon will go nowhere near the place. It is an unending storm with twisting winds that reach down from the skies to the ground and prevent all passage further east."

"Sounds as good a way to hide a race of man than any we have encountered yet!" Avrank said a bit too excitedly.

Orian nudged his friend. "You have a death wish Turd? Smaller winds would toss your minuscule frame to the four corners of the planet!"

"Bah! What is a little wind to the Zidu'Si?" Avrank said.

Shuran chuckled along with his friends. "I am glad you are in such spirits, but do not underestimate the challenges we face. We do not know how the Lil'Du will receive us and what challenge they may pose to my right as Shin'Ar."

Gregoran furrowed his brow. "I assume there is no avoiding this insanity? I suppose we should make first for the Drakkian settlements and leave from there. But I must warn you ahead of time, those we will meet at the settlement will not be what you expect of the Drakk people you have already met."

"How would they be different?" Vala asked.

"They have dabbled with their gifts far more than they should have. They are volatile and prone to fits of fire. And then there are the wild drakkon," Gregoran smiled in a mischievous manner.

Dara's curiosity was piqued. "How do you mean 'fits of fire'?"

"They sometimes spontaneously combust and become flame itself, or so I am told. We do not mingle with them much and it has been many generations since we have had dealings with them. Fallon may be able to enlighten you more, Shuran."

"We shall see what we find soon enough," Shuran began. "Let us prepare for the journey beyond the Drakkian settlements and have provisions prepared and sent to the Vault."

As the Zidu'Si and friends went about preparing for the journey to the Highlands, Shuran went to find Fallon to talk about what he might share regarding the Drakkians who settled in the Far East of Ersetu.

The Highlands were an unknown wild land that was created millennia ago during a sudden shift in the land that broke the earth and caused the creation of Hell's Mouth. During the volatile years of Hell's Mouth's eruptions and the upheaval of land bordering Aurderia, the Drakkians that lived in the eastern regions stayed there and became reclusive. Part of the reason they remained was due to the turbulent times and fear that their comrades in Drakk were killed during the initial destruction that followed. Later they remained solitary, taking the events as a sign from the Gods that they should remain pure and separate from the other races.

Fallon's forefathers and surviving members of the race that remained in Drakk found refuge below ground and remained to preserve their rights to the land. It was centuries later when the race was reunited during an expedition that took the Aurderia Drakkians out to the Highlands in search of surviving drakkon to replenish their failing stock.

"You know there has always been something that bothered me about our youth! Your father's and mine that is," Fallon said as he continued telling

Shuran of the Drakk history. "When my adda brought him to the family, all I remember is him saying that I had a half brother and he would be staying with us. I do not recall adda ever explaining anything else."

Shuran turned with a look of suspicion. "You mean he just showed up and you accepted him as sheesh, then no other details?"

"Actually yes, I remember growing up with Dalgon and our many exploits and trouble-making adventures, but I do not recall details of who his mother was or anything else. Adda is long past so there is no longer the option of asking for more specific details-"

"It does not matter uncle, I am afraid I already know the answers. It is likely that your father would not recall the manner in which he brought my adda into your home, Nagutan is likely involved with the introduction and magic would have fogged the details." Shuran was both understanding and upset with the realization that his father's origins were still leading to a mysterious beginning and more unknowns for the future.

Fallon took Shuran by the shoulders. "I know your adda boy! He loves you and would only stay away for good reason. Whether he is truly of my family blood or not, is no matter. He is my kin as are you!"

"Uncle, I do not doubt the ties that bind, whether they be true or only by association. I simply wish to know what is the true line of my blood and what all of this prophetic yak scat means!"

Fallon just laughed and slapped Shuran on the back. "Familial bonds or not be damned... You are Dalgon's son and the fire of Drakk is in your blood boy! Family is what you take to heart and by my count, you have a family the size of which the whole of Ersetu would envy!"

Shuran turned more serious in his demeanor when he spoke next. "Uncle, do you think the other Drakk stayed away on purpose or do you suspect intervention?"

Fallon looked surprised at first then narrowed his stare and moved closer to Shuran. "I always wondered that myself. It never made sense, as the Drakkians always stayed close. The separation was a tumultuous time for our people and we had many hardships with such a small population. It is said, by some, that the Gods kept us apart to create a new breed of Drakk."

"What do you mean by a new breed?" Shuran asked.

"A bunch of mystic, yak scat as you say, if you ask me, but some still believe that those in the highlands as the true Drakkians, the Ag'Lu, or fire people." Fallon said the last words in hushed whispers and then walked away with a wink to Shuran. He left one parting comment when he turned back. "When I look to piece together a puzzle, I seek out the most unlikely connections to the whole!"

Shuran was surprised by the cryptic comment since Fallon was not one to speak in riddle. His overall impression was that Fallon was attempting to share something that he could not speak openly about. Shuran would have to figure out this latest mystery once he arrived in the Highlands. As he pondered this latest bit of information, he decided to seek out Nagutan for guidance and any added knowledge the secretive old man would decide to impart upon him.

It did not take long for Shuran to locate his grandsire; he was settled in a comfortable seat near the fire inside the Drunkard Tavern. Avrank's watering hole was doing a splendid business, not in the least due to the fact he owned the only fleet of magurmu that supplied the city, but also because it was the only place where citizens of the mundane population were able to purchase ale for private or public consumption.

Nagutan sat back comfortably with a tankard of Avrank's best brew, regaling the crowd with stories of the old days and times lost to recorded history. He retold tails of the time before the Sikil'Mah and when the creation of the races of man occurred. It was no longer withheld information the fact that Nagutan was thousands of years in age and one of the Telukukal.

Shuran disapproved of the gatherings on principal. It was not that he felt the correct history of Aurderia not be told, it was more that his grandfather appeared to enjoy his drink and Shuran feared his tongue might loosen far more than was prudent. Just as Shuran learned a way to mask the scent of a shifter from Andra, others may have done the same. Shuran did not want to appear paranoid, but spies were a definite threat and Britengate needed protecting.

Shuran approached the crowd and joined in a hearty laugh at Nagutan's last quip. "Such a wonderful tail grandsire. I wonder that I might have a moment of your time, privately?" Shuran looked to the crowd as he said the last word and watched as they quickly nodded to him and dispersed. Once the last of Nagutan's audience left, Shuran accepted a mug of wine from a maid and narrowed his stare upon his grandsire.

"Are you certain this wise, telling such histories at this time?" Shuran asked.

Nagutan grinned and set his tankard down. "Oh, my boy it is quite the perfect time. These people need something to grasp onto. The very foundation of their faith has been shattered and they need something to believe in." Noticing Shuran's shift in position, Nagutan adjusted his explanation. "Do not get me wrong, my boy, the people of this city have more faith in you than you can imagine. You challenge the Gods they have believed in for all their lives and the lives of their kinfolk before them.

"But they see you also as just a man, not a God. Something has been taken from them and they must re-establish their faith. My stories are just a means to guiding them to decide that there is something more, but what that is we do not know and simply must believe in a greater power."

"And how are they to deduce that there is a greater power?" Shuran asked doubtfully.

"When they see you bring the Shadow to light and the Sumer are sent away, then they will see that there is power greater than their false Gods. The fact they already know you are just a man of Ersetu, be you a powerful one, most will begin to understand that there is always something greater and more mysterious." Nagutan just grinned and took another drink of his ale.

Shuran just shook his head. "I do not see this ending so easily but there are more pressing matters that bring me to your counsel."

"There always are these days I am afraid. I assume it pertains to your eminent visit to the Ag'Lu of the Highlands prior to your journey to the Pillars?" Nagutan inquired with a sly smile.

"I will not bother asking how you know that since you are as full of silence as you are secrets. What I would like is anything that you can share of these people before we encounter them?" Shuran asked.

After a long pause and mock look of contemplation, Nagutan returned Shuran's gaze. "As you might assume, there is much I could tell you but will not. But before you get upset I think there is something that I can share to help you avoid certain… un-pleasantries."

Shuran was all ears.

***

Dara and Vala, as the only female members of the Zidu'Si, had become steadfast friends and did everything together when not in the company of the men in the collective. They found company among most other women in Britengate intolerable, however, except for that of Moona. So that is where they found themselves spending their time, with Moona.

"Gather around girls, you are gonna learn things that them boys can' put in their think heads," Moona said as she winked and motioned for them to close in. "True use of the Essence ain' in whether you wield or weave, it be in the finesse of which you do it!" Moona then waved her hand over a pile of dirt and backed away as it grew in size and formed the shape of a man. With another word of command, the golem moved at the words Moona intoned.

"You see men may try to use their power to move mountains by force, but they never understand that ya get better results from asking. O'course womanly guile ain' a bad way to get what ya want neither!" Moona laughed.

"Moona, I do not mean to be short, but is there a reason you asked us here while we were preparing for our journey east?" Vala asked.

Moona just grunted and moved toward her workbench. "Always in a hurry, you young folk don' matter the race, ya'll are just wantin' to get going before yer heads are on tight! Now gather and pay attention girls!"

Moona motioned them close and pointed to another mound of dirt and rock on the bench where she created the golem. Around the pile of dirt she placed, had been carved a deep groove where she now poured water. "Dara, if you would please convert the inside of the trench to metal."

Dara obliged Moona's request with both humor and a bit of curiosity.

"Good, now Vala I want you ta make the water flow in time wise direction at rapid speed while Dara focuses on heating the metal lining."

As the two Zidu'Si women followed Moona's direction, she molded the mound of dirt into a miniature mountain range. While the two girls watched, Moona lit a clutch of sticks aflame and the smoke began to draw toward the small mountain and gather into a cloud over it. As the cloud condensed, moisture began to fall from the gathering and moisten the small mountain of earth. Quickly the mountain began to get pulled down by the flow of water that fell upon it and flow back toward the trench.

"Do you see? The fire evaporates the water, the water and heat change the flow of air to form the clouds, the clouds grab ahold the particles of smoke and rain upon the land, the land yields to the force of water flowing back to the deepest point it can reach!" Moona cried.

Vala and Dara looked at each other puzzled before Moona finally grunted again and explained. "The elements of Essence are all reliant on one another! You want to move a mountain you will need to use the other elements!" Moona was exasperated. "You two should understand better than most! You can' go out there thinkin' you can control everything alone. You need each other and I expect you girls to remind the thick headed men of your little group of merry wielders!"

"I apologize Moona," Vala realized. "We will maintain a more level head and will think things through and use what is best among our combined strength to accomplish the tasks at hand."

Moona was a bit set off at first since that was not what she was trying to convey. She was now unsure what she was trying to impart, but this sounded good enough. "Exactly my dear!" she said unconvincingly. "Now there is something else I would like your help with. I been thinking that bitch sister of Shuran's will soon find a way around the padiri'bur, so we need a back-up weapon."

Moona worked with the girls for several hours until they achieved what it was Moona was expecting. At her insistence, Dara and Vala kept their work a secret for Moona's fear of spies among the citizens. She said they could only speak of it in private among the Zidu'Si once they left the city for the Highlands.

Chapter Four

Bastien sat alone in the practice grounds thumbing through the Iniminim Ma and learning spells that would assist in the upcoming adventures of the Zidu'Si. He felt he had to prove himself and wanted to gain as much knowledge as he could before his first expedition with his fellow Zidu'Si. It was not a lack of knowledge in spell casting that worried him; he gained a great deal of knowledge while possessed by the Telalsu. That was dark magic or in the least used to achieve dark results. Bastien wanted to learn how to change the result of the spells he knew, but none was close to the contents he found in the spell book obtained from Andra so long ago.

The spells in the book were advanced for certain, but with his wand added to the knowledge Bastien gained while possessed by the demon warrior, he understood the spells and mastered them with ease. He found spells for healing of major injuries. There were spells for transmuting matter and affecting the weather. It was not until he came across a spell for transfiguration, that Bastien had reason for pause.

The spell words themselves were not beyond his understanding; it was the context and ingredients of the spell that befuddled him. There was a call for crystals and some sort of substance called primal Essence extract. Bastien could not determine what this was and inquiry to Mallick yielded no further answers. He decided to ask Shuran about the spell.

"Mallick was unable to identify the ingredient from his access to the Vault library?" Shuran asked later that day when he and Bastien spoke. "I have a recollection of the term but not the meaning. I am afraid that this knowledge is not among the memories left behind by Nergal."

Bastien opened the spell book to the page and showed it to Shuran. "No, Mallick found no information among the Vault library either. From what I glean of the spell, this is some means of creating a lasting morph into another form. It also calls for the use of some device with the seven crystals and the elusive primal Essence extract."

Shuran suddenly had a moment of clarity and dismissed the conversation. "I may know more about parts of this spell, but I do not think it the time or place to discuss. Besides, we have more pressing matters to attend at the moment Bastien. Have your things ready by dawn so we might leave at first light for the Highlands." Shuran took hold of the Iniminim Ma and instantly transferred it back to the Vault.

Bastien simply stood there, mouth agape and confused.

***

The next morning arrived with the same dreary darkness that accompanied most dawns of Utu since the Shadow arrived. With the murky darkness of the Shadow undulating along the shield, sunlight was shortened in the city. It was not until late morning through late after midday that the sunlight entered the city around the level of cover the Shadow caused.

Shuran performed his morning ablutions and dressed for travel into the vast wilderness of the Highlands. With the provisions safely stored in the Vault and his limited knowledge provided by Nagutan and Fallon, there was little else to prepare before leaving. He finished dressing in his traveling attire and headed off to the meeting hall to break his fast.

The Zidu'Si were already present and finishing their meals when Shuran arrived. He grabbed a bowl of porridge and joined them. "We will need to travel by Emmuku'Gu to near the Altar of Chaos," he said as he sat down.

"Will that not alert the Shadow of our exit from Britengate?" Dara asked.

Shuran nodded in response as he swallowed a spoonful of the bland mix of oats and milk. "It will, but I am hoping that will perhaps cause Ereshkigal to give up her senseless assault upon the city."

"Are you wishing that it follows our travels?" Orian asked in surprise.

With a wicked grin, Shuran pushed his bowl of porridge away. "I have learned from Nagutan something of great interest about the movement of the Shadow. It cannot pass beyond the cliffs that border Drakk and the Highlands."

"I thought the Shadow could travel anywhere the Emmuku'Gu flowed? Are you saying there is no flow beyond the borders or Aurderia?" Gregoran asked.

"Not necessarily, but it would be deep below the earth and the Shadow would need an easy path to follow to the surface. What I refer to, is the gug that lines the cliff face from the events that created the Highlands many millennia ago." Shuran saw the looks of understanding beginning to spread. "I see that you are all beginning to follow my words.

"By the time the Shadow senses that we have left and arrived in Drakk, we will be well on our way to the cliffs and making our way up to the plateau. We will take in turn the flight to the top. Once Moltar drops me and at lease two others, he can return for the remaining Zidu'Si."

"I have been speaking with some of the other Drakkon Riders Shuran," Gregoran interrupted. "Three of them have offered assistance to carry a passenger as far as the settlements."

"I thought most drakkon do not carry another rider beyond their Lugaldur?" Orian asked.

Gregoran shrugged. "Normally this is the case, however the desire to leave the confines of the city combined with visiting the Drakk of the Highlands has provided an incentive to the drakkon, seeing this as a mutually beneficial endeavor."

Shuran stood and gestured for the others to follow. "Shall we meet our obliging escort?"

The Zidu'Si all filed out of the meeting hall to find the three riders and drakkon awaiting them. They were already saddled with secondary harness and straps. After sizing them up, Shuran assigned Mallick, Orian, and Avrank to accompany the riders. Vala would ride with Gregoran leaving Dara and Bastien to travel upon Moltar with himself.

Avrank shuffled off toward his drakkon and rider with a look of disappointment upon his face. He looked back as Dara climbed upon Moltar with Bastien and Shuran. As Shuran caught his eye, he looked away.

Shuran snickered and patted Bastien upon the leg. "It would seem that Avrank is turning green of envy at your riding upon Moltar."

"Surely he must know that Dara is too large for the other drakkon, or is it perhaps he wishes to trade places?" Mallick said as understanding surfaced. "He has a warming toward the Gila'Lu? That would be as unlikely a pairing as dwarf and troll!"

Laughing, Shuran turned to Dara, who seemed oblivious to the situation. "Aye it would, and I will thank you not to put those images to mind in the future!"

Once everyone was settled upon the drakkon, they were quickly transported by Emmuku'Gu to just between what remained of the Stone Forest and the Altar of Chaos. The forest seemed menacing no more, not since the release of the Dryads from their deep slumber. Moons earlier, Shuran and the Zidu'Si freed the ancient creatures from the petrified remains of the forest, uncertain of what they could expect. What they found were beings of mysterious magic that had an uncanny immunity to the power of the Shadow. These same creatures turned on the dark wielders caught in the middle of their awakening.

Shuran had gambled on the ability to revive the Dryads based on a passage in Nergal's journal and a fractured memory left in the recesses of his mind where Nergal once resided. Shuran heaved a great sigh at the loss of Nergal's guidance. Though he did not realize at the time, Nergal was responsible for Shuran's innate understanding of powers he had only begun to understand. Once the shi of the once great leader of the Sumer left his mind, Shuran was left to regain the strength in abilities he previously wielded with ease.

Sensing his Lugaldur's emptiness, Moltar purred and sent thoughts to Shuran. "It will be well, Lugaldur. The power is in you, and together we shall gain the knowledge to wield it and chase the Shadow back into darkness!"

Shuran patted Moltar on the side of his neck and suddenly went still as he gazed upon the hairs of his arm standing on end. "It knows we have left the city! Let us be off quickly!" Shuran barely uttered the words as gloomy black tendrils of the Shadow sprouted from the broken earth.

The drakkon immediately took to the sky with thunderous bursts accompanying the frantic beating of their leathery wings. As they gained altitude and distanced themselves from the growing conglomeration of Shadow, Shuran looked back to find the smallest drakkon of their clutch, struggling to free itself of a vine that wrapped itself around a hind leg. It was the rider who carried Mallick, and the drakkon they rode did not have a spell to repel the Shadow's influence.

Shuran instructed Moltar to turn back and assist, but they stopped and hovered as Shuran could sense the spell forming on Bastien's tongue.

Bastien was closer and noticed the struggling riders before Shuran turned to intercede. Working out a spell he learned only that morning, Bastien instructed his rider to turn their drakkon to the side where he could aim his wand. With a thrust of his arm, he let the spell pass his lips and fuel the waiting power of his Gidri Zisura. "Bil-E Emmuku Te Gisnu!" Bastien shouted and sat back in shocked surprise at what happened.

As the last syllable of the spell passed his lips, a wave of power washed over his body and fed the waiting gugtu weapon in his hand. The wand hummed and glowed white, growing brighter as the spell built up strength. As the brilliant light neared blinding brightness, it finally winked out to become replaced by a burst of light from overhead that spread across the Stone Forest and bathed it in Utu's light.

The rays of golden light that hit the surrounding area were more intense and powerful than Utu on even the clearest of mid-summer days. It was not a natural light that began burning away the vines and chasing off the Shadow; this was an Essence born light that was burning the darkness.

Mallick and his rider held fast to the drakkon as its sudden release sent them flying high into the sky in an uncontrolled ascent. Once they finally eased into a steady lift, Mallick turned back to see the results of Bastien's impromptu spell. The once charred and lifeless forest was turning green with new growth, and there was no sign of the Shadow. "What was that?" Mallick yelled as they came up along side Bastien.

Bastien shrugged and looked at his wand. "Perhaps I misunderstood the precise meaning of the spell, but it seems to have done the deed!"

Shuran flew in near the two, having heard the exchange he motioned them onward and spoke to Bastien. "The meaning of the words is less important than the meaning of your heart and mind when you say them. What were you thinking as you spoke the spell?" Shuran was curious at the outcome of the spell he recognized but had not used.

"I wanted to burn away the Shadow and the vines," Bastien said with a confused look.

Shuran shook his head. "That is not all, what did you see in your mind?"

Bastien suddenly became aware of what happened. "I had a sudden wonder of what this dead forest had once looked like and if it could be brought back to life. I glimpsed a green and thriving garden and sprouting trees just before I spoke!"

Shuran nodded and flew ahead. He was beginning to see the potential power of the Zidu'Si to reshape the world. They could bring life back to the land with this kind of power. Then a dark thought came to his mind.

"You worry over things that cannot be stopped Shin'Ar. It is up to you to keep this power in balance, and I fear not of you becoming corrupted by that power." Mallick smiled and ended the mental communication.

The glow of Hell's mouth loomed to the North as they flew past Drakkfoth and onto the sheer cliff face of the Highlands. From a distance, the riders could make out the aged steps long ago carved into the land, allowing ascent to the lands above. They were seldom traveled and had fallen into disrepair, but the drakkon they rode made travel by land unnecessary. They continued their climb into the clouds until they could see the top of the plateau that stretched beyond the horizon. Onward toward the Drakk settlements they flew, not knowing the reception they would receive.

The settlement was easily enough found once they passed the initial stretch of deserted flat land where the Highlands began atop the massive uplift of land that bordered Drakk. Shuran could make out large buildings of stone from a distance but could make out no sign of the people who were supposed to reside here. Even through his enhanced vision and Essence senses, he could not make out any signs of life. Only stone, dust, and fire.

As the Zidu'Si and drakkon riders neared, they landed just outside the Ag'Lu city and walked the remaining distance to the center of the buildings. As Shuran had sensed, there were no Ag'Lu found present in the outpost. The drakkon took to flight in order to scout the area and look for anything that might provide a meal.

As a group, the Zidu'Si and riders entered a courtyard passing between two pillars of fire jetting up from basins in the granite floor that spread out before them. The dance of light from the flames cast a play of illumination upon the granite floors and pillars of the open structures before them. Night was approaching, and the increasing darkness set the stage for the eerie howling of the wind that blew in from the plain and pushed the flames into motion.

Shuran climbed the side steps of a two-level building that appeared to function as a massive platform of some sort. As he reached the top and backside of the platform, he turned to walk toward the front of the structure, is when he sensed their approach.

Chapter Five

The guttural rumble vibrated the foundations of the platform Shuran stood upon. As the roar escaped the immense maw of the green and tan lead drakkon, it was cut short as all the air was knocked from the beasts body by an upthrust of ground directly below it. The drakkon was much larger than any other the Drakk bred; it easily outsized the others by a full span of its leg. There was but one drakkon that outsized him and they were about to meet for the first time.

Moltar set down in front of the beast and billowed his wings as he towered over the other drakkon. His posture became commanding as he lowered his head and squared off against the threat to his Lugaldur and companions. "You were about to say something little one?"

The green and tan snarled and flashed forward over the rubble that earlier knocked the air from his lungs. "Be careful the little one's I always say, they can get to your soft spots!" In an instant he was beneath Moltar, rolling over and preparing to dig his claws into Moltar's underbelly. As his claws reached Moltar's soft scales, they met with a force of energy that sent spasms through the full length of the drakkon's body.

Moltar stepped back away from the recovering drakkon. "And you should understand what you are facing."

"Enough! You outsiders are not welcome here!" The shapely Ag'Lu woman stepped around the others and moved toward the Zidu'Si. "You Aurderian Drakk also do not belong here," she said to the Drakkians now showing their fire as a sign of blood ties. The other Ag'Lu left with their drakkon, leaving her alone with the unwelcome guests.

"We are kin mistress, Drakk blood fuels this fire!" one of the Drakkians said as the flames danced across his hands.

The Ag'Lu woman stepped closer to the Drakkian and paused before speaking. "We are not so close to kin as before the split, cousin." She stood there with her blue-black skin, hair the color of flames dancing in the wind. Her eyes began to shift from deep blue to a glowing bright bluish-white. Flames began to trickle and chase along her skin as she stepped out of her wrap. The instant her garment hit the granite stones at her feet, her body ignited and she become fire, pure and driven to burn.

The Drakkians stood in awe of the spectacle before their eyes. A living female form of smokeless fire paced before them. She alternated her colors from red and orange to green and blue, burning various elements in the air around her. As quickly as she transformed to flame, she stood before them again, picking up her garment and re-adorning it before turning back to them.

"After the upheaval, when our people split between the Highland tribes and those who remained in Drakk, we began to change in our isolation," the Ag'Lu woman spoke. "In our seclusion we have become more than the wielders of our forefathers. We have become more attuned to our abilities and honed them."

Gregoran stepped forward. "We have continued to strive for this ability as well, but have been unable. How is it you have become so adept with fire?"

"You are distracted by the ways of Aurderia and the troubles of man. The lack of discipline keeps you from true embodiment of your gift." The Ag'Lu woman made no expression or hint of any emotion on her voice as she spoke. She seemed completely indifferent. "It is late. You may rest for the night here at Drakkon Port, but you should be on your way at first light." She began to turn to leave when Shuran finally spoke.

"We do not wish to impose upon your grace however we are in need of guidance of your elders, if it please them." Shuran spoke humbly and with open palms of flame. "I am Shuran Shin'Ar. You have spoken kindly to our Drakkian friends, but the Zidu'Si wish to seek ukken ana su geshtu-bad."

The Ag'Lu woman stopped walking and gazed at Shuran with a look of suspicion for several moments before approaching him. "You speak the words of greeting from the ancients, seeking a meeting to share great wisdom. How is it you know of this?"

"As I have said, I am the Shin'Ar. I have vast knowledge that covers the ages of man and before, at my command. It is my hope that we might barter friendship with your people and build upon the kinship we have." Shuran then took a blade from his belt and opened a cut upon his palm to display his blood to the Ag'Lu. When he saw the quick look of understanding cross her face, he quickly healed the wound.

Surprised by more than just the markers in his blood, the woman shifted her emotionless gaze to one of curiosity. "I am Aglia. I do not know what this means, but I am certain that I will be able to bring one to you who will understand. I shall send word and we will have an answer by first light." With a smile, Aglia turned and left the group. She walked to a small hut and shortly afterward a young Ag'Lu boy exited, mounted a small drakkon, then flew off to the Northeast.

As the Zidu'Si and Drakkon Riders settled in and setup for the night with the provisions Shuran called from the Vault, the drakkon gathered on and around the bi-level platform. This platform, they realized now, served as a resting area for the drakkon. This settlement was nothing more than a resting point for traveling the vast expanse of the Highlands. The Ag'Lu must have a city or other settlements elsewhere.

Mallick joined Shuran near a fire where the evening meals were cooking. "Where did you learn that saying? I found nothing in the Vault library that references such a request or greeting," Mallick asked.

"Not everything is in those books, nor was it in Nergal's journal. Nagutan shared what little insight he was willing to part with before we left Britengate," Shuran said.

"I suppose he did not tell whether he had friends among the Ag'Lu or anything useful toward reaching the Lil'Du?" Mallick asked already knowing the answer. Nagutan was methodical in his interference and guidance equally. There was a plan in motion that started millennia ago, and the Zidu'Si all knew this now, as well as the old man's involvement.

"He shared little and even that was intentionally cryptic. I only know that his manipulation is nearly at an end. Hopefully when the time comes, my grandsire will be more open with information." Shuran shared the little information he was given. "I know that the elders of the Ag'Lu value information and knowledge of the ancient world, the times before the races of man."

"You have this information?" Bastien asked as he and the other Zidu'Si gathered and sat down.

"Very little at present, but I know where to gain insight and our friendship with the dryads will be helpful," Shuran started. "The compendium contains all the knowledge gathered from the Sumer when they arrived on Ersetu. Once we find it, we will have more than sufficient knowledge to share."

Dara wore a concerned look as she shifted in next to Avrank. "Is it wise agreeing to sharing this information? We do not yet know what this compendium contains or that we can even find its location."

"I have little doubt that it will be found, when the time is appropriate," Shuran said flatly. "The knowledge of its existence will provide the motivation required to elicit assistance from the Ag'Lu. Nagutan was most insistent that it would work."

While Shuran was speaking, Bastien had risen and stepped off a short distance practicing a spell. None of the others gave much notice to him as he took to practicing spells and fiddling about with his wand regularly. This time he took advantage of his sometimes-peripheral existence, and began speaking a spell and running his wand over his arms and body. With a last unheard mumble, Bastien transformed himself into a living flame.

"BASTIEN!" Vala screeched and burst toward him wrapping her watery, transforming arms around him. She surrounded him with her body as she transformed further. She only backed off when Bastien pushed her away laughing.

"Vala, STOP!" Bastien laughed. "I am not on fire, it is just a spell!"

Vala pulled back and reformed her body. "SORRY, JUST A SPELL?" she shouted. "Do you know how woefully inadequate that sounds? You are playing with something you are not meant to achieve. I believed you had..."

Vala stopped speaking, grabbed her clothing, and ran toward the closest rock outcrop.

Shuran stood to go after her, but Dara stopped him by placing her hand on his arm. "I will go after her," she said. Dara headed off to find Vala. She did not have to go far, Dara found her behind the same large rocks where she first escaped view. After helping Vala finish fastening her garments, Dara sat beside her and waited.

After several moments, Vala finally spoke. "I share my sorrow for speaking so rashly. I should not have reacted in such a way."

Dara waited to see if Vala would speak further before finally speaking up. "I understand. Bastien is not like us, he is not descended of Coosco, at least not as closely."

Vala looked at Dara with surprise. "You know?" She paused and thought about the fact that the Gula'Lu long ago separated from the races of man and lived in solitude with the elements. "Of course, your people are the same, and the Ag'Lu who separated from the other Drakk."

"Yes," Dara sighed. "But I think we should leave it alone for now. The others will not understand, except for Shuran. But that is a conversation for another time. Shuran has already shown he is touched by Coosco, it will not be long before he pieces things together."

"Are you speaking of the promise?" Vala asked excitedly.

Dara simply smiled and nodded before taking vala's hand and led her back to the others. "We will say you over reacted. You were concerned for Bastien's well-being is all!"

"Not a complete untruth," Vala mumbled.

"What was that dear?" Dara asked, smiling. She obviously noticed Vala's attraction to Bastien. Vala was the only one watching Bastien when he created his illusion. Vala always watched Bastien, with interest.

"Um… nothing really, as you said I was concerned. So how about we get the boys to show us a little war play. They need some practice with spells now that Bastien has bolstered our ranks."

Vala's poor attempt at changing the subject did not escape Dara, but she conceded. "Good thought, perhaps we can spar together." Dara adorned her most mischievous look.

Bastien fumbled to get up and approach Vala as she returned. "I apologize Vala, I should have warned you. Usually no one pays me much attention when I go off practicing."

Vala took Bastien's hand for just a moment before shyly letting it go. "I overreacted. I thought you set yourself aflame and just-"

"Let us just forget it and perhaps take the time now to practice some spells," Dara interrupted. "I thought maybe a little girls versus boys… on second thought that would leave us outnumbered six against two. Avrank and Bastien with myself and Vala, against the remaining?"

An agreeable nod was the sign to separate and prepare their list of spells for competition. Avrank and Bastien joined the girls wearing ear-to-ear grins.

The two groups now huddled separately deciding what tactics to use for their offensive and defensive spells. Moments passed as they worked out their strategies, so engrossed none of the Zidu'Si seemed to notice the return of several drakkon and Ag'Lu. The new arrivals settled in among the rocks to watch with curiosity.

Most curious of all was Aglia watching Shuran with intensity that crossed the line of mere inquisitiveness. She found a spot among the columns of the drakkon platform and watched the Zidu'Si practice spells and elemental magic, keeping a close eye on Shuran.

Chapter Six

The two groups barely finished their preparations before launching themselves into mock battle. Spells began flying through the thick hot air of the early night. For each offensive spell conjured and equal defensive spell was brought into existence, canceling each when they met.

As the exercise proceeded, Bastien and Shuran both stepped back from direct participation offering encouragement and suggestions. Of the Zidu'Si, Shuran and Bastien were most adept at weaving without thought. Although Mallick was a weaver, he relied upon the Mudutu'Har to access spells within the books of the Vault library. The delay in accessing spells, though minimal, was more than sufficient to allow the odd casting to reach close enough to nearly have effect. On more than one occasion Shuran would step in to deflect or neutralize any spell that threatened any harm.

After near half a turn, the others noticed Shuran and Bastien holding back and began goading them to spar against one another. The two equally matched in spell weaving, conceded and stood ready for a wizards duel.

"No using Moltar to strengthen your workings Shuran," Bastien warned.

Shuran grinned and held his hands before him. "I would not dream of such treachery. I shall not need the aid, my friend. I shall face you with nothing more than that which I have upon my person." Shuran pulled his half of the Mudutu'Har from his finger and handed it to Mallick.

"You may need that ring sheesh. I have memorized most of the Iniminim Ma," Bastien teased.

Shuran answered with a grin and a single word. "BADUR!" A watery sphere appeared in his hand and within a heartbeat it was launched toward Bastien.

Bastien laughed as he raised his wand and produced a wall of flames before himself. "Is that the best you can begin with my friend?"

"AB!" Shuran said as he pointed toward the wall of flame along the path of his water spell. A hole appeared in Bastien's wall allowing the sphere to pass and find its mark.

Dripping wet, Bastien held a look of both surprise and bewilderment. "How did you counter my spell?"

"It was not a counter Bastien, I used it as a focus of another spell. You will have to use your creativity to best me!" Shuran laughed with the others as Bastien dried himself with a weaving.

"Prepare yourself Shin'Ar. I am coming for you!" Bastien snarled raising his wand arm and charged Shuran.

"That would require finding me first," Shuran said as he reached into his pocket and wrapped his fingers around the green gem. Since Bastien's shi no longer occupied the stone, it worked again as intended and Shuran disappeared.

Bastien skidded to a halt near falling over as he passed through the space where Shuran had moments ago been standing. "No fair using the Emmuku'Gu!" Bastien shouted.

"Reach out, you will not find the flow of power nearby. I do as I promised and use only that which I have on my person." Shuran's voice echoed through the clearing, leaving no indication where he had moved.

"The stone! It works again and you said nothing, you sneaky son of a yak!" Bastien began looking around for any clue as to where Shuran had gone until he found the sign of dusty footprints trailing from a puddle left by Shuran's previous spell. Not wanting to let on he saw them, Bastien veered off a distance intending to circle back while he thought of a reveal spell.

As he circled around the columns of flame jetting from basins surrounding the court, Bastien readied the spell in his mind to counter Shuran's invisibility.

Bastien jumped around the last column where he felt Shuran was standing and released the spell from his wand. The spell met a pile of clothes.

Befuddled, Bastien kicked at the pile and began looking around for Shuran. Laughter again echoed through the grounds and Bastien ran back to the middle of the circular clearing to search out Shuran in earnest. He weaved his reveal spell in every direction. There was no sign of Shuran.

"So now we play a child's game of hide and find?" Bastien said under his breath. "Have it your way." Bastien waved his wand and lifted it above his head. "BUBULU GIL'SA," Bastien shouted. He created a spell to locate the gemstone. A wave of light burst from the tip of the Gidri Zisura and spread out in every direction. A moment later he found the location of the stone.

Bastien raced over to the column of fire where the gemstone now lay upon the ground. As he bent over to pick it up, he failed to notice that the fire was not erupting from a basin in the earth. This jet of flame danced upon the even granite floor between two pre-existing fires. Two fiery hands extended from the flames and reached over Bastien's bent form.

As the hands left the fire, they began to reform into man's flesh and small sparks of energy began to dance across the fingers. Bastien began to rise and went still in an instant as the sparks darted from the flame-born hands and into his unprepared body.

Shuran stood naked and calling forth his pile of clothes as the last of his skin rendered from the flames that slowly receded around him. As he dressed himself, Bastien began to gain his senses and the rest of the Zidu'Si gathered, grinning and giggling at the scene they witnessed.

"That was brilliant!" Mallick shouted.

Dara and Vala, though impressed and entertained, both held looks of concern as they watched Shuran gather himself.

Sensing their watchful eyes, Shuran looked upon them with a knowing smile and glanced back at Bastien offering a hand.

"That, Shuran, was not playing fair. This was a spelling duel," Bastien complained half-heartedly.

Shuran shook his head and grinned. "My friend, we did not set that as a rule when we began our face-off, only not to use aid beyond our own abilities and what we carried."

"That is bending the line to near breaking Shin'Ar," Orian said.

"Your enemy does not play by any rules, you must be prepared for everything imaginable." Aglia walked out from behind a column in the platform. Behind her the other Ag'Lu that witnessed the previous display stepped out and followed her toward the Zidu'Si. "You show ingenuity and fast mind work, Shuran Shin'Ar. It has been ages since one such as you have visited our people."

Vala was the first to turn at the approach of the Ag'Lu. "You do not have many visitors?"

"The Ag'Lu, entertain guests often enough, but none such as the Shin'Ar and the Zidu'Si. Only once in my time upon Ersetu have I witnessed ability with the Essence from an old man who once came to seek council with the elders." Aglia stopped in front of Shuran. "You carry much like this old man."

"I might wonder that his name was Nagutan?" Shuran asked.

Aglia nodded. "The Elders will greet you after Utu regains the eastern sky. You shall all break your fast with them in our central settlement. You should mount your drakkon and follow."

"We leave now?" Gregoran asked. He was excited at the prospect of entering the Drakkian settlement where the Elders resided. Not a Drakk from Aurderia has been allowed to know the location of their home let alone set foot upon their soil.

"Best to be in the shelter of Mikidisati Kitus when the dust storms arrive." Aglia walked off toward her own drakkon now waiting for her at the platform.

Avrank shuffled over to his rider along with Orian. "Dust storms? You think that torch woman would have left us out here without telling us about dust storms?"

"It matters nothing now as we are headed to shelter in their city," Orian said offering Avrank a hand climbing the drakkon.

"Some shelter, you do realize their city name is ancient tongue for 'Home of Burning Fire' don' ya?" Avrank asked.

Orian shuddered and climbed atop the beast and strapped himself in. "At least we will be warm for the night."

The Zidu'Si and Drakkon Riders took to flight and followed the Ag'Lu to the Northeast. In the full darkness of night, there was only blackness ahead and no sign of settlement. There was no moonlight this early in the spring evening to light their way and the enhanced eyesight of the drakkon did not help in identifying any landmarks. Only the general direction of flight provided any sense of where they now headed.

Moltar rumbled with a guttural roll of his innards. He held back a roar, as he did not understand the urge driving his instinct. His sense of urgency grew as a looming shadow began to stand against the darkness spread out before them. The feeling of coming home washed over the massive drakkon and he thrust forward and flew out ahead of the others, including the Ag'Lu.

"Moltar! What are you doing?" Dara yelled.

Shuran could feel the same thing Moltar did through their bond. "He is going home. Somehow he is linked to this place and knows precisely where he is headed."

The shadow that loomed on the horizon became clearer as they approached and soon they were landing upon a platform similar to that of the one in Drakkon Port. As Moltar landed, fire began to rise from basins around them. The Ag'Lu riders, followed by the Zidu'Si and Drakkians, all landed in the area surrounding the platform.

"Welcome to Mikidisati Kitus," Aglia said as she slid off her drakkon. "I will show you to a chamber where you may wash and rest until first light." Aglia turned and led them into the darkness.

Orian stepped back with Avrank and walked with his undersized friend. "Is it me or does a night back in the dust storm seem a better invitation than what lies ahead?"

"It's you," Avrank jested. "I have to admit I don' hold much hope for a comfortable nights rest."

Their worries were premature they discovered as soon as they entered the sizable cavern entrance Aglia led them through. They stood at the top of an ornate landing with stairs leading down onto a vast city of gleaming crystal buildings lining obsidian-paved walkways. Canals of liquid rock flowed between sections of the city and upon those fiery rivers, glided boats of black diamond with Ag'Lu passengers going about their business.

Dara and Vala stood at the rail of the landing staring out at the glowing crystal conurbation. Light from the lava flows shone upon the buildings and refracted color of every shade throughout the great chamber that the city spread through.

"Gigil'Sa," Dara whispered to Vala 'to transform to jewel'.

"You understand what we have achieved?" Aglia asked from behind them. She left them with a knowing smile and started down the expansive stairway leading to the city below. As the other's followed behind her, Moltar and Jade took to the air of the chamber, flying behind the other drakkon. Aglia noticed Shuran's confusion. "He will be well, Shuran. This is his home; all drakkon can trace their line back to this place. It is in their blood one could say." Aglia gave Shuran a mysterious look before continuing down.

"The Drakk of Aurderia have lost the truth of their origins, but all Ag'Lu came from this place and the breeding of the drakkon began here," Aglia continued as they all descended. "Over the millennia we who stayed and those who returned when Hell's Mouth erupted rebuilt this city and made it what you see today."

Gregoran was confused. "We have kept records of our history, but there is no mention of this place."

"Perhaps not of what it is now, but you will have a record of the caverns of fire, no?" Aglia asked.

"Yes, but we always tell the tales as myth. No Drakk truly believed that they were true."

Now it was Shuran who was confused. "The caverns of fire? What is this story you speak of Gregoran?"

"It is told that the Drakkian people first stepped upon the earth from pools of liquid fire from deep in the caverns of a place called 'Ka'Ag', the Portal of Fire. When the first of our kind gathered, they molded the flows of rock into dwellings and settled in the caves below ground. It was in this place that the drakkon were bred from crossing the great cave lizards with mighty flying creatures that hung from the ceilings of the caves.

"The stories say that some of the Drakk wanted to explore the lands outside the caverns, but others refused and decided they would not mingle with the outside world. This is where our history begins in Aurderia. We found other man beings out in the world and began trading with them. Eventually, we settled on the outskirts of Aurderia in what is now Drakk.

"Although we kept contact open with those Drakk who stayed in Ka'Ag, that connection drifted and we grew apart. The Drakk in Aurderia became more accustom to dealing with the humans. Eventually, the ties to Ka'Ag began to weaken and we lost that part of our beginnings.

"It was not until the balance first broke and Hell's Mouth formed that our history began recording the Drakk of the highlands. Those who fled or were in the uplifted lands when Ersetu shifted, settled in the Highlands and created a new tribe, or so we believed." Gregoran paused seeing Aglia wanting to say something.

"Those refugees found the original race, the Ag'Lu. We welcomed them home and slowly they returned to their natural state, becoming less human once again." Aglia felt she should interject this fact.

"We always knew there were others as we have traded with them in the past, but it would appear that the stories are true," Gregoran continued.

"Flawed and incomplete as you retell them," a gravelly voice sounded from the base of the stairs. Standing at the bottom of a long stairway was an imposing figure of an Ag'Lu man. He was dressed simply, with a pair of short pants and loose tunic. Around his neck, however, hung a large diamond pendant on a thick gold chain. A tribal marking of some kind spread across the left side of his face. "I am Magnar, leader of the Ag'Lu, welcome to our home."

"Magnar may I present our cousin Gregoran from Drakk. He brings other kin and the Shin'Ar called Shuran. The others are his Zidu'Si." Aglia gestured toward Shuran and the others, then stepped aside so that they could be greeted properly.

"It is true then, the legends of the Shin'Ar and his Zidu'Si? You all seem rather short lived by appearance to be those of the stories our elders have passed down through the ages," Magnar asked.

Shuran stepped forward and bent slightly in greeting. "These are but titles and roles that are placed upon us. There have been others in the past. We are but the next to carry the weight of these names."

"Great weight indeed as I have been told. Come we shall escort you to a place you may rest after your journey. In the morning, you shall break your fast with the elders of our people and speak to us of what is transpiring in the lands to the East." Magnar took the lead and the others followed.

"How do we even know when morning is down here?" Bastien whispered.

Dara pinched him.

"OUCH! What was that for?"

"You must not be rude to our hosts. I am certain we will know when the time comes." It was Vala who answered.

Bastien held his tongue at Vala's words. He stepped up next to her and continued their walk in silence.

In their speechless procession, the sounds of the deep cavernous city filled the silence. The low rumble of flowing liquid rock vibrated lightly against their senses. Falling droplets of water from gigantic stalactites met the ground, echoing drips off every polished jewel surface of the buildings. Water that fell to the flow of molten earth sent hissing sounds and steam through the air.

Gentle warm breezes gave way to alternating hot gusts originating deep in the earth and cool bursts from surface fissures high above. The constant ebb and flow of air kept the cavern at a bearable temperature for those not accustomed to the heat. None of the newcomers seemed to notice the temperature as they were mesmerized by the colors and sparkles of light that danced about the chamber more as they moved deeper into the settlement.

At long last, they reached the building where Magnar stopped their travels and stood beside the entrance. "You will find comforts for refreshing and resting within. I must part from you now but will return in the morning to escort you to breakfast with the others I spoke of. Good rest." And with a final gesture he turned and left them for the remainder of the evening.

Aglia saw them inside where they found fresh water running from a section of wall and into a basin mounted below. Fruits and bread were spread upon a table along with bottles of wine. A staircase led up to the second and third level where small rooms containing bedding were found.

"I shall leave you to rest as well. In the morning, we may speak again." Aglia left the dwelling and the Zidu'Si, along with the Drakkon Riders, helped themselves to food before washing up and lying down to sleep. None of them truly slept, as they were far too excited and nervous.

Shuran was more than a small bit perturbed knowing Nagutan had been here at some point. "What was that old schemer up to?" he thought to himself. As with anything his grandsire did, Shuran would be at the middle of it and nothing could change that now. Morning would bring with it answers and likely more questions.

44

Chapter Seven

Barurbe watched as the shifters returned to the clearing where Andra lay staked to the ground. She knew she must save Andra, but she could not afford to reveal herself to the others if she had any hope of infiltrating their ranks. She did not want to disappoint Shuran, and she felt she owed him much and needed to atone for her misguided involvement in Sulura's capture.

Wanting to know what they were about, Barurbe shifted into the form of an owl and quietly flew to a nearby tree so she might listen in on the conversations taking place among her kind. Only one shifter gave her a passing glance as she perched on a tree and pretended to ignore their presence. She was close enough to listen in the quiet of the forest, yet far enough that the shifters would not sense her true identity. Shifters could almost always sense the presence of another of their own kind.

One of the shifters, in the form of an elf, moved up to Andra and pulled down the collar of his shirt checking the glowing band around his neck. "Horrible business these restraints, I understand they cause great pain for the wearer. Are you in much distress Andra?" the false elf asked mockingly.

Andra stared blankly back at the shifter while ripples moved across his face. The gleaming green collar shone with a dull glow of power. It was plainly made, with no gems or elaborate decoration. The band itself was made of an unknown green-grey metal while the surface of the band was deeply etched with cuneiform symbols of the ancient language inlaid with black pigment. The only thing known about the mysterious band is that it prevented the use of Essence and the shifting ability for only certain shifters. For a shifter, that lived a life of moving between forms, it is the most excruciating pain for them, being forced out of shape and into their natural form.

A different shifter in the form of a human male approached as he spoke. "You are stronger than I assumed, Andra. The Nabusa was correct in assuming we would need the use of this ancient artifact in order to detain you. It will not be long before you are unable to resist the effects. You will tell us what we want to know, then we will release you from your agony."

Andra turned his attention to the new arrival. "What information could you possibly need from me that the Nabusa is unable to scry for herself?"

"The location of Durangug primarily, and then there is you having hid the crystal that opens the Vault," the man said. "The Nabusa would very much like to know what else is within the Vault you have omitted from reports, in addition to accessing the central chamber."

"The Vault contents are of no use to your movement, and the central chamber beyond your or Nabusa's abilities to operate." Andra was interested in gleaning information from the shifters as well. "What would you possibly have to gain by accessing the Shin'Ar's Vault?"

The elf shaped shifter moved forward and leaned in close to Andra. It whispered something in Andra's ear and then leaned back to enjoy the look of shock on Andra's face. As the shifter stood straight, it laughed deep and without restraint. "You see, there is no avoiding this and we will take our rightful place upon Ersetu."

Barurbe could not make out what was said, but from the look upon Andra's face, she knew that whatever was spoken, did not bode well for the other races. She decided that she needed to act quickly and flew from her perch back to her supplies.

Barurbe found a safe place to leave her belongings and quickly shifted into her favored form, the white wolf. Soon the members of her pack that had followed her from Britengate fell into close quarter. She had a close bond with the wolves, and they followed her thoughts as command. She sent them into the clearing to attack the shifters and draw them away from Andra.

The shifters were ill prepared for the convergence of the large beasts. Six great wolves leapt from the surrounding brush and trees. The shifters were surrounded. One after the other, shifters began morphing into forms that would afford them a chance against the grey and black wolves now charging them down. They did not shift fast enough.

It was over quickly for all but a single shifter. The elf had been at the center of the attack near Andra. The added moments allowed it to shift into a large cat-like beast. As the feline jumped over a mauling grey wolf, it was taken in the side by a swift racking of claws from one of the blacks. The cat quickly recovered but not without injury, a large gash spilled blood as the spotted beast recovered its feet and ran for freedom.

Two of the wolves gave chase but were quickly outdistanced by the faster animal. They stopped their pursuit and turned to the call of their mistress. As they ran back and entered the clearing, Barurbe was standing above Andra removing the stakes that held him to the ground.

Andra was near unconsciousness and unable to heal his wounds. If he had been fully aware, he would not have possessed the ability to heal at any rate because of the restraining collar he wore.

Barurbe attempted to remove the collar but could find no sign of fastenings. It appeared to present as a solid ring without any break. As she touched it, she began to feel weak and dizzy. The effects of the active collar worked upon her as well if she continued to touch it. She broke contact and sat back trying to gain her wits.

"Shuran," Andra mumbled. "Get me to the Shin'Ar." Then he passed completely into unconsciousness.

Barurbe sat there quietly for several moments before looking off in the direction the single shifter escaped. She was supposed to join the shifters, but she could not leave Andra out there. She sensed he would not survive his current state without her help. She also knew that Shuran was well on his way to locate the Lil'Du.

"Perhaps the old man Nagutan can help," she decided. Barurbe set about gathering long branches and limbs from nearby trees. She sent three of the wolves out to find some large game so she might skin them to make a gurney on which to carry Andra as comfortably as possible. The others she sent to track the injured shifter and watch where it traveled then meet her back at this clearing to take her there once she returned from Britengate.

It did not take long for the three wolves to return with two large stags and a boar. Barurbe worked meticulously to skin the beasts and remove the intestines. She left the remains for the wolves to feast upon so they might rebuild their strength after the attack and hunting. She would require their help transporting Andra.

Several hours past while Barurbe cleaned and dressed the skins to her satisfaction. She used the fire attempting to dry the skins as best she could but with time against her, she could not afford to trouble over details. After emptying the intestines, she twisted them into long cords, which she used to thread and secure the skins to the limbs and branches.

Once she was satisfied the litter would hold, Barurbe moved Andra onto the contraption and secured him to it with strips of hide after wrapping him in a blanket from her supplies. Using a rope she carried with her, she fashioned a handle stretching from one branch to the other at the lead of the litter. She did the same at the back end.

After securing her supplies to the gurney, Barurbe let her wolves know what she wanted and then shifter herself into the shape of a white wolf. Taking the rope handle in her mouth, she lifted the front of the litter.

One of the wolves took the back rope handle and lifted. Together, the wolves carried Andra and headed along the long path back to Britengate. Along the way, the wolves paused several times to take turns at carrying their charge while the others hunted small game to keep up their strength. It would be a long journey at the pace they kept, traveling too quickly would not be good for Andra.

Night fell, and morning had returned before they reached the North portal of the shield protecting Britengate. Though the Shadow and dark forces had retreated from the area, the city defense shield remained in operation. Shuran left instructions that it was to remain on indefinitely.

Still within the cover of the wood, Barurbe shifted back to her human form and carried the front of the gurney the remaining distance. She reached the gateway to find an asipu keeper standing guard. "I need to find the one called Nagutan, Shuran's grandsire. Andra is hurt."

Though he was leery of the unknown woman accompanied by wolves, the keeper moved forward to observe Andra laying upon the litter. He recognized

Andra and sensed no malice from the odd woman, so he called forth the gate to open. "PETA," he called, and the gate slid into position creating an opening in the shield.

Barurbe led Andra through the opening, followed by the wolves. She instructed them to stay just inside the gateway and not to bother the inhabitants. A nearby weaver came to take the other end of the gurney and together they continued to the center of the city where Nagutan would be found.

Nagutan emerged from the meetinghouse once Barurbe arrived outside. "What has happened?" he asked. Nagutan stepped closer and gasped when he noticed the collar around Andra's neck.

"You know what that is?" Barurbe asked.

Nagutan tittered and stepped around to look at Andra's wounds. "What caused these wounds in his hands?"

Nagutan's avoiding an answer to her question did not put off Barurbe. "He was staked to the ground and wearing that collar. Shifters were questioning him about a vault and a crystal. You did not answer my question."

"What information did they retrieve?" Nagutan asked without looking up from healing Andra's hands.

"Nothing that I could tell, Andra was more interested in finding out what the shifters were about. Now answer my question, what is that thing?"

Heaving a deep sigh, Nagutan finally looked at the collar and then at Barurbe. "It is certain death if not removed soon. It is a restraint created by our makers long ago, used to prevent the use of Essence in Telukukal."

"Shackles in other words? But how is that a death sentence?" Codger asked stepping forward.

"This device was made not of Sumerian magic alone. Something else was used, and before you ask how it was made, I do not know. My maker never told me of its creation. There would be a key of some sort to disengage it, but I doubt the shifters carried it with them." Nagutan continued to titter.

Now Moona was moving into the group. "What are ya gonna do 'bout this then? You must know something for all yer scheming and wonderin' these past millennia?"

"I will go to the source of this distraction and get the key. If I am unable to retrieve it and return within several days, you must contact Shuran."

"What can Shuran do? I know he is powerful, but you mention a magic that is unknown," Codger asked.

"The magic is not unknown to me, only the ability to wield it. Shuran will be his only hope." Nagutan stood and called for healers to come take Andra to the medical housing. "Make him as comfortable as possible, and do not touch the collar."

Nagutan turned to Barurbe. "You can do nothing for him here, I suggest you return to the task Shuran set for you." Not awaiting a response, Nagutan went back inside and gathered a few things before going back outside and walking past everyone without a word.

"Where are ya off to then?" Moona screeched after him.

"To see the Nabusa," was Nagutan's short answer before he disappeared in a swirl of light.

Moona turned back in a huff and started barking orders. "Get movin' with shifty here and take him to a bed and cleaned up! Have mundanes see to him, not like ta be hurt by that collar thing. Codger! See wolf girl to her pack and on their way!"

Barurbe followed Codger to the North exit from the city. She felt hurt by Moona's comments and it must have shown because Codger tried to comfort her.

"Ya mustn' take her words to yer heart dear, she's jus' old an' set in her ways is all. She speaks with venom ta everyone."

Barurbe forced a smile and nodded a farewell before heading out of the gate following her wolves. As she neared the woods, she began to sob and quickened her pace before transforming.

Codger watched as the beautiful young girl shifted into a white wolf and leapt into the forest and out of view.

Chapter Eight

It was midday by the time Barurbe made it back to the clearing where Andra had been found. The other wolves were already present and awaiting her return. Without stopping, she instructed them to lead her to what they found. Seven wolves ran into the woods and northeast after the trail of the wounded shifter.

The pack traveled throughout the day passing by the outskirts of Rivenwood. They found a calm area of water to cross the feeder river and followed the banks until they reached Elmwood. The former human trading town was destroyed when the death walkers attacked many moons previous. Now the settlement was almost rebuilt and inhabited. The pack stopped their approach when Barurbe halted.

From this distance, Barurbe could sense the town was full of shifters. There had to exist hundreds of them for her to sense them at her current position far from the border. She shifted into her human form and prepared herself as best she could for an unknown welcome. She sent the wolves back into the forest, not knowing if she would see them again.

Reluctantly the wolves departed, leaving Barurbe standing on the riverbank alone and shaken. She was on her own for the first time and facing her own kind. She was not sure if they would accept her or do as they had with Andra.

With a final deep breath, she strengthened her resolve to prove her worth to Shuran. Slowly at first she began the walk to Elmwood, before quickening her pace to a brisk walk. As she neared the outskirts of town she was greeted by two men, shifters, dressed in the garb of city wardens.

"Are you lost young woman?" one of the men asked. "You are not from here."

"I was sent away from my home," she sobbed.

A few tears, it seems, affects even shifter men.

The man who spoke pulled a cloth from his waist pocket and held it out for her. "You are one of us are you not?" He allowed his outstretched hand to shift into a claw and back to a human hand. "Where have you come from?"

"I was a ward of the Baron de Drakk. When It was discovered what I was, he forced me from the only home I have ever known," she poured on the tears and sobbing. "I have been wandering the forest for weeks, alone and frightened."

"Come with us child, we will take you in. You are among your own kind now."

Barurbe pulled back the forced tears and allowed them to lead her into town. As they walked the cobblestone streets, she wondered at how the place appeared complete and unmolested by the attacks that left it practically razed to the ground. She turned to one of the men. "What town is this? I thought this area was destroyed by some kind of monsters?"

Laughing, the man looked upon her kindly. "It was my dear, but you will find our people capable of a great many things when we wish. The former humans of this town abandoned it so we have claimed what was left for rot."

The man then stopped and pointed to a tavern and inn, indicating that was their destination.

She followed the men into the tavern to find it full of patrons drinking, eating, and making merriment. Barurbe could not help but smile back at the people who turned and greeted her in kind. A lifted tankard here and a welcoming smile there, she felt as though coming home.

"Dabnik, we have a newcomer to Elmwood. She arrives to us from Drakk where those who she thought family, turned here out for being their better."

The men smiled back at Barurbe at the words that she was better than the Drakk and other Aurderians.

A tall and lean man walked into the room from the kitchens and wiped his hands on the front of his apron. "Welcome home miss-"

"Barurbe," she offered.

"Such a lovely name, it suits you." Dabnik said.

One of the men that brought Barurbe into the inn took Dabnik to the side and conversed softly. Dabnik glanced over at Barurbe and smiled kindly. After they had finished speaking, the two men left and Dabnik escorted Barurbe to a table near the hearth.

"As you are new here, we should make certain you understand what it is we are trying to achieve here in Elmwood," Dabnik said as they sat. He called over a barmaid to bring them ale and plates of food.

"I am afraid I do not understand," she answered attempting to not already assume the plans of the shifters. "Are the shifters not trying to make a home here?"

"Shifter? Oh my dear, you should not refer to our kind in such vulgar terms. We are the Arakharat, the Eighth Race, those the Telukukal Seer, Nabusa created when the weaker seven races of man still crawled in the dirt of Ersetu and fought amongst themselves over pure 'unpolluted' bloodlines."

"Arakharat... I like the sound of that. It is nice to have a name for what I am," she admitted.

"What you are is a young woman new to this town and in need of a roof and occupation. What was it you did back in Drakk?" Dabnik asked.

"I was the ward of the Baron, I mostly looked after the affairs of the household and staff. I suppose I have little to offer." Barurbe had many skills that included hunting, tracking, and dressing game, but she thought better than to present herself as anything more than a pampered and lost child of Aurderia.

"Nonsense girl, you ran an entire royal castle, all be it minor royalty, but that is far grander than running a meek tavern and inn. You will have a room here and take over the running of this establishment," Dabnik insisted.

"Run this entire inn and tavern? I could not, is this, not your place now?"

Dabnik laughed lightly. "That it may be, but I am best suited for the kitchen and butchering of meat. I have not the head for figures and managing staff."

Barurbe took her offered plate when the barmaid returned and sipped her ale. "You are too kind Dabnik, I thank you for your offer and accept."

Dabnik caught himself from snorting out his gulp of ale. "Kind? You see me after a day of running this place and tell me I'm kind." He smiled at her quick loss of a smile. "Oh, not to worry, I think you will straighten this lot out," he said slapping the barmaid's rump. "You will have room and board along with a generous pouch of coin at the end of the week. I will leave all affairs outside of the kitchen to you."

As they lifted their tankards in salute, Barurbe smiled greater inward than out. This was going to be easier than she initially expected. There is no better place to listen and participate in casual conversation than an inn or tavern; she had the best possible position to hear all that went on in Elmwood. With any luck, Arakharats get as loose in the lips as any other race when plied with spirits.

After their meal, Dabnik showed her to a room and had one of the maids fetch her some clothing and personal items from a nearby shop. She was told her first weeks pay would more than cover the cost of the items. She freshened herself and decided to go to work straight away. She busied herself getting to know the staff and some of the regular patrons. It was mid Utu the next day when he walked into the tavern and Barurbe nearly dropped the tray she was holding.

Standing in the entry was the Arakharat, who persuaded her to help take Sulura away from Drakk Castle. It was unlikely that a shifter used the same face as another, and then there was his scent.

All people, be they human, dwarf, Arakharat, or otherwise, had a scent. Barurbe spent so much time as a wolf that it affected her sense of smell, making it acute. His scent was spicy as most other of her kind, but it was overlain with a sickly sweet smell like that of an elf. She wondered whether he spent much of his time in that guise. Then she noticed the limp as he favored his left leg.

When the wolves attacked the Arakharat in the forest glad outside Entensiama, the one that fled was racked in the left flank by the claws of one of the black wolves. Barurbe had to assume this was one and the same man. He did not favor his leg when last they met, but she had to be certain.

Without awaiting his discovery of her presence, she walked out from behind the bar and strode up to him. When he turned to face her, she slapped him hard across the face and stepped back.

His first reaction was to begin to reach for her, but then he recognized her. "Barurbe? What are you doing here?"

"I waited for you. You said you would come for me and teach me about my true people. You never returned and I was left to take the fall for your treachery upon my house." She spat at his feet and turned to walk away. She walked straight into Dabnik.

"What is going on here Barurbe? Has this man assaulted you?" Dabnik seemed to know the other man, but he did not favor him over Barurbe.

"He is the reason I was forced from my home, then he left me there to take responsibility for his actions against my steward the Baron. He spun his untruth and led me against my adopted family."

"Are you unhappy with your own kind?" Dabnik asked.

Taken aback, Barurbe was unsure what Dabnik was getting at. "I am more than happy to know my own race, but that does not excuse the circumstances that brought me here. This man was supposed to come for me and bring me to my people. He left me there to stand accused."

"What is it Tharell did?" Dabnik asked.

"I did as I was ordered before we broke from the Nabusa and her plans. I took the abomination's mother to his hellspawn sister," Tharell answered. "I am sorry I did not return for you, but I was unable. I was genuine in my offer."

Unable to perceive truth or not, Barurbe decided it was best suited to play along, but not too easily. "That remains to be proven," she said and then returned behind the bar.

"Dabnik, when did she arrive?" Tharell asked.

"Just yesterday, she was wandering along the river, tattered and weary. Why, is there something I should know?"

"No, no I only wish I had gone for her when I promised," Tharell said. He looked over at Barurbe with a glint in his eye.

Dabnik stopped Tharell as he moved toward the bar. "I know that look. Do not mess with my new manager or I will not stop her from slapping the snot out of you old friend."

Tharell laughed. "Not to worry, this is a different look entirely. You have no clue as to how valuable this girl is to our cause."

"I do not think I want to know, but I like her and I will not allow you to harm her." Dabnik gave Tharell a warning look that let him know there was business backing up the threat.

Tharell nodded his understanding and made his way to the bar. He took a seat near where Barurbe was sitting and placed a coin on the polished wood surface. "May I order a tankard of your best ale barkeep?"

Barurbe poured a tankard of ale and dropped it on the bar in front of him. She collected the coin and instead of leaving his change, she put the coppers in her bosom. "You can order a keg of our worst yak piss for all I care, so long as you have the coin to pay for it!"

As she turned and walked away, a satisfied smile spread from ear to ear. She could have fun torturing this man so, which would make her getting information from him that much easier. She treated Tharell with the same coolness all evening and instructed the other barmaids to ignore him altogether.

Throughout the evening, Barurbe played her game with Tharell. She could not help but feel sorry for him, but reminded herself that he deserved everything she could throw his way. She kept him waiting for drinks and mused at his requests for food. When she thought he might finally break and leave, she yielded and brought him a plate of food.

When she came out of the kitchen, she found he had moved to a table in the back of the common room. She walked over to him and placed the platter of mutton before him. Every piece of meat was cut from the rump of the beast that was roasted earlier that day.

Tharell scowled at the un-choice cuts of meat but said nothing.

"You have been an ass so I though best bring you a familiar platter," Barurbe quipped. She turned to walk away, but his hand gently reached for her as she expected.

"Please sit a moment and let me explain myself," he pleaded.

Reluctantly, or so she pretended, Barurbe sat down across from Tharell and looked him dead in the eyes. "So talk, I have other customers."

Tharell scanned the near empty room and grinned. "I can see you are in high demand at the moment." He took a bite of his food and chewed it with as much grace as he could muster. After a forced swallow, he cleared his throat and looked at Barurbe. "I would have come for you as promised, but my task was not complete and I was detained until just yestermorn. I was injured and required healing that is not yet complete as well."

"The limp? I noticed when you walked in," she said.

Tharell smiled at her admitting she watched him enter. "I am glad you are here now though, saves me a trip back into that wasteland Drakk. I know it was where you grew into the beauty I see before me, but it is dreadfully barren."

"Be that as it may, Drakk was my home and the Baron was good to me… until you took Sulura from his home and left me to blame." She had no need to act to add the venom in her response. Barurbe was still hurt by the way she was treated until the truth was told. Shuran was giving her a chance to prove her loyalty and now she had to walk the line of two fronts.

Tharell narrowed his gaze upon Barurbe. "It seems a waste, you working here in this place. You have far more talents that we could put to use… elsewhere." Tharell reached up to block the slap that was headed for his face. "I do not mean anything of impropriety, I speak of our cause."

Barurbe pulled her wrist from his grasp and sat back. "And what cause would that be then?"

"For now we gather here in Elmwood, then we will spread out to other towns and wait. Living among the Mundanes and other races of man, until such time when we will take our place, above all, other races and bring order to Aurderia."

Barurbe was feeling uncomfortable and it must have been apparent as Tharell leaned closer to her. "We are better than the others you know, they squander their gifts or hid from the rest of the world. We will not keep secrets or be unwelcoming to outsiders. We shall guide the others to our ways and they will be all the better with our ruling."

"Ruling? So you plan to reestablish the monarchies of old? How is that better, as I recall from lessons in Drakk the monarchs of old had no better time of it?"

Tharell leaned back and smiled. "That was because they could do nothing about the balance that was falling apart and destroying the land."

"And you… we the Arakharat, can do something about that?" Barurbe asked.

"No, not the Arakharat, but your adopted cousin Shuran, he will bring balance back for us, and then we can step in and put our plans into action." Tharell seemed pleased with himself.

Barurbe thought for a moment and then looked at Tharell. "If he is powerful enough to bring about a balance that none before him could do, then how will we take over Aurderia without him stopping us?"

Tharell glanced around and leaned close over the table. "There is a piece of the prophecy that few know. In order for the balance to return to Ersetu, the Shin'Ar must sacrifice himself." Tharell sat back and let Barurbe absorb what he just shared with her. When he felt that she understood, he placed his fork and napkin on his plate. "Yes dear Barurbe, in order to bring balance, Shuran must die."

<u>Chapter Nine</u>

As promised, Magnar and Aglia arrived in what was assumed as morning within the city, to escort them to break their fast and meet with the Elders. Once all were refreshed, dressed, and ready to leave, they exited the building to witness morning deep inside the caverns.

Brilliant white light radiated from the sides of every structure. Shuran noticed that it was not spelled light, but natural in origin. He followed the rays back to several openings high in the upper reaches of the cavern.

Aglia noticed his search. "The same fissures that open to the outside and bring in fresh air, also allow light into the chamber. The Ag'Lu that first began reforming this city, created crystalline surfaces angled to send the rays throughout."

"It is more beautiful than last evening," Vala exclaimed.

Aglia sidled up between Dara and Vala. "Come sisters, we will eat and let Shuran speak with those Elders who choose to attend." Aglia pointed out the tables where the Zidu'Si would sit at the breakfast feast and led them around the aisles of other tables.

"What do you mean those who 'chose' to attend?" Vala asked as she followed Dara and Aglia to a seat.

"Not all the elders are convinced that having the Shin'Ar among us is wise," Aglia said. "Their reasons are unknown, I am not among them nor are those who matter most."

Magnar arrived as the Zidu'Si were sitting down. He nodded at the others and took his seat, which was directly across from Shuran. "Please begin eating, the others will join us as the meal ends. They do not share in the community meals, preferring their isolation."

Shuran and the others helped themselves to the meal laid out for them and all the others in attendance. Unlike meals in the meetinghouse of Britengate, which were loud and lively, the morning meal among the Ag'Lu was quiet and reserved. The Zidu'Si ate with discomfort, feeling the eyes of all the Ag'Lu upon them.

Once the meal was finally at a close, Shuran and the others followed Magnar and Aglia outside the hall and into a chamber nestled behind a tapestry. Inside the room sat several ancient looking Ag'Lu, staring at Shuran with great interest.

Magnar stopped before the dais where the elders sat. "Great Elders of the Ag'Lu, I present for your consideration the Shin'Ar. Shuran has traveled far to request Ukken ana su Geshtu-Bad."

Low murmurs and a few grunts where the initial response to Shuran's relayed request for a meeting to exchange knowledge and wisdom. "What would a young man possess in wisdom that those of the Ad'Lu Elders have not already learned?" one of the Elders asked.

Shuran stepped forward and addressed the ancient men and women of the Ag'Lu. "History, the true history of the times before the races of man. Who the Gods of old were and what they did while they walked the face of Ersetu."

There was an uproar of voices at the mention of knowledge of the Gods. "You dare speak of the Gods as if you know them personally BOY!" the same Elder shouted. Flames began licking at his fingertips.

Shuran was not sure how yet to respond. He had to tread lightly if he expected any help from these people. He was not even certain what help they could give him. That is when the memory came to him, not a memory but a flash of understanding.

He stepped closer and took the hand of the Elder whose fire had spread up

60

his arm, but was not burning his clothing. Shuran's own hand transformed to flame and his fire danced with that of the Elder. In an instant, Shuran joined his shi to the Elders and initiated the Hala'Sa, the connection of souls. Shuran shared his experiences with the old man.

As they joined, both their bodies became flame and rose into the air as one. As the memories and past events flowed from Shuran to the Elder, the flame they created danced and swirled in the air around the others present. Their fires undulated and morphed into the faces and scenes that Shuran was remembering.

The Ag'Lu in the room stood in awe of the sight while the Zidu'Si beamed with excitement watching their Shin'Ar advance in his abilities without the aid of Nergal in his head.

Dara knew exactly what Shuran was doing; her people learned long ago how to achieve Hala'Sa. Though the Gula'Lu transformed into a mercurial state to do so, the premise was the same. Shuran would no doubt get the help of the people who now stood watching and hopeful to learn this state of joining.

The Ag'Lu began gathering beneath the sphere of fire that recalled recent history as well as ancient. Flames formed across their bodies and an expression of joy and hope painted their faces. As they reached up, trying to touch the joined fires, Shuran and the Elder parted and slowly settled back upon the polished obsidian floor.

As Shuran reconstituted his body, he looked down at his clothes lying scorched and useless upon the floor. He had not thought this through completely as he now stood naked before the room full of people. His face turned as red as his prior flame with embarrassment.

Understanding the situation, Bastien removed his cloak and quickly covered Shuran as best he could. He had to hide his smile however, Bastien wanted so much to make a wise comment and laugh but this was not the time. Shuran would hear of this again.

Shuran took the cloak thankfully and wrapped it around his waist. He tried to call a spare set of garments from the Vault, but was unable to get a mental lock on them. Something about the Ag'Lu city or perhaps the depth below ground prevented his getting to them and he scowled in frustration.

"What is it Shin'Ar?" The Elder said as he adorned his unmolested garment.

"I am unable to connect to the Shin'Ar Vault in Durangug to retrieve fresh clothing." Shuran said.

Understanding the reason, the Elder spoke to a page in the room and turned back to the Shin'Sr. "That would be due to the flow of molten rock and metal within the caverns. It produces a magnetic field."

Shuran understood immediately. "This flow must traverse most of the Highlands. That would explain the weakness I feel from the Emmuku'Gu and why the Shadow is unable to attack these lands."

The Elder nodded and then took a bundle of garments from the returning page. He walked out to Shuran and presented him the clothes. "If you find the need to become one with the fires again young son of Coosco, these articles of clothing would better serve, than the hides of your cattle and spinning of wool."

Shuran accepted the clothes gratefully and quickly adorned them. "There was a moment, while we were in Hala'Sa, where I recognized the face of my grandsire in your memories. Can you speak of why he was here and when?"

The Elder smiled and took Shuran by the shoulders. "He was among the Ag'Lu many generations ago. It is your grandsire Nagutan who first led our people on the path to Bartu Shi."

"Flames of the soul?" Dara asked.

The Elder turned to Dara and narrowed his gaze. "Yes dear, and from the sight of your own aura, I believe your people have achieved something much the same but by way of metal element."

Dara smiled back at the old man and nodded, as did Vala when he turned his gaze upon her and looked into her shi as well.

The elder turned back to Shuran and saw that he was fully dressed now and the redness left his face. "You will find that these articles will not burn, and so long as you learn to hold them while burning as living flame, you can carry them with you."

"What are they made from?" Shuran inquired.

"They are from the skins of cave beasts that live deep within the tunnels. They prefer the high temperatures of the deepest caverns and have been observed swimming within the flows of molten fire." The Elder now took Shuran's arm and led him back to the common hall where they first had their morning meal.

"You must tell me of this Compendium and more of the images I witnessed while in Hala'Sa," the Elder said. "I admit I was suspicious of your claims, but having witnessed them through your shi I cannot deny the truth. Others will come to understand soon when I spread what has been learned."

Shuran sat with the Elder as he ate food that remained on the tables. There were still Ag'Lu in the hall dining and they gathered closer to listen to Shuran's stories of the outside world and the history of Ersetu that he recalled from the journal and memories left by Nergal.

They sat in the Hall for several hours, as the events were laid out, starting from Shuran's birth up to the present. On occasion the telling would speak of times long before the races of man. This is when Shuran would recall memories of Nergal, Nagutan, or Gimagala. Since Gimagala and Nagutan were connected to Shuran by means of ancient ties to the Zidu'Si, he could gain access to memories of their times serving Nergal when he was the first Shin'Ar.

The Elders and others listened intently this entire time without interrupting until the point where Shuran spoke of the Urentel, Frost Demons. "What do you think they meant when they spoke of others and living where they were needed?" one of the Elders asked.

"Until recently I was without knowing, but after experiencing a conversation that Orian and Florisia, Queen of the Elves, had with the Dryads I have come to believe that their ancient magic and connection to Ersetu goes beyond the corporeal." Shuran explained what he thought it meant, believing that the Urentel and Dryads were in fact of the same kind of being and took whatever form was necessary to carry out the will of Coosco.

"The Urentel, or whatever they truly call themselves, made mention of there being something more when I claimed to represent the blending of the seven bloodlines. I was not aware of what they meant, but now I think it something to do with the fact I am related to Nagutan and through him Nergal."

The Elder who joined with Shuran stood and took Shuran's hand. "We may not be able to assist knowing the location of this Compendium, but we will help any way we can starting with joining in your fight against the Shadow."

Shuran accepted the aid with honor and the Elders departed to leave for a place to commune and work at mastering the Hala'Sa. Magnar and Aglia saw to gathering a force of Ag'Lu warriors and making preparations for when Shuran returned from the Lil'Du. It was decided that Moltar, Jade, and the other drakkon would wait among the Ag'Lu until the Zidu'Si returned for them.

The next morning, the Zidu'Si were ready for the journey to the Pillars of Wind and Aglia was there to see them off. "The winds shift unexpectedly and without warning Shin'Ar. This is what keeps outsiders away."

"Has no one attempted to fly over or around the storms?" Avrank asked.

Aglia laughed. "If only it were that easily done, the winds will reach out for you should you attempt this. If you were to fly around you would circle the great barrier. As far as we know this windstorm surrounds the Lil'Du City and to fly above would be higher than a living creature could survive as the air becomes too thin to breath and freezing cold at great altitude.

"You will make the Pillars by foot, by nightfall from here if you take the Eastern flow by diamond ship. One of our pilots will ferry you to the furthest point in the flow before he must turn back. The flow dives deep into the world soon after."

Shuran and the Zidu'Si parted from the Ag'Lu and boarded a large vessel floating upon the bank of a massive flow of molten earth. The ship was crafted of pure black diamond on the exterior hull. The interior was lined with the skins of deep cavern dwelling lizards, and benches were perfectly fitted into the curves of the vessel. The material used for the benches was porous and dark grey, volcanic in origin.

As soon as all were aboard, the Ag'Lu pilot un-roped and soon the boat was lumbering along at a steady pace down the lava river. The ship quickly picked up speed and soon they were gliding along tunnels burned into the world deep below the surface. The Ag'Lu city, Mikidisati Kitus, was far from view and before them was the eerie glow of menacing stalactite filled tunnels illuminated by the red glow from the molten-rock river. The Zidu'Si each imaged themselves traveling deep into the open jaws of some fiery serpent.

Several hours passed as they had traversed the winding river before they reached the port where they would disembark. The ship glided into a carved out slip and the Zidu'Si exited the craft, followed by the Ag'Lu pilot.

"I will wait here for your return," the pilot offered.

Shuran shook his head and placed his hand upon the man's shoulder. "That will not be necessary friend. If we are successful in gaining the Lil'Du's aid, something tells me we will return quicker than our journey here."

64

The pilot returned to his vessel and began the arduous trip back to Mikidisati Kitus.

Shuran and the others began the long walk up the stairs carved into the tunnels leading to the surface. It was nearly four hours before they reached the end of the tunnels and fresh air. The late afternoon Utu was still beating down on the barren landscape as they emerged from the fissure. Their destination was visible and immense even from the distance they still had to walk.

The Pillars of Wind were far more imposing than any of the Zidu'Si imagined. As they neared, the funnels of wind twitched in anticipation, as might a spider awaiting a fly landing upon its web. As far as they could see, the twisting winds stretched in each direction, standing in defiance of any who dared venture too near.

Shuran stretched out with his Essence fueled senses to see what he might in regard to the size and strength of the obstacle now keeping them from proceeding east. What he found was a confirmation of the tales relayed back in Mikidisati Kitus, by the Elders. The blockade was a deliberate border of protection that circled a structure within. Shuran was unable to penetrate the winds enough to get a better understanding of what lay within.

"How do you suppose we get past this blockade of turbulent wind?" Mallick asked.

Shuran scratched his head and shrugged. "We cannot go over or around it, perhaps the answer is to go under it."

Avrank took that as his cue. He stepped forward and focused his mind on the earth below and in front of him. At first there was a low vibration that soon gave way to a roiling and rumbling as the ground before him opened up and a mound of upturned rock and dirt trailed off toward the barrier. The tunnel opened up and continued on, past the funnels.

Finished and feeling proud of himself, Avrank walked up to the opening and turned to present it to the others. "You see, sometimes in order to accomplish something big, you must learn to think small." Just when he was beaming brightest, his expression changed as his feet started to slip toward the tunnel entrance.

Chapter Ten

A funnel of the twisting winds moved over the tunnel exit from the far side and was creating a vacuum. The force of the air was pulling in Avrank. As his feet finally lifted from the ground and he began flying into the opening, a flowing metallic hand wrap around his wrist.

Dara stretched out her form, having converted her lower extremities into heavy metal and used her upper body to stretch out as mercury and grab hold of Avrank. "Quickly, someone collapse the interior of that tunnel. I cannot hold him for much longer."

Shuran reached out with the Essence and pulled at the interior of the tunnel. As the tunnel fell, the debris was getting sucked out the other end from the force of the funnel. "I need help, the vortex is pulling the rocks out as I collapse the tunnel."

While Orian, Mallick, Gregoran, and Bastien chose areas of the tunnel to collapse, Vala took hold of Dara around the waist to help hold her as she started to slide forward. The tunnel began to fall in several parts and the funnel strength was defeated. As the vacuum decreased, Avrank was pulled free of the opening and Dara recomposed herself.

Everyone sat upon the ground panting and catching his or her breath. Each of the Zidu'Si stared at the clouds and funnels reaching down, ready to take them in turn and toss them to the far reaches of the world. They looked defeated.

Bastien was the first to stand. He looked at the twisting winds and took out his wand. He contemplated a moment before looking back at the others. "I have an idea but I need some help."

The others stood and gathered around him so that he could give them each a task. Bastien asked Vala to pull moisture from the air and clouds. Mallick needed to retrieve a spell from the Vault to form his own cloud. Avrank needed to break down earth and dirt into dust particles while Orian charged them with electricity. Dara was to reform the minerals in the ground into a metallic track that took a specific path into the barrier of twisting winds.

"What do you need me to do as help," Shuran asked.

"You are the only one of us with a measure of air abilities, we need to try and push our own little storm into the Pillars." Bastien held a grin on his face that said, 'This is going to work'.

Once all the pieces of his plan were ready, Bastien gave the signal for everyone to do their part. As Vala called forth the moisture, Mallick cast his spell to collect it and formed a cloud. As the moisture fed it, Bastien began his spell that lifted the cloud and then lifted the electrically charged dust hovering in front of it. Shuran began pushing their storm cloud toward the route Bastien planned and where Dara created a track of metal upon the surface of the ground headed for the center of the Pillars.

With a last wave of his wand, the dust entered the cloud and Bastien sent the cloud to spinning in the opposite direction than those in the Pillars of Wind. As the dust swirled in and the funnel began to form, bolts of lightning crackled and threatened to strike down. As the cloud gained in speed and the funnel reached the ground, Bastien let go of the spell and it moved of its own accord.

"Explain to us how this is going to work," Mallick said.

Bastien put his wand away and turned. "As the storm gains in strength and charge, it will continue to follow the metal trail Dara set. Once it reaches the Pillars, the opposing rotation will break apart the storm where it hits. Then we can pass through."

Everyone was impressed and turned their gaze upon the collision as it began. Just as Bastien predicted, the storms colliding caused a large gap to open in the Pillars and they could see a large mountain beyond. Atop the mountain was a lush and vast forest with waterfalls that cascaded down to disappear within the creases of the mountain.

As they began their fast walk toward the opening, they noticed the storm begin to close. They all took up running and Dara grabbed Avrank.

"I apologize, but I think your legs might not carry you fast enough Avrank," Dara said.

Avrank smiled and said nothing.

They all made it just before the storm closed behind them. As they caught their breath, the group turned to observe the mountain before them. There did not seem to exist, any stairs or other means of reaching the top easily. Everyone was having the same thought, but it was Avrank who spoke.

"I don' suppose we could simply make our own steps to the top could we?" Avrank said from the comfort of Dara's arms.

Suddenly embarrassed for not remembering to put Avrank down, Dara turned a shiny red in the face and quickly set Avrank on his feet. "Sorry, I was caught up in the excitement."

"I have that effect on the ladies, worry not my fair maiden," Avrank said.

Orian stepped up and cracked Avrank in the back of the head when Dara turned away. "More likely she was reminded of holding someone's swaddled sprat, Turd!"

Before they could continue the bantering, a charge in the air alerted them to some sort of presence. An enormous face shimmered into existence and looked down upon them.

"Welcome Shuran Shin'Ar and your Zidu'Si, we have been expecting you. We would thank you not to deface our home with the creation of steps we would only wear away with the winds. Please gather close and we shall lift you to our city." The face then dispersed as the winds began to swirl around their feet.

Shuran and the others gathered close just in time. The air pushed below their feet and began to lift them skyward. As they looked down, the ground grew further away with every breath and Avrank lost the contents of his stomach. The air lifting them caught the vomit and lifted it faster than the Zidu'Si and it sailed up into the air.

"Sorry, I dislike heights," Avrank said as he closed his eyes.

Their ascent began to slow quickly as they neared the top of the mountain. As they approached, they began moving in toward a ledge where they could see two frail looking figures staring down at them.

Once back on the ground, Avrank cleaned himself and looked up wondering what became of his sick. He did not have long to wonder about it as Orian stepped over to him red-faced and covered in Avrank's released lunch. "I was wonderin' where that went."

Orian was not amused as he cleaned himself.

The other Zidu'Si were having a good chuckle when the two Lil'Du approached them. They were excessively thin and narrow framed. Their skin gave off a glistening shine and was slightly transparent. "Welcome, the Shin'Ar and his Zidu'Si less one. The Chancellor is awaiting your arrival in the city center of Aluanu, City of the Sky." They turned and walked back to their stations watching over the Pillars.

The road leading to Aluanu was a winding path through forested land that grew unnaturally lush atop the plateau of the mountain. The elevation the Zidu'Si now found themselves would normally be far too high to provide breathable air let alone support the abundance of plant life that seemed to thrive in the Lil'Du home. Above them, they saw airborne vessels of a strange kind that floated through the skies like enormous bladders. From a distance, they could see people within the carriages beneath the massive balloons.

Shuran was not the only one among the Zidu'Si to appear confused at their situation. Orian and Avrank both stepped off the path and into a wooded area to examine the plants and trees up close. What they discovered was that the fauna and flora were unlike any known throughout Aurderia. Though there was nothing obviously foreign in the foliage, it somehow seemed ancient.

There were also dangers to poking about with plants that were unknown, as Avrank quickly observed when he witnessed a small insect fly into a brightly colored flower to partake from its nectar.

The flower closed its petals around the insect in a flash of movement that caused Avrank to draw back in surprise. As the petals constricted and twisted, the buzzing resistance of the insect within halted and the flower opened again. Two tiny wings gently fell from the stamen and flitted on the breeze.

Avrank made his way back to the safety of the roadway. "I would not suggest picking the local flowers, they are a bit aggressive."

Orian nodded in agreement as he stepped up beside his friend, having witnessed something similar in his exploration. "The trees do not seem all that agreeable either." Orian picked the last bit of vine from his arm as they continued to walk toward the grand domed city before them.

"I think it best we stay on the paved road and not disturb the native plants," Shuran said. He watched both his inquisitive friends as they explored the area and was amused by their observations. As amusing as it had been to witness Orian, a former Forest Ranger, wrestling with a vine that threatened to drag him to the waiting maw of some carnivorous tree, he sensed the danger that lay in wait beyond the safety of the road. "It would appear that the vegetation is not vegetarian."

As the eight of them walked the path toward the city, they observed the dome that covered the center of the plateau and completely encased Aluanu. The shield did not give the charge of an Essence energy barrier as that of Britengate. It did not have an energy signature at all, which added to the mystery of the Lil'Du home.

Shuran and the Zidu'Si made their final approach to the glistening dome of the city, Shuran was able to reach out and physically touch the barrier. "It is glass," he said. "Nothing more than clear glass formed into a stupendous dome over the city. A sizable strike of force would likely break such a structure. What on Ersetu would possess a race to construct something so weak as a defensive shield of glass?"

"Why would you assume it is a shield for defense," came a soft voice from behind them.

Shuran and the others turned to find the lithe and thin framed Lil'Du girl who spoke to them. Shuran moved toward the girl in greeting and she stepped forward to be met. "I am Shuran, Shin'Ar and this is my Zidu'Si."

"I am known as Coralil among friends, are you here as a friend Shin'Ar?" Coralil asked.

Shuran was put off by the question after the warm greeting by the guards and the apparition that lifted them from the plains below. "The Shin'Ar and Zidu'Si are friends to all who align themselves with all that is good in the world. Am I wrong in assuming the Lil'Du follow the Light?"

Coralil smiled and bowed her head. "You have a friend in me Shuran

Shin'Ar." The doors to the main gate began to open and Coralil disappeared into the surrounding wood. She called back to him as she departed. "Trust your instincts and beware the one who would keep you nearest."

Shuran turned back from looking upon the open gates to find Coralil gone, but heard her departing words. He faced the gates again and took the lead entering the city. "Keep your eyes open, something is not right here," he said to the Zidu'Si mentally.

The Zidu'Si followed Shuran into the city of the Lil'Du, mindful of the concern that Shuran held. Though there was something amiss, they all could not help but be sidetracked by the beauty that met their exploring gaze.

The light entering the great domed city played upon the gleaming glass surfaces of the buildings that stretched skyward. Every building was constructed from crystal of various colors and shined with a radiance that took their breath away. From every window, the slender and statuesque Lil'Du stood waving and calling out greetings to the arrival of the Shin'Ar and his Lil'Du.

While the Zidu'Si delighted in the welcoming, Shuran sensed an underlying unease coming from the people as they passed. Something was wrong here in Aluanu and Shuran felt that somehow, his presence was related. He put those thoughts to the back of his mind while they approached the center of the city, where an ornately dressed Lil'Du man stood upon the steps of a towering citadel.

The man raised his hands to the sky. "Welcome Shin'Ar and the Zidu'Si, we have awaited your arrival." He lowered his arms and beckoned Shuran closer. "Come, you are among friends and we shall celebrate. I am Chancellor Ugamma."

Shuran stepped up to accept Ugamma's hand. "I am Shuran. How is it the Lil'Du knew of my coming?"

"Why it was my advisor Kettanu who met with the asipu Nagutan some eight years past. Word of your birth brought hope to the Lil'Du that we might once again serve the Zidu'Si." Ugamma said.

Shuran narrowed his gaze. "It was thought the Lil'Du never left this place but to trade with the Ag'Lu."

"Though we restrict our exposure to the lesser peoples, Kettanu has taken the risk of venturing the lands to provide me with updates of what transpires in the savage lands beyond our city. He takes a great risk for our people."

Shuran heard the slight and felt the old prejudices from this man, but underneath he felt something else from Ugamma that he could not quite place. "I would like to meet this Kettanu and hear what he thinks of the current state of Ersetu."

"All in good time Shin'Ar, first we shall allow you rest before the ceremony." Ugamma motioned for the attendants behind him to escort the Zidu'Si and Shuran to guest rooms in the citadel.

As they left, Ugamma walked down the street and greeted Kettanu in the shadow of a neighboring structure. "Is this necessary Kettanu?" Ugamma asked.

"The Shin'Ar must remain among the Lil'Du if he is to survive. We must keep him here for the sake of all Ersetu," Kettanu said, and then watched as Ugamma returned to the citadel. He stepped back into the shadows and lifted a scrying dish to his face. "The Anzillu is among the Lil'Du, it shall happen this night."

<u>Chapter Eleven</u>

The ceremony was scheduled to commence in two days time. Shuran and the Zidu'Si were to the honored guests of the Lil'Du and were given full tours of the city. Though they were afforded every courtesy by their hosts, many of the Lil'Du they encountered during their walks through Aluanu seemed to hide behind a facade of indifference. Not all the Lil'Du appeared to welcome the arrival of Shuran and his comrades.

While walking the open market, Shuran stopped at a stall providing fresh fruits and vegetables. He marveled at the fresh and strange items that were laid out by the farmer behind the counter. As he perused the selection, a Lil'Du shopper openly snubbed him and walked away from the stall with a look of disdain.

The seller tittered after the citizen and called to Shuran. "Do not judge us all by the faults of the few, Shin'Ar. We do not all fall prey to the words of the pretender."

Shuran saw both fear and hope behind the eyes of the stranger. "I am afraid that not all the Lil'Du are as welcoming as we had been led to believe. Is there something I need to know?"

"A great deal you need to know," the farmer said. "This is not the place to speak freely, but I would caution you to beware the pretender. He has the ear of the Chancellor and stirs the people of Aluanu."

"I have heard of this pretender, who is it that you speak of?" Shuran asked.

Before the farmer could answer, a city guard began to approach his stall. "Thank you for your compliments Shin'Ar, I grow these delightful plants in the eastern fields outside the walls. One could see my fields best from the weeping stone." The farmer glanced from Shuran to the guard that approached.

Shuran noticed the guard watching their conversation with more scrutiny than should be necessary of an honored guest and mere farmer. When he turned back to the farmer, he was gone. Shuran took his parcel that the farmer left him and headed back to his lodgings to await the Zidu'Si and attempt to contact Nagutan. Shuran delighted in the delicious fruits the farmer gave him and pondered the worries that cracked on the edge of the old man's voice when he spoke of the pretender. Shuran pulled up his sleeve to reveal his communication stones secured to a silver arm brace. He tapped the red stone that would connect him to friends in Britengate. Of all those who might answer, Moona was the one whose voice he heard.

"What is takin' ya so long boy? Ya need ta get back here soon," she shouted.

Shuran grimaced at her loud voice. "Moona there is no need to yell. I need to speak to Nagutan."

Moona explained that Nagutan had gone to look for something, but she did not elaborate. She advised that the Shadow had not returned and that Barurbe had reported that she was heading back Northeast toward the river villages. Moona did not advise that Andra was returned wounded for fear Shuran would abandon his quest to return and help prematurely.

When the Zidu'Si returned, Shuran had finished speaking with Moona, and he advised them that Nagutan had left Britengate. The Zidu'Si shared their experiences through the day, being snubbed and welcomed in equal measure.

"I do not understand what the issue of our presence has presented," Vala said.

Shuran shook his head as he eyed the parcel from the farmer and looked closer. He noticed a folded slip of paper in the string on the bottom of the bundle. "Perhaps this may shed light upon the subject." Shuran opened the note and read its contents.

"The note says only, best seen from the weeping stone at dusk," Shuran said.

"The man said something similar when a city guard became far more interested in our conversation than seemed necessary. I think I must visit this location to get answers."

Shuran had time before taking evening meal and being subjected to the Chancellor's ceremony that evening. He decided to seek out this Kettanu fellow. As he walked the citadel, he found no help in locating the man who seemed to pull the strings of the Lil'Du government. When he came across the Chancellor, he was assured that he would meet Kettanu that evening.

As the day wore on, Shuran paced his room much to the aggravation of Bastien and Mallick who kept him company.

"Shuran! Would you please seat your backside down. You will wear a groove in the glass floor," Bastien complained. "If the farmer meets you at this 'weeping stone' place, then perhaps you will get the answers you hope to find."

"I wish you would let one of us accompany you Shuran," Mallick said. "I do not like you going out alone, what if it is some sort of trap?"

"I am confident the farmer was sincere in his warning, it is not the first time we have heard about this pretender." Shuran replied.

"It would be far less obvious if one of the Zidu'Si slipped away after dinner. You would be missed," said Mallick.

After a lengthy debate, Shuran finally relented and agreed that Bastien would meet the farmer in his stead. He would carry a crystal and use its power for a transport spell in case of emergency.

The evening festivities finally began with a dinner in honor of the Shin'Ar accompanied by music and several long-winded speeches by various important houses among the Lil'Du citizenry.

When he inquired about the point of these speeches, Shuran found that these were the families that hoped to gain favor with the Shin'Ar in hopes that a suitable member for the Zidu'Si would be found among one of their households.

As the meal drew to a close, the ceremony began. The sun was setting quickly as evening approached. The altitude of the city provided for longer exposure to Utu's rays than would normally be experienced upon the lower plains and valleys. Bastien quietly took his leave and slipped away with only a thought. "I will keep you informed," he shared with the Zidu'Si and Shuran.

As Bastien made his exit, he cloaked himself and skirted along the walls to avoid the many Lil'Du that gathered in the halls for the ceremony planned to welcome the Shin'Ar. He quickly found a doorway out onto the walkway that lead off toward the eastern exit of the city walls. Passing through the gateway was easily accomplished as there were no doors or guards at this side of the dome.

While Bastien was safely away and searching for the farmer, Shuran and the others were enduring an oratorios opening to the ceremonial welcoming of the Shin'Ar. Once the extended narrative describing the times of peace and hope that accompanied the first Shin'Ar ended, Shuran saw the man who must be Kettanu.

Mallick also noticed the man whispering in the ear of Ugamma. "Do you suppose that man is Kettanu?" he asked.

Kettanu stopped speaking and spared a glance in their direction. Ugamma then looked as well and smiled as Kettanu stepped around the Chancellor to approach Shuran and the Zidu'Si.

"Greetings and welcome, Shin'Ar and Zidu'Si. I am Kettanu, advisor to the Chancellor. It is a true honor to meet you," Kettanu managed. "Not since the wielder Nagutan visited our city, has there been such occasion to celebrate."

Shuran did not miss the undertone of disgust as the man labored to get the words free of his tongue. He also noticed the peculiar and unmistakable smell. "Kettanu, please call me Shuran. You are equally well met. I had hoped to speak with you of Nagutan's visit. You are a busy man as I have looked to speak with you before this eve and found difficulties in locating you. Have you only recently returned to Aluanu as well?"

Noticing Shuran's ploy, Kettanu smiled and excused himself. "Perhaps we can speak of his visit here another time. I must return to my Chancellor's side for the ceremony. I do hope you will accept our hospitable offers this evening." Maintaining his disingenuous smile and demeanor, Kettanu slinked his way back to the Chancellor's table and resumed whispering in Ugamma's ear.

"He seems rather tall for a Lil'Du from those I have encountered," Dara said.

Shuran nodded back at Kettanu, who continued to watch the Shin'Ar closely. "That is because he is not a Lil'Du."

Surprised by this revelation, the Zidu'Si all looked at Kettanu out of reflex.

Kettanu's expression changed to one of concern and he spoke one last thing to the Chancellor before retreating from the hall.

Bastien made his way through the throngs of vegetation and trees leading in the assumed direction of the weeping stones. Earlier in the evening he spent time scanning the outskirts of the city to the East from atop the towering buildings of the city center. There was but one outcrop of stone and boulders that were viewable, though the trees and plants could easily have hidden others from view.

More than once, he was required to spell vines of trees that threatened to drag him off into the brush. When he finally made it to the rocks, he found he must have the spot they were to meet right. Water poured steadily from cracks in the rock face as though the stone was crying. From the opposite side of the weeping stone came a young woman.

"You are not the Shin'Ar," she said. "You are the one they call Bastien, the human weaver of the Zidu'Si."

Bastien approached the female Lil'Du cautiously. "And you do not appear to me the older gentleman farmer that Shuran met in the market. Though I do recognize you as she who shared a warning word upon our arrival."

"You are observant, that is good. I am Coralil. You will need to use that skill to see past the lies of the pretender. My father was the farmer this day and he has disappeared, so I came in his stead." The Lil'Du girl stifled a cry at the mention of her father being missing.

"What is happening in this city?" Bastien asked as he tried to comfort Coralil.

Coralil told Bastien of the calm and secluded times that preceded the twin stars. Until such time the Lil'Du learned of the prophecy and the coming of the Shin'Ar, they lived in peace in their city above the clouds. Other than the rare occasion when a contingent would visit the Ag'Lu for trading, only one ever ventured outside the city, Kettanu. Once the stars appeared, he left the city in the still of that night. When he returned the many moons later, he brought news of the birth of the Shin'Ar. His excursions into the realms of Aurderia increased and the Chancellor became all the more paranoid.

"Not all Lil'Du welcome your arrival, Bastien. Some among Aluanu would remain hidden in seclusion until the other races wiped one another from the face of Ersetu," Coralil said.

"I take that you are not among those people?" Bastien asked.

She smiled and looked up at Bastien. "We have kept ourselves hidden for too long. The shame of our race upon the first Shin'Ar must be reversed and the pretender be removed from our company."

"Who is Kettanu?" Bastien asked.

"That is a very good question, young human weaver," Kettanu said as he approached the stones. "And who is this young Lil'Du whispering upon the wind?" His hands raised and a glowing blue orb formed.

Bastien immediately grabbed the crystal in his hand and hooked his arm around Coralil's. He spoke his transport spell quickly as the orb hit his hand and the crystal was lost from his grip. The spell however took them as far as the outside of the city where they then began to run for the citadel.

Kettanu retrieved the crystal where it fell. As he rolled it around his hand, a smile spread across his face and he vanished.

<u>**Chapter Twelve**</u>

The celebration was in full swing when Kettanu finally returned to his Chancellors side. Moments earlier, Shuran received thoughts from Bastien as he ran for the building with Coralil. Several times they were delayed as they waited for guards to run past. Something was stirring and Bastien had to make it back to Shuran.
Shuran watched Ugamma and Kettanu closely as they returned his stare.
Ugamma stood and raised his hands. A strong wind blew over the crowd, immediately silencing the revelry. "We have come to the time of the evening where we must extend our most honorable guests the gift most befitting their station."
Ugamma walked down to the center of the hall and beckoned Shuran and the Zidu'Si join him there. Once they approached, Ugamma turned to Shuran and narrowed his eyes at him. "Where is the human weaver Bastien, I do not see him among your Zidu'Si Shin'Ar?"
"Bastien will be among us momentarily, he returns from-" Shuran was cur off by Kettanu still standing upon the dais.
"Spying and consorting with a dissident!" Kettanu yelled.
"Is this true Shuran Do you plot against us?" Ugamma said as he stepped away from Shuran and the others.

They were now alone in the center of the hall and surrounded by Lil'Du. Shuran started toward the Chancellor when he felt the pressure from all sides that prevented him from moving. The rest of the Zidu'Si were likewise held in place.

The Chancellor resumed his seat next to Kettanu. "And here I thought us friends, Shin'Ar. We would have offered you a safe haven among the clouds until such time that the people of Aurderia were erased from the world by their own hatred and greed."

Kettanu moved toward Shuran now, allowing Shuran to catch a glimpse of the Abnu Emuq in his hand. "Perhaps he is no different from the Anzillu of the Sikil Mah." He then crept closer to Shuran and whispered so that only he could hear. "If it were up to me I would have these fools kill you where you stand."

Shuran tried to speak, but the wind was taken from him by a wave from Kettanu's hand. He wondered how the shifter had mastered the air elemental magic. He must have Lil'Du blood running through his veins. Shuran was not able to move, but he could reach out with his shi. He reached for the mind of Ugamma.

"You must listen," Shuran sent him. He could see the Chancellor raise his brow at the intrusion. "Kettanu is not what he appears."

Ugamma wavered in his hold on the Zidu'Si and Shuran.

Kettanu sensed this and moved to take control of the situation. "Do not be swayed by these abominations, my Chancellor."

"You must listen to the Shin'Ar, the pretender must stop whispering in your ear," Coralil shouted as she and Bastien entered the room.

Kettanu raised a hand to Bastien and sent a concussive wave of air at him. "You see they move against you with the dissidents."

Ugamma weakened his hold on Shuran as he struggled through the fog that coated his mind. Eight years of the building influence of Kettanu peeled away from his consciousness and anger began to replace the spell of compulsion and persuasion. "What have you done Kettanu?" He shouted and moved his influence from Shuran and the Zidu'Si to Kettanu. "What would compel my closest friend and counsel of the last hundred years to conspire against the edicts of the Lil'Du?"

Kettanu responded with a wicked laugh. "You think us friends you fool? I spent the last century swallowing the bile that accompanied every word I spoke to you and your inferior kind. Once news of the birth of the children was approaching, I finally saw the light at the end of the cavern."

"You will not see the light for a very long time where I plan to see you placed," Ugamma promised.

Again Kettanu responded with a maniacal laugh and spit upon the floor. "You will not hold the likes of the Arakharat!" Kettanu gripped the crystal and abruptly disappeared leaving nothing but particles of the shattered crystal dropping to the ground.

Shock and surprise waned and Ugamma ran down from his seat to where Kettanu stood moments before. "Find him! I want answers for what all that has transpired."

"You will not find him in the Lil'Du lands Chancellor. The stone he carried was an Abnu Emuq. It is likely this Lil'Du impostor used it to power his transport back to his people," Shuran explained.

"How would he accomplish such a thing, the Lil'Du have no gift for spell casting," asked Ugamma. "And where would such a powerful stone have come into his possession?"

Bastien approached with Coralil. "I am afraid Chancellor, that is the fault of my own. The Arakharat attacked Coralil and me as we met in the shadow of the weeping stones. His spell knocked the stone from my hand as we escaped using a similar weaving to return here."

Ugamma shook his head clear and began pacing the floor. "Weaving and subterfuge, I am only now coming to realized the influence that 'thing' had over me for all these years." Though his anger abated, the leader of the Lil'Du became overcome with remorse and embarrassment for being led astray and endangering his people.

The celebration no longer held the joyous atmosphere and the guests quickly dispersed as Ugamma, Shuran, and the Zidu'Si left the hall to confer in the Chancellor's chamber. "What I wish to know is if this shifter or Arakharat being, was Kettanu from the start or if the man who was my friend was at some time replaced."

"How long do you feel that you were influenced?" Shuran asked. "That may provide some point in time to think upon. Perhaps you may remember a time when this Kettanu changed, but I think it likely the shifter was among your people for some time before the birth of myself and sisters."

"Sisters?" Ugamma asked. "I was told that it was twins of prophecy?"

Shuran explained how the prophecy was interpreted many ways. The twins were actually triplets and of the two girls, one was sacrificed while the other was now a tool of the Shadow. While he retold the events of his birth and the time leading up to his arrival among the Lil'Du, Ugamma listened intently without interruption. When Shuran spoke of Nagutan's visit to the Lil'Du is when Ugamma paused Shuran's story.

"Nagutan, now that is a name I have not heard tell of in many centuries. I am afraid that he was never here among the Lil'Du. I have no doubt that he shuns our kind since long before the time of the Sikil Mah."

Shuran was confused by the story of Nagutan having visited the Lil'Du. "I was led to think he had been here, the Arakharat said as much as did you."

"I am afraid that was the influence of the spell. I would not so easily forget facing Nagutan again after the last time we spoke." Ugamma said. "He requested the assistance of the Lil'Du in some plan to defy the Gods. When we refused, Nagutan placed the winds upon our borders."

"Nagutan created the Pillars of Wind? What purpose would that serve, you are air element Essence wielders?" Bastien asked.

Ugamma grunted as he poured himself a glass of wine. "We were not always as strong of wind as we are this day. When first the winds gathered, the Lil'Du could not manipulate them as we learned to do over our millennia of isolation. They were designed to imprison us until we learned our lesson."

"And what lesson was that, if I might inquire without offense," Shuran asked.

Again Ugamma grunted. "I am afraid you would have to ask Nagutan to find an answer to your question. It was not until after we learned to manage the winds well enough to begin venturing from our city, that we saw Nagutan again. He was there, at the base of our mountain waiting as though he knew we would escape.

"He advised me that the debt of my forefathers would need to repay one day and that it would be the Lil'Du who would hold the last piece to rebuilding the Zidu'Si. I think this Kettanu must have wanted to prevent our people from assisting. He wanted us to keep you here in Aluanu."

Shuran pondered what Ugamma said and tried to make sense of the words. He also thought back to the last words Kettanu had said about not being up to him that Shuran should live. "I wonder who exactly these Arakharat align themselves?"

"Are they not agents of this Shadow?" Ugamma asked.

Shuran shook his head. "I do not believe they are in league with the Shadow and the darkness it creates. They perhaps colluded in some respects, but I think it is only to further their own agenda, whatever that may be."

Before they could discuss matters further, a guard entered the hall in a panic. "Kettanu, he has been spotted entering the Bitilu'Bir," the man shouted.

Ugamma gasped in horror. "No, it cannot be! Quickly we must get to the Temple of Light and stop him before he kills us all."

Without asking questions, they all ran after Ugamma. The man moved quickly for his advanced age, which Shuran was uncertain of but estimated at least well over a millennia. As they ran for the temple, Shuran and the others began to struggle as the air seemed as though it were getting thinner. Shuran soon realized the Bitilu'Bir must be where the Lil'Du maintain their elemental hold on the air that allows them to survive at this great altitude.

When they finally arrived within the temple, they found Kettanu attacking the Lil'Du inside.

Within the central chamber was a grand statue of their Goddess Hebat, Lady of the Sky. Encircling the statue was twenty-four platforms on which lay Lil'Du men and women, their soul purpose to maintain control of the winds and air over Aluanu. They worked in shifts and would rotate duties only a few at a time. Until they were relieved, their work kept them in a trance and completely vulnerable.

"The creature has already killed ten of the watchers, maintaining the system requires no more than five be replaced at any time. Lady Hebat, what are we to do?" Coralil cried.

It was Ugamma who answered. "We need to get watchers in to replace those who have been slain. I need aid in getting every last Lil'Du into the city dome and we must seal the gates."

Shuran nodded and looked toward Kettanu. Ugamma grimaced at knowing what Shuran must do, and he left the temple with the others, leaving Shuran to the business of dispatching the shifter.

Kettanu glared at Shuran with hatred and rage as he approached the next Lil'Du. "I will destroy you all and prevent the Zidu'Si rising again. My mistress will not be pleased but since I could not return to her with that inferior Emuq Abnu, I will do what I must." Kettanu inched his way toward the Lil'Du lying vulnerable upon the platform. He had great difficulty moving as the winds we quickly being pulled from the chamber.

The Lil'Du on watch were struggling to maintain their hold on the great elemental working that provided breathable air for the city. As they writhed and convulsed in obvious pain, Kettanu sent a charge of energy into the next man. As the man died, the remaining hold on the winds weakened further.

Shuran was swept off his feet as the gusts of wind in the chamber increased. He grabbed hold of a spire as he slid past and was able to anchor himself. He steadied in time to find Kettanu advancing on the next watcher and raise his hands. Shuran thrust out his own hands toward the watchers as Kettanu released his assault. Shuran erected shields over those who remained to fight the winds escape.

Kettanu raged against Shuran's interference. "You should never have been allowed to live. I do not understand what possessed the mistress to allow your existence, but I will do what she is unwilling."

With the Lil'Du watchers protected, only Shuran remained as a target in the central chamber of the Bitilu'Bir. Shuran and the Arakharat stalked each other in the chamber, throwing bolts and spells.

Outside, the air was getting thinner. As the Lil'Du scrambled to reach the expected protection of the dome, Zidu'Si were stationed at the two gates helping them fight against the debris that was being sucked out the gateways. As they threw spells and elemental forces at the objects, the Lil'Du pouring in fought to hold back the winds that threatened to push them back out the way they came. The temperature outside the dome was falling fast.

As the last of the Lil'Du managed to enter the city's main dome, the Zidu'Si worked to create a shield over the eastern gate that did not have doors to close and seal. Once sealed, the winds died down considerably, but there was yet a whirlwind surrounding the temple. The Zidu'Si made their way back there as quickly as their feet would carry.

When they arrived, they found Shuran pinned to the wall by the force of air. Kettanu, if that was his true name, laughed and teased Shuran from a safe distance. Shuran was weakening as the Arakharat slowly siphoned away the air from Shuran, causing his breathing to become increasingly labored.

The Zidu'Si were forced to watch, unable to help as the wind and air within the chamber prevented them somehow from entering. They stood pounding against an invisible barrier, helpless to enter.

One person there was not helpless; Coralil lifted her hand to the barrier and pushed through without impediment. She raced toward Kettanu readying to force him back with her own winds, but he saw her coming and reacted with a force she could not battle.

Lightening struck at her and threw her, flailing across the room, to join Shuran pinned against the far wall. She was struggling to keep hold on her consciousness and was bleeding from a cut on her head.

Shuran used what strength he had to reach out and take her hand. He poured healing power into her body and closed the cut. "Thank you for trying Coralil, but he has the one gift I lost when Nergal left me. I cannot control air as he has learned while among your people."

Coralil squeezed Shuran's hand. "Then let me help you in return."

At that moment, Shuran accepted Coralil among the Zidu'Si. Several things occurred in response to her bond with the rest. The Zidu'Si held beyond the room all entered without protest and advanced on the platforms where six of them took up stations and joined in the watch over the city's winds. Shuran raised his hand toward Kettanu and knocked him into the opposite wall, forcing the wind from his lungs. The gate to the city opened and the Zidu'Si shield to the East dropped, allowing fresh air to enter the dome to the relief of those within.

Shuran finally answered the nagging at the back of his mind that had begun when Kettanu first attacked him and started suffocating Shuran. "I am well, my bonded. We have won the day and shall see you soon enough." He turned and approached the spot where Kettanu still held fast on the wall, a large spike of metal protruding from his mid-section.

Ugamma entered the chamber with twenty-four Lil'Du watchers, who began replacing those who suffered the ordeal of Kettanu's attack. Five at a time the Lil'Du were rotated out until at last the Zidu'Si who took places were also relieved of their watch.

The Zidu'Si reached Shuran, who had taken the Arakharat down from the wall where he had been spiked. Shuran's hands lay atop the shifter, attempting to heal the man.

Coralil did not understand why Shuran would heal this creature. "Why do you not let it die, Shin'Ar?"

"I fight with that question myself at this very moment, Coralil. If I let this thing die however, we may not get the answers we need," Shuran fought the urge to allow the shifter to expire, but he wanted to know things only the Arakharat called Kettanu could answer. Shuran was loosing the battle to heal the shifter, however, and it began slipping away. "There is something different about this shifter's anatomy."

"Why do you trouble yourself ANZILLU, you will only be destroyed in the end? It is the prophecy!" Kettanu coughed and was nearing his death.

Shuran quickly placed his hands on each side of the shifter's head and sent charges of current into its body and pulled its mind into his own. There Shuran waded through mist and fog, flashing scenes and past events, all memories of the soon to die Arakharat. Shuran searched for anything that would provide an answer to his questions. He found only one image that sparked his thoughts.

It was an image of a joining ceremony. The Arakharat was there in the shadows watching. At the altar stood Nagutan performing the rituals. The maiden was his own mother Sulura. Standing before her was a man who was just out of a full view. It must be his father, the man was turned away though, and Shuran could not make out his face. But then the man began to turn around and then Shuran saw… "ANDRA!"

Shuran fell back in shock and the shifter began to convulse and smoke. As everyone backed away, the creature that had been Kettanu melted into a pile of gelatinous mess and rags.

Bastien helped Shuran to his feet. "That was not Andra was it?"

Shuran shook his head, "No, I have melded with Andra and that is not him. It was something in the shifter's memories. I think Andra is my adda."

<u>Chapter Thirteen</u>

Nabusa was unable to reach her agent in Aluanu. She already heard of Shuran's arrival in Aluanu, from the Arakharat that was living among the Lil'Du for over a hundred years. She knew from reports days earlier that Shuran and the Zidu'Si had made their way to the summit of what millennia ago had been Mount Aris. It was the highest peak of the Orenthal Mountains and location from which the pure crystal for the Altar of Creation was found. After the Lands had lifted and shifted during the eruption of Hell's Mouth, the mountain was raised higher still and shifted far to the East, taking the home of the Lil'Du along.

She laughed openly at the memory of the event and Nagutan's reaction. "It serves them just for abandoning the Shin'Ar's last requirement of them," he had said. That is when he set upon the great storm to encircle their remote home and keep them secluded and cut off from the rest of Ersetu. An attendant entering the chamber interrupted her walk down memory lane.

"Yes, what is the matter?" she asked.

The attendant stuttered and wavered, not saying anything intelligible.

She noticed the ashen look upon his face. "For Damkianna's sake, spit it out!"

"How interesting you should call to that particular Sumerian, I once thought it was I who could claim your support and servitude," Ereshkigal said as she drifted into the chamber unannounced.

Nabusa stood straight and attempted to compose herself. She was not shocked to see the shadowy form of her former mistress. She was not prepared for this alteration in her detailed plans. "To what do I owe the pleasure of your presence, Queen of the Netherworld?" Nabusa slinked back to her chair and waited until allowed to sit. She was not sure why she still carried such fear for her one time matron.

Laughing at the title, Ereshkigal indicated Nabusa should sit. "I am no longer relegated to such a low and undesirable station, my dear… Nabusa is it now? I prefer Queen of Shadow at present, it suits my current manifestation do you not agree?" The misty formation of the Queen drifted in and around the Arakharat, who currently provided the vessel in which she walked the corporeal plain.

"I was led to understand you had taken as a host the twin female of prophecy, Salmetu? Why have you changed your vessel?" Nabusa inquired.

Again Ereshkigal laughed and smiled at Nabusa. "The child needed time with her mother, beside I wanted time to speak with my old apprentice, and who would know best where to find you than one of your little pets." The shadowy limbs gestured up and down the body of the shifter she currently held. "I am afraid they are not quite up to standard. This one is nearly dead on its feet and I fear will not hold me much longer."

As she spoke the last word, the shifter melted into a pile of mess at her shadowy feet. "Oh, this will not do, you must do better next time Nabusa if you wish to walk in your makers' shoes."

Nabusa was loosing her patience with this intrusion. "What is it you want Ereshkigal, I have my own business to attend?"

"To the point and fresh as you ever were my child, as you wish." As she waved her now fully, Shadow formed arms, several kashshaptu appeared behind her. "You remember your sisters of the coven do you not? They have something you must help them with."

Nabusa cringed at the site of these witches who Ereshkigal brought into her home. She looked them each in the eye, remembering each and every one of them along with the looks on their faces the day she turned on them. She could see in their eyes that they were aware of her part in their curse and banishment. "What do you want of me?" she asked without remorse.

"You will create a spell as only you can, not like that of the kind you placed on those in the coven who chose Penelle to lead," the witch said. "We had come to terms with the fact you only turned over the spell to the council when we betrayed you and placed Penelle as the Grand Kashshaptu. That time has past, do this and it will be forgotten."

"And what type of spell do you require?" Nabusa asked as she took the pouch from the witch. Inside she found several large thin disks. She took one out and held it before the light and saw the fire dance within the scale. "Drakkon scales," she said.

"Not just any drakkon, these were gathered in the Mist Swamps before we left. We used them to manipulate the drakkon, but he has grown too strong now. We want you to help with this problem." The kashshaptu hissed and laughed. Though her body was repaired and restored to a state before the curse, she was no beauty, and her breath still reeked of the swamps.

Nabusa did not like this turn of events, but she had not thought of an alternative than to comply. She gathered the scales, save one, into a poultice and pounded them into a fine powder while pocketing the last scale. She continued by pouring the scale dust into a bottle and mixed with it several other ingredients that she did not explain to the gathered witches. She completed the mixture and then poured it into a gugtu vessel, then sealed and handed it over.

"It is complete, say the words when you wish to use the curse. You will get, but one attempt and the beast must be within one hundred paces." Nabusa looked after the small talisman as the kashshaptu stepped away and vanished, leaving only Ereshkigal's shadowy form.

"You have done well today my child and so I shall reward you." Ereshkigal moved closer to Nabusa and whispered in her ear.

Nabusa turned and grabbed a large crystal from a box on her table. She gazed at the radiant stone one last time before turning it over to the Queen. "It is the last, make sure Salmetu uses it wisely. Once they are free from whatever prison Shuran has placed them, I will expect what you have promised."

Taking the stone, Ereshkigal drifted away and into the darkness. "You will have the means to your end game, this I promise," her disembodied voice said as she disappeared.

Nabusa called her attendant back into her chamber. "Gather the council, and get me the Guardians."

The council gathered in the hall outside the Nabusa's chamber. She took her seat at the head of the table and looked down the table at the few who chose to attend. She was not surprised, most of the Foresworn had retreated deep into the land as far as possible from the strife in Aurderia. Those who attended her were old beyond usefulness except the two Guardians who had yet to return to the Shadow infested land in search of more mixed-bloods.

"We shall soon have a location and access to the chamber of the Shin'Ar, where we will find the proper means to finish what we started so long ago," she said to the Guardians while ignoring the older members. "I shall prepare to leave the territories at once."

"We shall accompany you to the settlement in Aurderia when you are ready," the guardians said as they stood and left the hall.

The others in attendance grumbled and argued but did not contradict their mistress. "What will you have us tasked with Nabusa?"

Nabusa stood and sniffed at them. "Go off deep into the Territories with the others or stay here and rot if you like, it is of no consequence to me any longer." She left them there in silent surprise and returned to her chamber. As she went about gathering what she required for her journey, the closing and locking of her door startled her. She turned to find Nagutan standing behind her.

"What are you doing here, after all this time?" Unable to maintain her stance at Nagutan's sudden arrival, she sat upon her lounge chair and attempted to look unaffected.

Nagutan began a slow and methodical walk around her chamber, occasionally glancing down at the various items laid about the many surfaces. "I have been feeling my years of late. Time has not been so kind as to leave me with unattended business or unfortunate histories."

Nabusa watched him closely, trying to determine his true purpose for being there. "Get to the point old man, I have business to attend."

Nagutan turned to her and looked at the bag she was packing. "Going on a voyage? Are you sure your health and constitution are up for travel? You know I am not the only ancient bag of bones in this chamber." He shuffled closer; looking like the old man she labeled him. "As it happens there is something that you may be able to help me with before you go about your escapade."

"A favor of me is what you seek, you have changed little since I last saw you. Though your body and face have sagged and pruned, you are yet the same scheming and self-absorbed dur you always were. Still chasing the Shin'Ar and looking to finish some age-old conflict." She stood and continued gathering her things.

Nagutan continued to snoop through her belongings as he strolled about her chamber. "You did not always think so lowly of me, nor I of you. There was a time when one might say we shared a feeling of companionship."

"I loved you and you returned that love by turning your back on me," she spat at him through hurt and anger. "You went off to chase that fool Nergal and his ill-minded notion of fixing what was not broken. He should have let things alone and we would not be in the mess we are this day. How many lives have been lost, how much more suffering will the world face before you realize you cannot stop this? I will carry forward with my own plans and shall see the return of the times before the inferior man races crawled from the mud!"

Nagutan finally gave up his ploy and faced her. "You cannot hope to achieve what you plan. You should already have given up with your first failure. The Arakharat will never be what you hope despite what you may think you have learned."

Nabusa was surprised by his words. "What do you know of them?"

He only tittered at her and stepped closer. "My dear, I know everything you have been setting about and meddling with. The creation of a chamber that failed, your pursuit to gain access to the original one in Aurderia, all in the hopes of bringing about the rebirth of the Telukukal. Pure folly, you are no Sumerian and could not possibly hope to achieve what they created in us."

"And you are any better? You and your manipulation of the boy Shuran; you hope to make him your Shin'Ar, Nergal returned?" She waited to see the surprise in his eyes but saw only mocking. "You are not the only one who can keep a watchful eye on events."

Nagutan laughed at this. "You speak of your visions and telling of prophecy? Who do you think sent you those visions you foolish old hag? Your gift of sight was always short, yet you convinced yourself this had changed. You are blind to your own shortcomings. Now give me the key."

That was what he wanted Nabusa now knew. She had him now and would not let this bastard son of Nergal get what he wanted. "You will not get what you want from me, I destroyed the key. Andra will die in that collar and the boy will rage against the world once Sulura and his drakkon are destroyed as well. The kashshaptu have a means to control the mighty flying beast bonded to Shuran, they hold the talisman now!" She watched the color drain from Nagutan's face. "You know Andra is your son, but did you know it was I who released the Gizzu'Su?"

Nagutan had enough and grabbed Nabusa by the throat and let energy pour from his hands into her, causing convulsions, choking off her air, heating her body, draining her fluids, turning her skin to stone, and her bones began to turn to metal. "I planned for you to steal him away from me so long ago you short sighted witch. Everything that has happened over the eons has been by Nergal's design and my hand. The only wrinkle was your failed attempt at recreating the Telukukal."

"It would have worked had it not been for the poor sample. Your child was not as pure as I had thought and he spoiled the results. Once we have control of the chamber in Durangug, we shall succeed. I will use my own blood to repair what was caused by your boy's inferior genes." Nabusa was goading him purposely. She hoped to break down his walls and gain the upper hand. Meanwhile, she fought with all her strength to counter the effects of Nagutan's spells upon her body.

"Your failure was your arrogance. My son was purposely spelled to protect him. You spoiled your own experiment and were playing games of the very Gods who were using us as playthings," Nagutan said. "You will fail again, since you are not but third generation and not true Telukukal."

Nabusa began to lose her struggle and Nagutan only grew in strength. Fear for Shuran, Sulura, Moltar, and his son Dalgon clouded his judgement and released his primal instincts.

"Shuran will see to the true abominations you have created in the Arakharat, and bring the balance of Essence back to Ersetu as Nergal had wanted before the dark Sumer plotted against him. You will not have any more visions sweet Nabusa, just as you did not see this as your last day to live." He dropped her and allowed his Essence wielding to take her.

As she fell, a single gleaming red scale fell from her pocket.

Nagutan retrieved the scale and quickly disappeared at the sound of approaching footsteps.

The Guardians entered the chamber to find the Nabusa, dead and laying on the floor of her laboratory chamber. They looked at each other and moved about the room collecting items of worth and then turned to leave. "Saves us the trouble of dispatching her later, now we will not have to keep our own work secret from her," one said to the other, and then they were gone.

<u>Chapter Fourteen</u>

Ereshkigal returned to the Academy to find Salmetu sitting in the corner of her room, still and silent. A ghostly apparition hovered above her vessel's head. "Why do you still trouble this realm spirit, you should be feeding the Shadow?"

Tianna turned at the words from the Queen of Shadow and fled through the wall.

The misty matron of malice floated over to her young host and began to fill Salmetu with her dark essence. As she disappeared into Salmetu, she began to stir and the dark fire returned to Salmetu's eyes as she stood. "That is better, I missed you my sweet priestess. Did you miss your Queen?" Ereshkigal's laugh echoed from Salmetu's mouth.

Sulura sat in the chair opposite her daughter's possessed body. "You play with us as a child would a toy, are you any different from those you rebelled against so long ago?" she asked.

Ereshkigal turned Salmetu's body around to face her vessel's mother. "What did you say woman? You know nothing of our history."

"I am afraid I know a great deal more than you might image, Ereshkigal. I am aware of your failure to follow the edicts of your people's ruling council the ME." That got Ereshkigal's attention. "I am further aware that you chose to follow your own dark desires and decided to twist the Netherworld of Ersetu even though Nergal forbade it. He turned you out and imprisoned you and the Gizzu'Su."

Long before the Gizzu'Su became as dark as they were when imprisoned by Nergal, they had already split from the group experiments and started their own workings throughout Ersetu. While some set about creating ogres and leviathans of the deep waters, Ereshkigal took her apprentice, Nabusa, to the land that was now the Foresworn Territories, and began delving into the darkness that existed deep beneath the surface.

There they performed rituals and spells to try and extract power from the dark flow of energy that kept pace with the Emmuku'Gu. Ereshkigal could sense the power within, but could not conquer it until the day she first took a third generation Telukukal and turned him into something otherworldly. She created the first Telal.

Now that she created a demon warrior that could flow from the confines of the corporeal, Ereshkigal sent him into the depths of the world to investigate the dark flow. What the demon reported back was a Netherworld of dark shi that were trapped within the blackness. The demon could enter, and since he was the servant of Ereshkigal, she would gain power from the intrusion into the shadow cast by the light. Ereshkigal soon became the Queen of the Netherworld when by proxy of her Telal, for she created more, was able to connect to the darkness and strengthen her own power.

The other Sumer, who began following darker plans of their own, soon congregated to her side, including her choice to have become the leader of the Sumerian presence upon Ersetu, Uggae. Together they formed the Gizzu'Su and created a force of Telal to fight for them in the wars that would precede their eventual capture and imprisonment. Those memories all flooded back to Ereshkigal as she turned on Sulura.

The Shadow filled Salmetu's face, twisted with anger. "He had no right to do what he did. He locked me away, but my faithful Telukukal servant freed us and we became the Shadow." She moved closer still to Sulura with darkness seeping from her every orifice. "You will know the truth of my power, I have suffered your presence long enough. You weaken my host and I will not tolerate you in my presence."

Ereshkigal used Salmetu's Essence to draw upon the power of Ersetu's dark energy that carried the Shadow and readied a strike against Sulura. She released the flow but before it reached Sulura, she disappeared in a blast of white light. The dark flow filtered through the light and hit the next target available.

Nagutan stood behind the spot where he reached out to send Sulura to safety. He fought against the Shadow as it attacked his entire body looking for a way inside. His body and mind were unprepared for the assault. Nagutan fell upon the floor with convulsions while coming to realize that his body was being taken over.

Ereshkigal lifted and floated Nagutan's body into the room and crept closer to watch the struggle for the old man's shi take place. Her borrowed face split into a toothy grin and her soulless black eyes reflected the Shadow within Salmetu's body, swirling in excitement. "It has been millennia since one of your kind has fed us, Telukukal. We shall savor every moment of your agonizing struggle against the inevitable."

Nagutan's mind was reeling as he battled the darkness that invaded every corner of his consciousness. Of all the possible things that could have happened during the countless millennia of his manipulation of events, Nagutan did not consider the strength he would need to resist a direct attack from the Shadow. He imagined the possibility but in his event managing of the last several years, he forgot to prepare himself properly.

Every mental shield he erected was shredded by the Shadow converging upon his mind. Had he been prepared for the assault he may have stood a chance, however the Shadow took hold and began feasting upon his shi.

Ereshkigal squirmed and rolled her head as she gained access to him and the information he held within the deepest recesses of his being. Memories of eons spent manipulating lives and scheming to bring about the return of the Shin'Ar, were all racing across her own incorporeal essence. As she accessed his innermost thoughts, Salmetu's face twisted and contorted with the semblance of Ereshkigal delighting in her victory over the son of Nergal.

"Your adda would be disappointed in what you have been up to in his absence," she whispered. "I find it remarkable that the Telukukal pet of the glorious Nergal, who not only turns out to be of his own blood, manages to break nearly every edict of the ME."

She moved closer to within inches of his face. She was enjoying his agony and his submission to her control. She found the retelling of his deeds both entertaining and insightful.

Nagutan replayed his efforts, dating back to the fall of the Zidu'Si and Nergal's plan to bring balance. They manipulated the bloodlines after persuading the races to intermingle. Those first two children were used to power the altars and ultimately sacrificed themselves. Nergal's first plan was flawed and it failed in the end. The balance did not restore and a new plan was created.

Over the centuries that followed the Sikil Mah, Nagutan sat by and watched his wife Penelle's banishment to the Mist Swamps. He used the same blood magic that condemned the kashshaptu, to craft his own spells, which furthered his and Nergal's plans. He used the darker magic to create his imp and then to conjure the Telal calling himself, Telalsu. His plan was to use the demon to chase Moona, carrying Shuran, to Middleton where she would encounter Codger. Dalgon by guise of Andra would then lead the demon warrior on a merry chase for several years. His plans adjusted to the events that did not proceed to his precise plan, such as Bastien becoming possessed.

The Telal was supposed to attempt to possess Shuran while Nergal was still present in his mind. This would have driven the demon out and back to the Netherworld. As it worked out, Shuran was able to free Bastien of Telalsu in the end and Nagutan's plans fell back into line with what he laid out.

 Visions of the remaining events leading to the current attempt at bringing balance floated freely from Nagutan to the Shadow. The creation of new children to blend with the races was methodically planned and carried through to the birth of Shuran and his sisters. He shared information on the whereabouts of Shuran and the Zidu'Si and what they had been doing.

A smirk spread across her borrowed face. "So the Shin'Ar spawn has thought to repurpose the prison that failed to hold us. I should have figured that out myself. I suppose I have been distracted with my pets, and this one's mother," she said gesturing to her current host, Salmetu.

Now Ereshkigal knew where to find her Gizzu'Su. She was troubled by the fact that Shuran had nearly finished the Zidu'Si and was in the Highlands now enlisting the Lil'Du. Though they were currently beyond her reach, the Zidu'Si and their young leader would have to return from the Highlands. She planned on having a welcoming committee awaiting them on the way back to

Britengate.

Ereshkigal wanted more, but Nagutan slowly regained some ability to block her out. She pressed him harder, but his mind was blocking a portion of his memory from her.

"What are you hiding from us Nagutan?" Ereshkigal moved back from her newest servant. "That problem with resisting us is that when your walls finally fall, and they will, the agony will be that much greater. We shall have all your secrets, in time."

Nagutan stared at her expressionless. All his remaining shi was focused on holding himself within his body to prevent eviction by the Shadow. He had to hold on to the most critical pieces of his mind if there was yet hope left at defeating the darkness and restoring balance. He was, therefore, physically at the mercy of Ereshkigal and her control over the Shadow now taking up residence within him.

Salmetu's features began to return to her face as Ereshkigal loosened her grip on Nagutan. He was her tool now and she could pull a part of herself back into the conflagration of hatred burning within the Shadow.

"Now my new pet, you shall accompany me to the chamber and help free my Gizzu'Su. With your power added to mine, and that of the crystal Nabusa provided, we shall make short work of breaking through the walls. Then we shall take Nergal and strip his shi of energy and feast upon him." Ereshkigal wavered and caught her balance against a chair.

"You shall then gather my mother and bring her back to me." This time it was Salmetu speaking.

Ereshkigal gathered her composure and stood firm. "You will leave the woman for now and only after you have assisted to free my followers and then take me to the chamber in Durangug, will I consider going after the mother. It will not be a rescue effort, but one of complete annihilation of every living thing in Britengate," Ereshkigal said as she regained full control of Salmetu.

Nagutan looked up at Salmetu with a knowing in his eyes that spoke of a chance yet to see his plans unfold as Nergal instructed. He fought the Shadow bravely but with that small intrusion of Salmetu's consciousness, there was greater hope.

Chapter Fifteen

Mallick was the first to recover from the shock of Shuran's announcement regarding Andra. "I thought you said that the shifters, or Arakharat rather, were unable to procreate?"

Shuran shook his head as he called fire to incinerate the remains of a man who was Kettanu. "I said they were unable to claim a recognizable form of their own. I know nothing of their abilities to have offspring." Shuran continued to wonder at the things he learned while connected to the Arakharat. "If this man was indeed who he claimed, then I believe Andra represents something entirely different. Andra had something different in his genetic buildup that was lacking in Kettanu."

"So then what is he then, your adda?" Avrank asked.

"I only think there is a possibility, not a certainty that Andra is my adda. The vision I glimpsed from Kettanu was that of a life joining ceremony. In this vision was Nagutan presiding over my mother and Andra, or at least the appearance that Andra favors when not mimicking another." Shuran attempted to place doubt to his vision, but he felt somehow that it was the truth.

Bastien stepped up beside Shuran and placed a hand upon his shoulder in an effort to support his best friend. "You will simply have to ask him. But until then, did you happen to get any useful spells from the shifter?" he grinned.

After a well needed laugh by all the Zidu'Si, they left the citadel with Coralil to go meet the Chancellor. They walked through the city receiving well wishes and small tokens from everyone they passed. Word traveled quickly among the Lil'Du since they were known as wind whisperers. The Zidu'Si saved the city along with the Lil'Du people and they were showing gratitude far beyond what would be expected.

Shuran called for Coralil to step to his side. "Cora, your people seem more enthused with our presence than a day previous?"

"Shin'Ar, they are indeed thankful for what the Zidu'Si did in saving the city, but moreover, they wish to show their readiness to follow the Shin'Ar and Zidu'Si," she answered.

Coralil explained to Shuran how the Lil'Du have waited many millennia to become once again placed in the service of the Shin'Ar. They paid their penance secluded among the clouds for all that time, working to better themselves in hope that one day the Shin'Ar would welcome them back into service. Now that she was a member of the Zidu'Si, their prayers to Hebat were answered and they could prove their loyalty and worth.

"They must learn the truth of Hebat and the other Gods, Cora. Now that you share the bond you must understand the fallacy of believing the Sumerians were nothing more than advanced beings from another world." Shuran left the truth telling for Cora; he felt it best shared from only those among the Zidu'Si. She would share her knowledge by explaining the bond and how this information was passed to her from Shuran. "You must not share the details of my lineage at this time, however, I do not think it prudent."

"You don' wish to be a god among the Lil'Du. Shin'Ar the Almighty?" Mallick cracked.

Though he grimaced at the thought, Shuran laughed off the jest. He had no desire to become raised any higher than had already happened. To aspire to anything beyond a man, no matter how powerful, was to invite the darkness by breaking the edicts of pride set by the ME. Though he was not a religious man, Shuran felt that the basic laws the ME established became gospel for a reason. They made sense and if it took the people believing they might be smite by a God for breaking them, then who was he to say otherwise. Pride would lead to other deadly sins as they had with Vardoran.

"You are not Vardoran, sheesh," Bastien said. "You also have the rest of us around to smite you, should you need it." Bastien shared a broad smile.

The Zidu'Si bond that Shuran altered, allowed them to share thoughts, and Shuran often forgot this, much to his chagrin. "Yes, and since you are all able to dance around and peer through the windows of my mind when I leave them ajar, I shall be ever watched and kept in balance. If only it were so easy a watch, keeping balance with Ersetu." Shuran wondered at his final statement.

When at last they arrived at the Chancellor's chambers, the trail of followers waned. The Zidu'Si were welcomed into the Chancellors room where he sat behind a desk with piles of papers and a defeated look upon his face. "There is no choice but to have a selection ceremony," he mumbled without looking up. "I see no other option with this many submissions."

"Is there something we can assist with Chancellor?" Shuran asked.

The Chancellor jumped with absentminded surprise. "Oh my dear boy yes, yes indeed! I should say you can." The Chancellor took Shuran by the shoulder and led him down the corridors to the central hall. "Since you accepted Coralil and, therefore, the Lil'Du as a people into your service, there have been countless inquiries for leading the armies into battle against the Shadow."

Shuran was confused. "Armies, I did not know the Lil'Du had armies. What need you of an army in a city that only you and the Shin'Ar could enter?"

"We created the air corps for the day you returned to us. Those flying vessels are not there for decoration Shin'Ar, they are unable to leave Aluanu due to the Pillars and we can only control one long enough to lower ourselves to the plateau, never mind a La'Bun Masua."

"Forgive my ignorance, but how exactly are these air-bladder ships useful if they are unable to leave the city?" Avrank asked.

"One thing at a time my little friend," the Chancellor said. "First we must choose Sutresi to lead the Gardu'Lil." The Chancellor pulled back the curtain of the balcony they found themselves standing upon. A chorus of cheers sounded that threatened to break Shuran's eardrums. The whole of Aluanu crowded the streets below them. They were gathered to find out who would be leading the troops of Lil'Du in the coming war against the Shadow.

"It would seem the Lil'Du are expecting you to choose who will be the commanders of the Air Warriors, Shin'Ar," Coralil said and smiled. Shuran exhaled deeply and scratched his head. "Perhaps the Chancellor is correct in his assessment of the complexity involved with the selection. There will be no easy way to decide."

"A contest," Shuran suggested.

The Chancellor smiled with relief. "Yes, a show of skill and strength."

Bastien was first to question the change in attitude of the Lil'DI. "When first we arrived, there was equal parts distaste and welcome at our arrival. How is it that so many changed their view of the Zidu'Si and Shin'Ar, surely not for simply saving them and the city?"

The Chancellor was thinking of how to respond, but it was Shuran who answered. "Kettanu was not simply attempting to destroy the city when he attacked and killed the Lil'Du who were channeling Essence in Bitilu'Bir, he was attempting to destroy evidence of a spell he placed on the pedestals they laid upon. The Lil'Du were inadvertently whispering upon the wind and spreading subliminal thoughts of distrust."

"Why are we only hearing about this now?" the Chancellor asked.

"The spell was broken when Kettanu died, I had hoped to spare you of further distress over the man's influence," Shuran offered as an excuse.

The Chancellor smiled and took Shuran's hand. "Thank you, but there is no need to spare my feelings in the future so always speak frankly with my Shin'Ar."

The rest of the afternoon was spent making plans for a tournament of skill and ability. The victors would be chosen to lead the Lil'Du Air Warriors, Gardu'Lil. Once the plans were set, the announcements were sent out upon the wind, that the following day would be a festival and tournament, both celebrating the end of the Lil'Du seclusion and the selection of Sutresi. When evening came, it was time to rest for the busy day ahead.

As the Zidu'Si left to have dinner and retire for the evening, Shuran stayed back with Coralil. "Would it be possible to take dinner aboard one of the La'Bun Masua?"

"I am sure I could find someone to arrange that. Do you wish an areal tour of Aluanu?" Coralil asked.

"I was hoping you would join me for dinner so we may speak and get to know one another better. Of all the Zidu'Si, I have spent the least time with you before induction." Shuran had a difficult time maintaining eye contact with her.

Coralil was lithe and statuesque as could any Lil'Du be described, but she also exhibited a strength that contradicted the outward appearance of weakness. Her blonde locks cascaded down her back and wisps of strands fluttered before her face as she stared back at Shuran with equal shyness. "I would greatly enjoy being your guest this evening at dinner. I do not think anyone has ever thought to dine aboard an airship, but I am certain that any captain would welcome the Shin'Ar aboard for such a..." she could not finish her thought.

Shuran looked into her eyes for several moments before speaking. "I shall leave the arrangements in your more than capable hands. Shall I meet you at...where do the La'Bun Masua dock?"

"I shall retrieve you from your chambers at two hours past dusk." Coralil awkwardly bowed to Shuran and quickly skipped away while Shuran remained transfixed, watching after her.

"SHURAN!" Mallick shouted. "Is that what you plan on wearing at the time of your first courting?"

Shuran turned at Mallick to find the other male members of the Zidu'Si mocking him. "THIS... is simply a dinner with a new member of the Zidu'Si. I know nothing of Cora before accepting her into-"

"CORA? See you already call her by a familiar name. Shuran and Cora sitting below a tree, k-i-s-s-" Avrank started before a burst of wind knocked him to the floor.

Dara and Vala entered the room with a bundle and stern looks.

"You scoundrels can leave. Vala and I will see Shuran off on his... dinner of acquaintance with Coralil," Dara said looking down on all the male members in the Zidu'Si.

The men quickly exited the room and after Dara had helped Avrank back to his feet, he scuttled off after them.

"Now, as much as it pains me to say, Mallick was correct in his assessment of what you are planning to wear. That is entirely inappropriate for a first date," Dara said.

Shuran was shocked silent and turning red.

"You are not going to become a flame are you Shin'Ar? Because that outdated jacket you chose from the Vault could use a good burning," Vala added.

"It is NOT a date," Shuran managed.

"Right, so Dara and I chose to go down to the market and select something more appropriate for you to adorn, something more fitting the mood," Vala continued. "Yes, I know you say it is not a 'date' but you forget the mental link we have."

Shuran immediately closed off his connection to the Zidu'Si, much to the disappointment of the ladies.

"Fine, have it your way. Just wear this and we shall pray to Damkianna you do not say anything foolish," Dara said as she followed Vala out of the room.

Shuran quickly adorned the clothing that the ladies chose. Once he checked himself in the mirror, he admitted to himself that they had been correct in their decision to assist. He looked much better in the Lil'Du clothes than what he had chosen from the Vault, even if they were a bit snug. After a final adjustment, he headed out to the sitting room where he found Coralil already awaiting him.

Shuran stopped in his tracks. Coralil drove the air from his chest by her striking beauty. Where before she had been lovely, she stood in rival to any vision he had seen in his own living memory or those left behind by Nergal, Nagutan, and Gimagala. Her golden locks were held back in fishtail braids intertwined with delicate ribbons and lace. Her elegant yet understated dress accentuated her lithe frame. When she smiled at him, her eyes sparkled as her face blushed.

"Are you ready Cora?" Shuran managed. After she had nodded, Shuran offered his arm and they left the apartments set aside for the Zidu'Si.

The Zidu'Si all gathered at the windows to watch them walk down the streets of Aluanu.

Shuran and Coralil reached the docks for the airships to find the captain waiting along with his crew. They were all dressed in formal attire and standing at attention. As the two walked past each man, eyes followed their progress with approving looks. Shuran was more uncomfortable than he had ever felt in his life.

The carriage for the airship was simple and efficient. At the front was a pilot deck, where the controls and steam engine sat. The engine served as both power to the spinning blades that propelled the ship, and provided fire to heat the air within the bladder that lifted the vessel. The center of the carriage was spacious and open to allow the transport of many Lil'Du warriors. This night, however, it contained only a finely set table with two chairs.

Shuran and Coralil took their seats at the table and began their meal in awkward silence as the La'Bun Masua, eased into the air and began drifting on the winds around the city. The crew set about bringing them several dishes from which they shared. The food was artistically presented and consisted of vibrant and delicate plants, vegetables, and fruits.

The Lil'Du, Shuran discovered, did not eat meats. It was not from a purposeful abstinence but from a lack of game in the heights of Aluanu. Thought there were birds, small reptiles, and insects that inhabited the surrounding forests, they were maintained to pollinate and control the plants rather than to be hunted regularly. When the reptiles procreated too extensively, their numbers would be thinned and used for their skins while the meat would be fed to the carnivorous plants.

"I believe that Orian encountered a tree that may have liked very much to taste him," Shuran laughed. He was beginning to relax as he and Coralil chatted and enjoyed one another's company. It was not long before the meal was complete and the two stepped up to the side of the carriage to view the city from above. "It is quite magnificent, your home."

Cora rested her hand upon Shuran's at the railing. "We take great joy in the building of our home. It has taken many generations to establish what we have here in Aluanu, which was nearly destroyed by Kettanu. But thanks to you and the Zidu'Si, my people are safe and our way of life protected."

Shuran sobered at the thought of protecting their way of life. All life on Ersetu was still in danger from the Shadow. "That way of life is still threatened, Cora. Kettanu was but a small conflict in a greater war brewing in the lands to the West."

Coralil understood and sighed, then turned back to the view and allowed herself a respite and feeling of peace before her imminent departure to battle the Shadow as one of the Zidu'Si. "Tomorrow we shall have the tournaments and then begin your training in air Essence. For now, let us simply enjoy the view."

Shuran did not take his eyes off of Coralil for most of the remaining night aboard the airship.

Chapter Sixteen

It was late in the evening when Shuran finally made it back to the apartment, where he found the boys waiting up in the sitting room. He tried to play smooth and collected, but his boyish grin gave him away.

"Looks as though someone had a pleasant evening," Bastien said. "What is she like then?"

"Glorious," was Shuran's single word response.

Avrank smacked Shuran on the rump and laughed as he passed. "Off to bed then lover boy, you've got a big day tomorrow choosing your army."

Shuran sobered at the reminder. Tomorrow he would be witnessing the selection of those wishing to battle the Shadow at Shuran's side. He wondered at how many would be returning to their home in the clouds.

Morning brought a renewed sense of urgency to Shuran. His dreams during the night were filled with scattered images of battles taking place throughout the realms. Death and destruction spread across the world as the darkness of Shadow enveloped all life upon Ersetu. His fitful night showed upon his weary expression and slumped shoulders as he made his way to the sitting room where the others were already eating a light breakfast.

"You look as though you did not sleep well Shuran, more visions?" Dara inquired.

Shuran shrugged and helped himself to juice and a pastry. "Not visions, normal dreams I think though they were foreboding and unpleasant. They begin to fade from memory now so I am not overly concerned with them becoming anything more than just dreams."

"You do not seem convinced," Orian said. "Perhaps you are simply worrying about the future, Shin'Ar. Why not focus on the gift of the present?" Orian glanced from Shuran to Coralil and back with a devious grin. His smile faltered when the biscuit Vala threw at him made contact with the side of his head.

Breakfast finished, the Zidu'Si and Shuran made their way to the open fields of the warrior training camps just outside the city. The back exit was already busy with people heading out for a good seat within the pavilion and those wishing to participate in the games. When at last the Zidu'Si arrived and made their way to where they would observe and participate, the arena was full of would-be commanders getting in last minute practice.

"How will this work then?" Bastien asked. "If we are to choose commanders, why do they combat one another? It will be entirely different when battling the Shadow."

Coralil answered. "The first rounds will be battles to determine who shall have the right to request a command in the final round. When the Gardu'Lil battle one another, they are evenly matched in most cases. It is through cunning, fast action, and perseverance, that a Sutresi stands out among the others."

Shuran nodded and continued the explanation of what would be happening during the competitions. "Once the first rounds have finished, those who earned the right of Sutresi will select among the air warriors and form his or her regiment. The Zidu'Si, because of their ability to counter other elemental Essence and weaving of spells, will then test the regiments. We shall choose the best among the regiments, and their commanders will then become the Sutresi that will report to me through Coralil." Shuran finished his explanation and turned back to the Gardu'Lil practicing in the arena.

Orian nudged Avrank in the side. "He seems to be comfortable with this whole thing as though it were normal."

"I think Shuran is simply accepting the Lil'Du warriors with grace rather than see them off on a fools quest alone," Avrank replied. "From all Coralil has said, I think the Gardu'Lil would do whatever it took to fly those balloon ships over the Pillars for a chance at redemption." He nodded back to Orian and they joined the others in spectating as the tournament began.

Throughout the morning and into early after mid-Utu the warriors were paired and duels played out many dozens at a time. The victor was determined when one of each dueling pair managed to knock the other off their feet and pin them with the use of air Essence. As the fifty Gardu'Lil, who earned the right of Sutresi, selected their warriors, the Zidu'Si made their way to the arena to take their places around the field to begin testing the quick thinking, effectiveness, and length of time they stood against the Zidu'Si.

Each regiment was tested once against each of the Zidu'Si. So that others would not gain insight and prepare better than previous contestants, the Zidu'Si would alter their methods. Mallick relayed mental tactics he accessed from a book on the history of wars located in the Vault. The tests went on until late in the evening before drawing to an end. The Zidu'Si would discuss their individual assessments and reach decisions by the next morning when the announcements would be made.

For his own part, Shuran spent the time during the tests, observing. He watched every mock battle and took mental notes on how each Sutresi and their warriors reacted. Though most were clear-minded and focused on their test, Shuran wondered at how any of them would truly perform against the Shadow. It did not play fairly or with restraint. He only hoped that these Gardu'Lil would stand as strong and not decide to retreat to the assumed safety of their city in the clouds.

That evening the Zidu'Si discussed their assessments and shared opinions on who they felt best suited the positions of Sutresi among the Gardu'Lil. Shuran for his part agreed with most of the decisions and only a few times guided the discussion toward specific individuals. They finally had their decisions and finished eating before heading to rest for what remained of the evening.

The next morning saw an early start. Not only was it time to announce who the Sutresi would be, but those commanders would be instructors in the Zidu'Si training of air Essence wielding. Although they gained the power and knowledge when Coralil joined the fold, practical experience and use was required to learn, to what extent each could wield. Though they were not true wielders of air Essence, such as those of the Lil'Du, each of the Zidu'Si, beside Coralil, were strengthened by the bond Shuran created for them. This bond would fortify their abilities and amplify them many times over.

Shuran, already having the markers of the Lil'Du race in his blood, had the ability, but lacked the knowledge without Nergal guiding him. He took his instruction directly from the knowledge Coralil brought to the Zidu'Si while she guided him in his efforts. He was a natural and required less instruction than the others, so he left with Cora to have a light breakfast and observe the others from stands. This did not go without notice from the Zidu'Si.

A flashing on the red gem of his bracer interrupted Shuran. He immediately thought of Britengate coming under attack while the Zidu'Si was away. He was both relieved and surprised when finding it was Moona on the other end. "What takes you so long Shuran? We been waitin' for word and you forget ta contact your Moona again," she scolded. She assured him that the city was safe at that time, but Andra was brought to the city wounded and restrained with a collar that none could remove. Nagutan had left to attempt to acquire the means to remove it but had not yet returned and was likely in danger. "Your mother was suddenly sent to the city by Nagutan when he rescued her from certain death by Ereshkigal. It would seem that yer sister is bein' consumed by that Sumer witch!"

"We will leave for Britengate at once. It may be that Nagutan is no longer alive or worse, taken by the Shadow. In either situation, Ereshkigal likely knows of the prison where her Gizzu'Su await her freeing them." Shuran closed communication after advising of the new alliance with the Lil'Du and the fleet of airships that will accompany them.

The Zidu'Si finished their practice session at Shuran's sudden entrance to the field. Once he advised what had happened, they all understood the need to return to Britengate immediately. Not only was the possibility of Ereshkigal freeing the Gizzu'Su soon on his mind, but the fact that Andra was in trouble and quite possibly Shuran's father was driving a feeling of absolute resolve through the Zidu'Si from Shuran.

The airships were stocked with gear and supplies for the one hundred troops each would accommodate. Twenty vessels in all were created for the purpose of Gardu'Lil transport. Though they could control the wind, they employed the steam engines to engage propellers to allow them to save their strength. The airships were aloft and heading to the barrier, where a portal was open to allow them exit into the open. They approached the Pillars when realization came to them all. In the haste to leave, they forgot the fact that the Pillars of Wind prevented the ships departure due to size, and the strength of the Lil'Du combined would not hold the winds long enough, nor could they fly high enough.

Shuran held out his hands and focused on the winds. As he gathered the Essence around himself to form an air attack, the words of a weaving left his lips. "Si'Il Te Im Zi Gub," he intoned. Part the winds to allow us passage. He let go of the spell and joined it to the air with a push of force that sent the combined weaving and wielding into the Pillars.

The Pillars of Wind parted at his command allowing safe passage beyond Aluanu. One by one the La'Bun Masua passed through the gap opened by Shuran, and out into the Highlands where they found Moltar and Jade flying in circles.

Shuran knew that Moltar would be present waiting for his Lugaldur, which meant Jade would accompany him. What Shuran did not expect was the host of Ag'Lu that were also in a formation hovering before the airships as well. Shuran dove from the vessel and carried himself on the wind to the back of his bonded drakkon, as did Gregoran. He flew out to meet Aglia, who led the Ag'Lu squadron of drakkon and riders.

"Well-met Aglia, I see you have brought some friends," Shuran smiled and nodded. "We travel to Britengate in great need."

"So your mountainous friend has informed us. We have decided that this battle would not be well won without the aid of the Ag'Lu," she said. "I believe it is time we join in the battle for all of Ersetu. May we be accepted among you?"

With a nod of acceptance, Shuran expanded his Zidu'Si to include the forces of the Ag'Lu and acknowledged those of the Lil'Du. They each became extended members and with that the power of the Zidu'Si grew. Shuran shook with the surge of power but regained his purpose and turned Moltar to the West and led his army of air and fire toward Britengate.

It was already near dark when they all flew off toward the end of the Highlands. By the time the boundary was in reach, Utu had fully set, and only the stars and waning moons had illuminated the way. It was then when the first drakkon went down.

From below sounded the cry for blood and the night brightened with the launch of an attack from both sides. The enemy lay waiting the eventual return of Shuran and his Zidu'Si. Ballista and drakkon guns were spread before them, blocking the way west. Balls of energy, fire, water, and air-launched toward the ground as it rumbled below the feet of the dark weavers and kashshaptu. The Zidu'Si were in full attack of the foe, except one.

Jade had taken a projectile launched by the enemy in the opening volley that caught them by surprise. Gregoran knelt at her side as he struggled to heal her wounds while ignoring those he took himself when they crashed to the ground.

One of the airships landed and Dara crawled from the carriage ushering the Lil'Du Gardu'Lil out as well. She took hold of Gregoran and as the Lil'Du carried Jade into the carriage, Dara checked on Gregoran. "Are you badly wounded?" she asked.

"I will be well, it is my bonded I need to see after." Gregoran struggled to free himself of Dara's grasp. "Let go, I am no use until I know the state of my drakkon." Gregoran took the Mi'Ib Ag from his holster as Dara backed away. "Take this to Aglia, she will stand in my stead until I might rejoin the fight." He threw the sword up to Dara and then ran to follow Jade into the carriage. They lifted off and headed back toward the Ag'Lu settlement.

Dara found Aglia and gave her the Sword of Fire with Gregoran's blessing. As she accepted the sword, an eruption of light and heat filled the night sky as though Utu had returned and day was upon them. As Aglia and Dara turned to see what caused the light, they felt the rage and anger radiating from the fiery drakkon and rider.

Moltar had been in a rage at the injury of his mother Jade, but the moment Aglia took the sword of the Zidu'Si wielder of fire, that added power rolled over him and into his shi. Shuran's deeper bond with him, cause the same intense desire and fuel. They turned to living flame both drakkon and Lugaldur, and they wanted for destruction.

Shuran leaned into Moltar and they streamed down toward the drakkon guns and incinerated them all, followed by ballista and anyone caught in their path. They began chasing down any dark weaver or agent of the Shadow they could find, but they were retreating. Shuran knew that they would be heading back to Britengate now that they knew the Zidu'Si were returning. He needed to beat them there, but to do so he would have to challenge the Shadow itself that he knew would be blocking the Emmuku'Gu in the Stone Forest.

Shuran realized there was another way. There existed another entrance to the Power Rivers of Ersetu, and it was closer than that of the forest. As he sent thoughts to the Zidu'Si to continue on to Britengate, he turned his flame consumed form and that of Moltar toward the only other fiery red glow in sight, Hell's Mouth.

The volcano bubbled and burped with magma that threatened to burst forth at any moment. Since his last visit when he dropped the ogres into their fiery grave, the mountain seemed to have awoken. Shuran and drakkon dove straight into the flaming maw of the volcano and glided through the lava directly to the Emmuku'Gu.

Kashshaptu were waiting outside the shield protecting Britengate when news from the Highlands arrived that Shuran and Moltar were on their way. The talisman began to glow a deep red as the words of incantation were spoken. The witches were taking control of the mighty drakkon as he traveled the lines of power back to the city.

Shuran felt the changes as they exited the Emmuku'Gu. His mind felt a grip take hold of a part of his conciseness. A piece of himself that was separate but joined to his being became twisted. It was being pulled from him as he fought to hold on. In his fight to wrap his will around that part of his mind, he fell from Moltar's back as they entered Britengate from the power flowing into the Altar. When he hit the ground and the wind was knocked from his lungs, he lost his grip on that part of him that he centered his strength around. Moltar was lost to him.

Chapter Seventeen

Shuran gained his feet in time to only take a glancing blow from the swipe of Moltar's tail. His beloved drakkon was blocked from his bond and thrashing around in agony. Shuran could see the confusion in Moltar's eyes as he turned to face his Lugaldur. Shuran tried to reach out for him, but Moltar backed away as though being struck.

The kashshaptu were repeating the spell to take control of the beast. It was not working as expected and they continued to weave their dark blood magic with the talisman. The bond between Moltar and Shuran was such that had never been before and was not so easily broken.

Moltar roared out in agony, fear, and confusion as the spell battered and tore at his connection to Shuran. The bond was weakening but not yet severed. Disconnected voices whispered in the back of Moltar's mind, offering freedom from the pain. He heard them telling him to remove the obstacle keeping them from bringing him peace. They told him what needed doing, and he turned around to face the Altar of Creation.

Mouth wide and eyes narrowed, Moltar tried to call forth the power of fire Essence to melt the crystal stones, but he could not wield. His wings flapped forward and hurled toward the altar, again without the result he expected. He was without the power of the Zidu'Si or his bond with Shuran. His fear turned to anger at what was happening to him and he let out a sound that had never before escaped his mighty jaws.

Shuran stood powerless watching Moltar, and feeling the walls closing around that part of him that was the bond of Lugaldur and drakkon. He never registered the hands that gripped him and dragged him back away from the altar and out of Moltar's reach.

Elves and weavers worked Essence in an effort to subdue the massive beast. The efforts were having an effect, but it was small and requiring all the strength they had. When Moltar was finally beginning to fall to the spells and influence of the elves, he let out a final screeching call of protest. Everyone that was not engaged in restraining Moltar covered their ears in an attempt to block out the cries.

The sound began to reverberate around the altar stones. The high pitch caused the vibrations to increase and cracks began to form on the uprights ringing the center structure. As the sound finally halted, and Moltar fell into unconsciousness from the elves and weavers, cracks continued to form in the altar. The damage was done and the altar stones were unable to maintain the power of the Emmuku'Gu flowing into them.

There was a blinding pulse of light that followed Moltar's fall to the ground, accompanied by fine shards of crystal, as the Altar of Creation burst apart. The shield that protected the city of Britengate fell the instant the altar shattered. The dark forces gathered outside the city grimaced at the bright flash of radiance, they gathered themselves quickly, however, and prepared for the assault.

Shuran snapped out of his trance after the smack to his face from Moona. "Ouch! What is happening?" Shuran was dazed and not entirely certain what was transpiring around him.

"Your monstrosity of a pet just blew up the Altar of Creation and the shield is down, how was yer day?" Moona answered. "What jus' happened?"

Shuran shook his head as he walked back to where Moltar lay sleeping under the influence of the elves and weaver's spells. "Something disconnected our bond." He staggered as he took each step. He could not clear his thoughts.

Moona grabbed Shuran by the arm before he could take another step. "Let sleeping drakkons lay, boy. We got bigger problems." She turned him toward the West where the Shadow was beginning to form and dark weavers were entering the city. "Where are the rest of the Zidu'Si?"

"They are coming from the Highlands by drakkon and Lil'Du airship. We were attacked at the borders upon return." Shuran could not stop looking back at Moltar, laying in forced sleep. Somehow the forces of darkness had done something to Moltar and his bond. He suspected the kashshaptu had something to do with this. "Where are the thirteen sisters, I think they may know what has happened to Moltar?"

"No need to look, Shuran," Penelle said as she ran toward him from the West. "It would appear as though the sisters who left my coven, have found the means to create a talisman. I could feel the blood magic in the Essence."

"How do we counter this kind of magic?" Shuran asked.

Penelle cast her eyes toward Moltar. "It is difficult to say. One would have to know how the talisman was created to devise a way to destroy the talisman's magic."

"Can't ya just destroy the talisman?" Codger asked.

"Unfortunately that will not work with blood magic. Unlike a weaving that is powered by the human casting the spell, the use of blood magic is powered by the subject of the spell." Penelle turned back to Shuran with a look of sorrow.

Shuran had no time to think on this more as the first volleys of dark energy began to sail over the city. Shuran had barely enough time to put a shield over Moltar before the attack moved into full battle. Those who were capable began defending the city in earnest.

As the dark weavers and witches began to gather at the trenches and file toward the areas where the water tunneled below the earth, they found they could not cross the open water. This delay in the advancement afforded the Britengate fighters time to gather and halt their advancement over the bridges at the gates.

The Guardians of the Altar, though weakened by its destruction, still had a connection to the Emmuku'Gu thus able to wield their spells of light against the Shadow. As much as they halted the advancement of the Shadow, several dark weavers and kashshaptu were able to transport through and into the city. Shuran called, by communication stone, to the other races for any to come to aid. He hoped that the Zidu'Si along with the Ag'Lu and Lil'Du would be arriving soon.

More dark forces were making their way into the city and began attacking the citizens who could not defend themselves. Most of those who could come to the aid of their fellow Britengates were only new to weaving and outmatched by their foe. For every one agent of Shadow that fell, three of the Britengate weavers fell to their attackers.

Shuran, followed by Moona, Codger, Penelle, and several elves, made their way through the city finding dark weavers and dispatching them as best they could.

Shuran tried to become living flame more than once but could not achieve it fully due to his lack of control. The effect of having his bond with Moltar blocked was causing him pain as well as grogginess that he could not afford the time to ponder. He moved in automatic response to the threat against his friends and followers. As he and the others moved through the falling city, Shuran called for everyone to make their way to the barracks and medical building. They would have an easier time defending a single location, than attempting to battle on multiple fronts.

The drakkon riders already in Britengate had their work cut out for them as they battled with conjurations of the same black flying beasts that Salmetu called forth at the Altar of Chaos. They threw Essence born flame to little effect on the evil beasts. The best they could accomplish was to keep the creatures busy and away from attacking the city below. They only broke off when they saw the approaching Magurmu of Aknard's fleet.

The ships did not bother with cloaking and only engaged the shields until they readied their first assault of padiri'bur. PAD TEGA NERU, the weavers spoke as they set the first triggers of the 'evil exploders'. When they loosed the explosives on the black beasts, the blasts rocked their ships from the concussive waves. A cheer went up aboard the flying ships as the creatures that did not disappear, retreated back into the Shadow surrounding the city. More blasts sounded in the blackening night as the magurmu continued to drop padiri'bur into the dark forces below.

Shuran was weakening as the fighting to defend the small section of Britengate pressed them tighter. As he tapped into the force of the Emmuku'Gu, he found it increasingly difficult to concentrate. He was beginning to feel the effects of whatever controlled Moltar. "The secondary bond," he realized. He could not fight the Shadow and its agents while

122

protecting himself from being taken by the same spell as his bonded.

Before he could decide what next to do, a strong wind began to swirl around the perimeter of their defense. The la'bun masua had arrived along with the Ag'Lu as Shuran heard the steady roars of drakkon adding to the cacophony playing both in his head and throughout Britengate.

Lil'Du warriors began lowering themselves down from the airships alongside the Zidu'Si. They fought back their dark opponents with fierce determination.

Badur'Lu began to arrive in the artificial river surrounding the city and sent powerful thrusts of water, ice, and steam at the dark forces attempting to enter the city.

Shadow agents began to retreat from the renewed defense by the citizens of the once center of worship for the Light and Creation. The Shadow was not giving up so easily. It roiled over the trench bridges and began filling the dark weavers with power to stand against the combined forces of the Zidu'Si and their supporters.

The once renewed defense began to weaken at the increase in power of their attackers. The immeasurable power of the Zidu'Si alone was unable to withstand the pressing attack of the Shadow since Shuran was now concentrating on blocking the effect of the kashshaptu spell placed upon Moltar. It was all they could do to keep the dark energy and influence from taking hold of them.

Ogres began to push forward through the Shadow, carrying large clubs made of twisted gug. They began swinging the clubs at the Zidu'Si shield, which would have destroyed the defense if they had made contact. As soon as the ogres attacked, a green glow formed over them and they froze in mid-swing. The clubs hit the ground as the ogres began to twist and shrink. Where the ogres once stood, small fur covered creatures hopped away.

Through the murky blackness of the Shadow, could be seen the approach of walking tree-like creatures. The Dryads had come to the aid of Britengate. They walked unmolested through the Shadow as the foggy wickedness pulled back from the Dryads when they approached. The first one to arrive looked down upon Shuran and touched him with an outstretched branch.

Shuran immediately felt a wave of relief as the effects of Moltar's spelled mind, was walled off from Shuran's own conciseness. "What have you done?

I no longer feel the connection."

"You are still connected Watcher, we have only prevented the dark spell from reaching you," the Dryad said.

"Can you reverse what has been done to my bonded?" Shuran pleaded.

The Dryad shook its branches. "Not without killing the beast, you must find a way to release it." The Dryad swung another branch out that held a talisman on a chain. The gugtu container held upon the chain was cracked and leaking a viscous liquid. "The tool of the spell is destroyed along with the witch that wielded it. You will need to undo the damage."

As Shuran stood, the air surrounding him and the others began to cool. While the temperature dropped, Shuran felt the presence he had only once before felt, that of the Tal'Ba-ad. The dropping temperature had a slowing effect on the Shadow as its advanced slowed to a crawl.

The Lil'Du warriors wasted no time in sending winds to push back the Shadow. Winds came from all around them and funneled the Shadow back out of Britengate. The dark forces that were within were frozen solid and shattered in place as the Shadow retreated. Those that remained outside the city border disappeared in swirls of a brackish smoke.

Chapter Eighteen

The Tal'Ba-ad stood before Shuran and the city defenders, icy forms of man and animal alike. The animated ice sculptures began to disperse leaving only one behind as a frosty dome began to form over the city where once the Altar powered shield previously existed. "You will not be safe here long Watcher, you must leave and prepare for what is to come." The demon dispersed and joined the others of its kind in the new shield over the city.

"Our cousins will not hold long Shuran, Shin'Ar. You must take your people away soon," the Dryad said before it and its companions dispersed as well and passed beyond the shield.

Shuran gathered himself and went to check on Moltar's condition. He found him much in the same state he was in when the attack began. He did notice that he seemed less restless than before. Perhaps the dulling of their link assisted, he could not be certain, but he could not dwell on that currently. Andra needed his attention.

Shuran made his way to the medical facilities where Andra was being attended after instructing the Zidu'Si to make preparations to leave Britengate. He found the mysterious man who had been in and out of his life since birth, lying in a cot pale and still as death. He approached without caution as he replayed the vision he took from Kettanu in Aluanu.

Moona stood to stop his approach. "Don' touch that collar," she said before stepping back from his path.

Shuran stood over Andra and eyed the collar with a hint of familiarity. "Shackles," he whispered before reaching his finger down to trace the glowing runes upon its surface. The strange marking protested his touch with a flickering glow, but Shuran did not seem to fall to the same effects the others who had touched it did. "Gub'ba Dur Gu'gal."

"Gabba dur what?" Moona asked.

"It is a restraint to transfix those who have been claimed into service. The Telukukal used them on those who served the Dark Sumer." Shuran reached down and gripped the collar. "Su'bar Tu," he said. The collar flashed briefly before opening.

Penelle and Sulura stood behind Shuran and stepped closer at the sight of his releasing the collar from Andra. "Nagutan said you would be able to open it, but I do not understand how?"

Shuran handed the device to Dara while glancing at his mother. "Please take this to your people and see if they can duplicate it. I would like four more of them if possible." He then turned to Sulura and the others. "The memories I have of this device are that of their use by the Sumerian and Telukukal forces in their wars. They would be used to keep prisoners restrained. They only work on those with specific markers in their blood, and without an unlocking device can only be disengaged by another with the same blood."

Moona was the first to realize what Shuran was saying. "Are you saying that you and shifty here are somehow related?"

"I believe that Andra is not an Arakharat at all, but a Telukukal offspring and possibly my adda." Shuran looked back at Andra or perhaps Dalgon if the stolen memory should be believed. Questions would have to wait as his possible father needed time to regain his strength after all the time spent in the collar. "We shall speak later mother." Shuran kissed Sulura on her cheek as she knelt beside him.

Shuran stood and led everyone out of the medical building that was not attending to the injured or sick. "We need to finish preparations for evacuation of the city. This place will not stand against the coming battle."

Avrank steeped forward. "We could go to the mountains or perhaps back to the Highlands where the Shadow cannot go."

"The Shadow would find a way, of that I have little doubt. We must go to the one place I am certain the Shadow is unable to go. We will go to Badgaldingir." Shuran instructed the Lil'Du and Ag'Lu to return to their cities and prepare, then wait until Shuran sent for them when the time came.

All throughout the evening, Shuran and the Zidu'Si began transporting people and supplies from Britengate down to the ancient city buried deep below the Orenthal Mountains. The first groups to go had only what supplies they needed and carried on their backs. Avrank and Orian took those first to evacuate.

When they first arrived in the courtyard of Badgaldingir, Avrank expected to catch the Caretakers unaware. He was surprised to find Zak waiting with carts and lines of other Entar'Lu awaiting their arrival. "Zak, you do not seem surprised by our arrival."

Zak smiled and nodded. "They told us the Zidu'Si would be bringing refugees from the devastated city of Britengate. We have been preparing for some time." Zak finished his greeting and motioned for the other Caretakers to begin showing people to their new homes. He then turned back to Orian and Avrank. "I will not keep you, there is many more I expect and we will keep others here to greet you as they arrive."

True to his word, Zak or Dravard were always available and waiting with other Entar'Lu, ready to usher off the latest arrivals to safety. No questions were raised. No protests were given. No warnings not to touch anything were spoken.

On the sixth trip back to the city Avrank finally had held his tongue long enough. "Zak, what is the matter here? I was led to believe this place was some religious refuge and only those within your order or the Zidu'Si were welcome?"

Zak smiled and pointed at the barrels that arrived with the latest group. "Pour me a tankard of that and I will explain." Taking the brew and drinking, he smiled broad and told his tale. "The voices have spoke at length of a time when the city would be needed again. This is part of the reason we Entar'Lu have been here, to look after things. This is no religious order or sanctuary, it is an ancient city of the Sumerians and now it will be put back to use for Shuran the Shin'Ar and his people."

More Zidu'Si transferred refugees of Britengate along with many supplies and animals. The Entar'Lu had accommodations for all including the livestock. Dravard more than once repeated to all that would hear, that the city provides for all needs. None of the Zidu'Si including Shuran had spent a great deal of time in the city to understand precisely how vast it actually was.

Within the borders of Badgaldingir was the outward appearance of a large city with every imaginable structure for living and trade, but there was more to the city than met the eye. While animals were taken to fields that none knew existed until now, people were shown to living quarters in lower level apartments that were spread throughout beneath the surface of the city, yet they had windows that provided fresh air and light.

The apartments were already filled with comfortable and functional furnishings made from materials and designs unknown to the new inhabitants. Though they settled restlessly, more out of fear from staying in Britengate, the new surroundings somehow made them feel at ease.

The evacuation was steady but slow moving, as many inhabitants needed medical attention prior to being moved. Others required time to gather their belongings which required sorting through rubble and debris from the destruction wrought from the battle. It was unfortunate that much of the devastation was a result of the padiri'bur loosed from the magurmu of Aknard's fleet. None of the survivors held any ill for the friendly fire, they felt as though they may not have survived without the weapons and things could always be replaced.

As the evacuations continued, Shuran left the others to attend the refugees after he transported Moltar to a secluded area near the tree he first met Zak below. He stroked his bonded's chin and forced himself to leave and head back to the Ag'Lu City with Aglia, he needed to check on Gregoran and Jade. There was no word as to their condition.

Shuran transformed to fire along with Aglia and her drakkon, Thyrin. They entered the Emmuku'Gu, exited from Hell's Mouth and headed immediately for the Ag'Lu City after reforming flesh. Shuran was thankful for the gift of clothes made from the hide of the 'lava lizards' as Avrank named them. He was feeling a wash of dread the closer they flew to Mikidisati Kitus. He could feel the connection to Gregoran fading. He felt it for some time but refused to acknowledge the loss.

Jade had already passed by the time they arrived in the city. Drakkon were rumbling a guttural cry of mourning that echoed throughout the night. She lay curled in a position that made her seem asleep and peaceful. Shuran held his head low as he dismounted Thyrin and walked toward Jade. His bond to Moltar may have been blocked, but his heart was breaking for his bonded as though it were his own mother lying dead at his feet. Shuran fell to his knees and wept.

Shuran was so grief stricken he did not sense the approach of the drakkon. They moved to surround he and Jade in a circle of mourning. When Shuran finally raised his head he found that he was encircled by drakkon, heads raised and wings extended. They roared out in the night and let fire stream into sky. When at long last they completed their tribute to the loss of one of their kind, Shuran stood and asked to be taken to Gregoran.

He found him weakened to within a breath of separating from his body and giving up his shi to the Essence. Shuran ran to his side and immediately began exploring his body to attempt healing his friend and Zidu'Si.

Gregoran stopped his effort with a touch. "It is far to late to help me Shin'Ar. I spent my strength attempting to heal my bonded to no avail."

"I do not accept this my friend and sheesh. Too many are lost I will not accept your passing as well," Shuran protested. His argument was weak as he already felt that Gregoran was beyond saving. Too much of his shi was spent in attempting to revive his drakkon. "There is only one thing I could do for you at this point in your passing."

Gregoran nodded, already knowing what Shuran was suggesting. "Transport my shi to the Emmuku'Gu, I will not allow the Shadow a chance to claim my Essence."

Shuran held back his tears as best he could and closed his eyes. "You have been brother, friend, servant, and family to the Zidu'Si. May your Essence blend with Coosco and nourish Ersetu until such time as you are reborn." Shuran said the words without realizing where they came from. A green glow emanated from his down-turned palms over Gregoran's chest that penetrated into his friend's body. An outline of Gregoran emerged as a final breath escaped his body.

The ghostly green form of Gregoran separated from his body and stood before Shuran. He laid a hand upon Shuran's shoulder. Causing a spasm of grief in his Shin'Ar, before walking to the laid out body of his bonded. As he reached her, his phantasmal form buckled in a final show of loss and grief before turning back to Shuran.

Shuran nodded in shared thought and watched as Coosco extended her reach of power up from the center of the planet and gathered Gregoran's shi. He was surrounded with pure white light for only a moment and was gone, leaving Shuran facing Jade. He reached toward the drakkon and began to chant a silent spell and call upon the Essence.

Jade's body began to glow and sparkle as he continued his casting. Her body began to burst forth with green light and became semi-translucent. As Shuran completed the weaving and wielding, he stood before the now precious stone sculpture of Jade, the remnants of her shi remaining held within to maintain a soft glow within the majestic beast that was a part of his family.

Aglia walked up beside Shuran to comfort him. "You have bestowed honor beyond any could have wished for Shin'Ar, their sacrifice will never be forgotten."

"Then why do I feel so empty Aglia? It is not fair. I asked for none of this but accepted it as my duty and destiny. All others have walked in my steps to stand beside me and face the same fates," Shuran cried out.

"The Gods have set a path-" she started.

"GODS BE DAMNED! They are not Gods. They are arrogant and prideful beings of another world, set upon this world to create us as toys in their games of dominance in the name of learning. I will entertain them no longer." Shuran was turning his pain into anger.

Aglia reached her hand to Shuran to join the fire he was becoming. "Shin'Ar, I speak not of the Sumerian pretenders who molested this world and transformed this world into a laboratory for experimentation. I speak of whatever Gods saw fit to create this world and all the other worlds that might exist among the heavens. I have faith in destiny and a path set before me. You should as well, for without faith in something greater, no matter how you choose to name it, then there is nothing to seek beyond the fleeting time we have in this existence."

Shuran stuttered, as did his flames at her words. "Aglia, how can you still hold onto faith when a piece of your heart has been torn from you?"

"Because the heart can heal as can the shi, so long as you believe in what is true and good."

Shuran calmed himself at her words and embraced her. "You will stand best in the place of Gregoran, should you choose to maintain the position. I only hope I am able to stand firm upon the ground beside you."

Aglia allowed the discomfort of the embrace for as long as she could tolerate. The Ag'Lu were not openly affectionate or emotional as a rule, but times were changing and they were adapting to the outside world. "We must return, Shin'Ar. The others will want to discuss what has transpired and there is yet more to prepare for."

Shuran separated from Aglia, feeling her stiffness at his familiar touch. He spared her an apologetic glance before turning to Jade and then felt the Emmuku'Gu below her that now connected the Ag'Lu home to the rest of the world. "I will take Jade back to the city with us. Moltar will need to mourn and pay tribute to his mother once I am able to break the spell that troubles him."

Aglia agreed but continued to look at Shuran as though there was something more. "My drakkon friend, Thyrin has asked if he might be accepted into the Zidu'Si as well, Shuran Shin'Ar."

Shuran was at first confused until he remembered that the drakkon of the Highlands did not bond with Ag'Lu as happened with the Drakkians. "You would require a bonding which I understand your kind do not normally accept since you have developed the ability to wield fire without such constraints."

Thyrin approached and laid his head down at Aglia's feet. "I am already bonded to this one in heart if not in Essence. I would join you in honor of the drakkon Jade, mother to Moltar, mightiest of our kind."

Shuran nodded to the drakkon and Aglia and advised her to lay her hand upon Thyrin's head. The acceptance of bondage was instantaneous and the flood of strength into the Zidu'Si was immediate. "You have a strong will, my friend. I welcome you to our family."

Thyrin moved for Shuran and Aglia to climb upon his back before Shuran indicated that it would not be necessary this trip. "In joining Gregoran to the Essence and transforming Jade to the emerald green likeness of stone she is named after, it would seem I inadvertently invited the flow to reach through the earth and join your home to the Emmuku'Gu. We will be back with the others in a beat of your majestic heart."

Chapter Nineteen

The Napalkua River took very little time in reclaiming the sloped lands where the Zig'Mada once plunged hundreds of feet over the hidden caves. Now that Shuran and the Zidu'Si pushed the land back down, none would otherwise know of the chamber that existed deep below.

Salmetu stood before the gentle slope of cascading water that remained where the falls once dominated the area. She turned to Nagutan and, by means of her Shadow influence, commanded he bring the chamber hidden deep in the ground up to the surface.

Nagutan did not fight or show any sign of protest. He extended his arms and called forth the power of the Essence to move rock and dirt. The waters of the Napalkua parted before the rise of earth that preceded the appearance of the gugtu chamber prison that held the Gizzu'Su. Nagutan began to strain under the pressure of moving the prison. Had not the Shadow been bolstering his power, me likely would have passed into unconsciousness long before the chamber surfaced. Nagutan fell to his knees in exhaustion.

Salmetu patted him on the head and moved toward the chamber with the crystal in hand. As she stepped closer, she called upon the power of Shadow to infuse the stone with dark energy. The battle for dominance within the stone caused it to pulse between deep red and bright white. When at last she reached the outside of the prison, Salmetu pushed the stone against the wall and forced it into place with a spell.

As she stepped back in haste, Ereshkigal momentarily began slipping free of Salmetu's body, causing her to stumble. She rejoined with her vessel and scrambled to her feet and continue running, but was not far enough when the crystal finally exploded. Salmetu flew through the air from the concussive wave that accompanied the blast.

An entire section of wall was blown open, exposing the white light emanating throughout the interior of the gugtu prison. Screams of agony and bewilderment echoed throughout the space and escaped the newly made breech. The Gizzu'Su inside could sense the way out but were being held back from departing by the wall of light.

Ereshkigal had been expecting the Gizzu'Su to become released as soon as the walls were breached. She was beginning to understand what was occurring. Nergal contained them and now she must lend her power to assist in their release. "I am coming for you Nergal," she screamed as she hurled herself from Salmetu's scorched and tattered body.

Her Shadow enriched shi streamed into the white wall of energy that separated her from her followers. She met resistance against her forceful attempt at entry.

Nergal slowly began to open a section to allow her inside. He hoped she would join her comrades in their prison. As he opened the hole wider, Ereshkigal's tainted dark shi began to slip through and into the prison. Nergal could sense her coalescing with the Gizzu'Su, and once she was fully integrated he would seal her in.

Ereshkigal eventually pulled her entire Essence into the chamber and Nergal began to close her in, but something stopped his sealing the wall of his energy. He focused his energy on forcing closed the wall when he felt the familiar presence. An arm was extended into the chamber through the hole, an arm he recognized as Nagutan's.

Nagutan, still under the influence of the Shadow, watched as his Queen entered the Gizzu'Su prison to retrieve her family. He also noticed the wall of energy begin to close behind her. Without thinking, his body reacted of its own accord and brought him to his feet and into a fast floating motion toward the wall. He shoved his arm in at the last moment, preventing his former master from sealing the prison.

"Dalgon no, you must remove your arm," Nergal called out from the ether. But Dalgon Nagutan was beyond his Shin'ar's reach. Nergal sensed the Shadow within his former Isten and knew his effort was in vain.

Ereshkigal felt the bridge to freedom the moment Nagutan reached his arm into the chamber. She wasted little time on thinking and immediately joined with his hand and used it to funnel herself and the Gizzu'Su through his body and out of the chamber. When the last thread of darkness passed through Nagutan, a boisterous scream of victory sounded through his head and the power of darkness surged, including that in Nagutan's body.

Nagutan pulled his arm free of the chamber that caused a blinding flash of light when at last he was free of the wall. He fell over in pain and writhed upon the ground in fits of spasm. A dark shot of power from his Queen brought him out of the agonizing episode.

Ereshkigal knelt beside Nagutan, having regained her vessel. "Are you still with us my new pet?" she asked. "I would hate to have lost a new one so quickly. This vessel has never been very good with her pets and I fear I am following suit."

Nagutan struggled to regain himself but eventually sat up and Shadow crossed his eyes. "I am well my Queen and prepared for what next you wish of me."

"You will go to Durangug and prepare for our arrival. My Gizzu'Su and I will not tolerate being kept from entry. We have vengeance to enact," she said before she turned away and disappeared with the billowing Shadow forms of the Gizzu'Su.

Nagutan turned toward the North and disappeared as well in a swirl of darkness that crackled with white lightening.

The Shadow converged on Britengate where the icy shell of odd energy replaced the Emmuku'Gu shield that prevented them entry. Ereshkigal spared only a moment before assaulting the barrier with dark energy and sending the Shadow to engage the ice. Pulse after bolt of darkness flowed and blasted the shell to no discernible effect. The Gizzu'Su and Ereshkigal were not deterred and increased their efforts.

Eventually, the shell began to waver and steam misted away from the barrier in a hazy green stream that gathered and moved off to the North. Slow at first the shell began to melt away from the top most point.

The Shadow surged over the top of the dome and poured down into the city. As the dark and foggy mass passed through the opening, it widened and melted away the dome exponentially fast. Soon there was nothing left but the retreating green mist.

Though she sensed something strangely familiar about the green mist that drifted away, Ereshkigal screeched with delight as the ice shield yielded and she floated her vessel Salmetu over the West bridge and into the city. Her joy at entering Britengate was cut short as she realized that the place was deserted. Salmetu looked in all directions to find that not a living thing remained. The buildings that stood were silent and empty. The Altar of Creation was naught but a pile of dust. Rage overtook her Shadow filled body and exploded in a burst of red plasma and streams of darkness.

The Shadow leveled the entire city. Every brick or stone was pulverized to dust and sent to fill the artificial river that surrounded the city. Wood was burnt to ash and blown away on the wind. Every last reminder of the people that only recently huddled behind an Essence shield of the Light was erased from existence, but the Shadow did not stop there. Trees, plants, bushes, and life of all kind was decimated in a final blast of force in every direction reaching several times the distance from the former city border.

Salmetu's body shifted with the influx of Shadow that poured into her as Ereshkigal pulled back her strands of Shadow. "We will find them and destroy every last one including those who harbor our enemy. I will have Shuran's head on a pike outside the Academy castle." She floated upon the mists north over the blackened lands that were once Britengate. The Shadow was going to advance on the elves in Entensiama.

As the wall of darkness advanced toward the tree line that marked the boundary of the forests around the elfin capital. The air began to haze over with a green glow that grew in brightness as the Shadow neared. Movement on the opposing side caught the attention of Salmetu.

She narrowed her eyes with recognition. Ereshkigal fed her memories of the ancient magic that resisted the Sumerians when they first came to Ersetu. "We thought you long gone from the world when your precious forest turned to that garden of stone," she mocked.

The Dryads lumbered around the interior of the shield they created to prevent entrance to the forest. "We are eternal, wraith. Unlike your kind who feeds from the living, we are life itself and are not so easily taken."

"Is that a challenge, or is your bark worse than your bite?" Salmetu echoed in a hundred voices. "Let down your barrier and stand against us or let us pass and we shall leave you to your precious trees."

A raspy and hoarse laugh emerged from the Dryad addressing Salmetu. "Your darkness will not pass into these lands, they are under our protection. You should return to the depths from which you came."

Rage returned to the Queen of Shadow as the defiance of the Dryads prevented her vengeance upon the elves. In an exercise of futility, she loosed blasts of energy upon the shield that only glowed brighter in defiance of her attempts. As quickly as her fury boiled over, it abated and she withdrew to the South with her Shadow.

Ereshkigal called out to her dark forces to spread out and find where Shuran and the people of Britengate had gone to ground. She felt the dead or dying bodies of many Shadow Walkers, Kashshaptu, and weavers at the border of the Highlands and Drakk. She disappeared in Shadow as the clouds of darkness entered the ground.

The Shadow emerged from the cracks in the dead earth of Drakk around Hell's Mouth. Every agent of the dark that remained, both dead and dying, were filled with the evil power and brought back to full vitality and power. They all gathered before their Queen and awaited instruction.

"Spread out and find any that remain in this land. I want an army," Ereshkigal told them. She then focused her attention on the caves along the side of the fiery mountain. Borrowing Salmetu's ability for sensing life and shi, Ereshkigal extended tendrils of power to ferret out what was hiding within the caverns. She smiled and Shadow swirled in her eyes. "Take the drakkon and fill them with darkness."

Salmetu also felt another presence that moved closer to where she stood. It was attempting to take her unaware. She turned in a blink to catch the dagger filled hand of Fallon. "Now Baron is that any way to treat family?"

Fallon spat upon Salmetu's feet. "You are no family to me, underworld filth. You have destroyed what was the girl who would be my niece."

"Perhaps... but now you have the opportunity to serve the Shadow and

become closer than family," Salmetu said with her own voice. "One of my Gizzu'Su could take you as their vessel-"
Fallon cut her words short when he reached up with his free hand and dragged it across the poisoned blade he held within the other hand of his restrained arm. The quick reaction caused foam to begin forming upon his tongue as he dropped to the ground at Salmetu's feet.
Shadow filled his dying body just the same. "It will not be so simple to escape us Baron. Ninagal will have your body since you choose to end its use."
At her instruction, one of the amalgamations of man shaped Shadow surged forward and slipped into Fallon's dying body. The body began to spasm and twitch as each vein bulged below the skin from the flow of darkness. The poison that Fallon took from the blade began to pass out of the body through a wound on his hand. As liquid spilled forth, it bubbled and steamed as it was expelled by the Shadow and twisted shi of Ninagal. As the murky blackness clouded over his eyes, Fallon was no more and the ancient false god Ninagal was reborn.

Chapter Twenty.

Ereshkigal helped her Gizzu'Su up from the ground at her feet. "How do you feel my child?" A smile of a proud mother watching her baby take its first steps formed upon her borrowed face.

Ninagal stumbled over the tongue of his vessel. After several attempts at speech, he was able to respond in ancient Sumer. "This body is stunted and lacking, my Queen."

"It will suffice for the time. We shall soon have new bodies that better suit our power and status. Once Nagutan has prepared for our arrival, we shall begin to reclaim this savage world and bring order." Ereshkigal preened and fawned over the being now occupying Fallon. She turned to the remaining three clusters of Shadow hovering near. "You shall have bodies as well."

Ninagal steadied in his temporary host and turned to Ereshkigal. "There are but few Telukukal remaining among the children of Ersetu, and the old man Nagutan is surely too weakened."

"Telukukal," she laughed. "They, like these we use to carry our shi are diluted and impure. Blended in blood as this Salmetu is who ferries me around, she too is not pure enough and something within her is strange and undesirable for permanent use."

"It is unfortunate that our bodies were destroyed in the prison chamber,"

Ninagal said. "Had they not been pierced by the Mi-Ib Simshi, we could return to our own flesh."

Ereshkigal slapped him, sending him back to the ground. "Had we not been released you mean, fool. We would yet be locked away in those shells, had my apprentice not freed our shi. We shall have proper flesh from which to retake our former shape."

The three Shadow forms, spread out from Salmetu and located their own bodies to inhabit. Once they located suitable hosts, they adjusted to flesh and revitalized the necrotic tissues of their dying vessels. One by one they rejoined Ereshkigal and Ninagal. The kashshaptu that two of them found were more suitable than the dark weaver found by the last Gizzu'Su. The witches were much older and closer in lineage to the Telukukal than the weaver who was likely less than a century of age, being a human. They would only be temporary hosts.

Five Shadow infused beings stood at the base of Hell's Mouth. Screams and roars of agony sounded over the low steady rumble of the volcano. Streaming flows of Shadow began billowing back toward the Gizzu'Su dragging with them a sizable clutch of drakkon.

The drakkon struggled against the inevitable, thrashing, clawing, and flapping wings in an attempt to break free. The Shadow had already begun to enter their un-bonded bodies and twisting them to serve Chaos. Bright and vibrant scales dulled and lost their shine as the changes began to mutate them into something menacing and evil. Scales flared out and grew to razor-sharp points. Tails malformed at the ends to include clubs, spikes, or multi-sided blades to mangle, maim, and eviscerate the enemy.

Ereshkigal moved Salmetu to the largest and most maniacal beast and stroked its chin. As her flesh shredded on the scales, she sent darkness to heal and stitch the skin until her hands were callused. With a wave and a word, a saddle and harness appeared on the creature that could no longer be called a drakkon. She levitated into the saddle. She created the same for the other beasts and her Gizzu'Su and army of Shadow Walkers all took to saddle before they took to the sky.

Darkness claimed the night and blotted out the moonlight that was illuminating the road to Middleton. The Shadow pulled along behind the clutch of Chaos ridden beasts, carrying along the beginnings of the Queen's dark army. She would take them to Middleton and bolster her force that she would then take to the enemy in a final battle for control of Ersetu. The citizens of Middleton, who held out hope and refused to leave when Salmetu took control of the Council naming herself Queen would have regretted that decision had they knew what was to come.

The twisted drakkon landed upon the town's cobbled streets with a force that blasted shards of stone and clumps of earth in every direction. Deep red and black plasma streamed from every sharp-toothed mouth and melted wall and roof of each structure throughout Middleton as the Shadow poured in to claim every last man, woman, and child.

Infants transformed into wicked little hunchbacked monsters. They emitted ear piercing screeches as they hopped along the streets, drooling and slobbering. Women twisted into winged harpies with claws for fingers, fangs, and soul penetrating hollow eyes. The men ambled forward in varying heights, covered in vein popping muscles, thick necks and mindless obedience to the Queen of Shadow.

The Queen of Shadow was enjoying building her army of darkness to take into battle against the Shin'Ar and his followers. They traveled from Middleton to Two Bridges and Castleton, gathering what few people were still in the towns and not already working for the Shadow. Once they returned to New Draven, The Gizzu'Su gathered at the Academy while their flying beasts circled the castle.

Ninagal, who had taken Fallon's body, stood at a window in the Academy grand hall looking out into the night sky. The twin stars shone bright through the cloud cover. "What does this mean for our plans, Ereshkigal?"

She shifted in her throne, discomfort hidden beneath the mask of Salmetu's face. "It is uncertain why they are here, but I suspect Nergal may be involved. Nagutan does not appear to know the ultimate cause for the arrival, though there is something within him that resists."

The Gizzu'Su all began debating and arguing over their situation. "What if they mean to put a stop to what we have been planning?" asked one of them. "Will we be stopped?" asked another.

"Silence," Ereshkigal shouted over them. "This means nothing for us or our taking control of Ersetu. Do you forget the last time these two same bright lights dominated the sky? For twenty millennia we have been left upon this world, forsaken and forgotten by our own people. The twins stars of some prophecy will not be the end of our work.

"When last we saw them, they arrived and did nothing. Nergal warned of destruction and failure of our task. Punishment for breaking the laws of the ME would be swift, he said. Then nothing happened. The night sky was again dark and the wars continued until we were imprisoned in that chamber. I see no reason this time would be any different. Nergal is in no place to use them against us."

Ninagal was not convinced. "Do you know what became of Nergal when you freed us from the prison? He has the same capability to take possession of another as do we, he could place himself in a better position to interfere."

"Nergal is no longer a threat. He used up his shi in the effort of holding you within the chamber. Once Nagutan reached in and allowed your escape through him to the outside world, Nergal lost his battle to hold you." Ereshkigal tried convincing herself as much as the others. The truth was that she had no idea what became of Nergal, but she would not let the others know this.

"All of this talk is irrelevant. Soon Nagutan will regain access to Durangug and through him we will be able to once again step within the control room. I am certain that we will find the means of sending those lights back into the darkness of space." Ereshkigal took in a deep breath and closed her eyes. "It is time to leave, Nagutan has entered the Vault."

Nagutan stood outside the Vault entrance in Durangug. He attempted many times without success to enter the chamber directly by way of the Emmuku'Gu. That way of travel was now closed to him. Neither did he travel the Shadow path of darkness. When he disappeared to carry out Ereshkigal's will, he moved through the world in a new and unexpected way, somewhere in between the light and the dark.

He did not wish to do as his mistress bade him, but the compulsion coursing through him was driven by the Shadow that would not let him loose. Somewhere deep within, Nagutan knew he could enter the Vault but was attempting to keep this from the Shadow. He was weakened by his struggle to protect his own shi, and this allowed the Shadow to find a way to gain access.

Nagutan placed his hands on the cover-stone to the entrance and sent a surge of electric force into the slab. With a word, he reversed the charge in the stone and stood back as the Vault opened before him. He moved with slow and forced steps through the entrance and down into the tunnels that led to the central chamber that housed the Shin'Ar's Vault.

One laborious step followed the next as he approached the door to the Vault. When at last he arrived, he no longer fought the urge and raised his hand to the door and sent the energies and spell to open the way. When he entered, the door closed behind him and he moved to find the objects of his task, the Mi-Ib twin daggers.

He found them resting upon the table where Shuran created his communication stones and would sit reading from the journals and scrolls that recorded the long history of the Sumer since the time of their arrival on Ersetu. He spared himself several moments to wonder over how he had manipulated events and guided destiny along to reach this point in time. The Shadow allowed him this time of reflection and fed upon the anguish Nagutan released at facing his failure. The mistake was soon realized when the Shadow attempted to regain control and reached for the first blade.

Nagutan held onto the Mi-Ib Simshi but would not lift it from the table. His will to protect the blades was strong and he was asserting what strength that remained of his own shi. The blade would not lift from the table, but it was not necessary to raise the dagger to destroy it.

The Shadow pulsed in his hand and began to wrap around the hilt, sending flashes of deep red light along the blade. The blade began to heat and warp as it melted in Nagutan's hand. Soon all that remained was a hardening pool of metal upon the table. Nagutan may have been unwilling to destroy the blade, but the Shadow did not need him for this one. The twin Mi-Ib Karshi would be the one it could not touch.

Nagutan sensed the Shadow's unwillingness to wrap itself around the Mi-Ib Karshi as it backed away from the hand that Nagutan reached out to take hold of the dagger. He grabbed the hilt of the blade and lifted it from the table and stepped back toward the center of the room and awaited the arrival of the Gizzu'Su. He did not have a long wait.

Through the link of the Shadow within Nagutan, Ereshkigal and the rest of the Gizzu'Su swirled into view from the murky dark cloud that appeared before him. As each of them arrived, they backed away from Nagutan, seeing and sensing the blade he held within his raised hand.

"What are you waiting for, destroy that blade?" Ereshkigal demanded. She looked closer to see Nagutan's eyes shifting and the Shadow twisting around, fighting for control. She did not anticipate the possibility that Nagutan would have been able to fight back. She moved to intervene, but backed away when Nagutan raised the blade higher. "Leave the Telukukal to me and take the bodies of the Sumer in those alcoves," she instructed the Gizzu'Su.

While Ereshkigal stood before Nagutan, the Gizzu'Su left the bodies they were inhabiting and flew around the Vault in search of a new and more suitable body to take. They would not simply possess these bodies since the shi of the previous owner was now trapped within the Emmuku'Gu. The Gizzu'Su would take complete ownership of these bodies encased in gugtu. They first had to twist the stone so they may absorb into the surface, but they soon discovered that they had another obstacle, the pendants hanging around each neck was also a ward.

A burst of white light shone from each gem on the statues that cast more light than mid-Utu against the reflecting ice sheets of the Frozen North. The Shadow shrank back toward Ereshkigal, who stood stunned into silence. She did not understand what was happening as she watched the light grow intense and hot.

Nagutan began to laugh through the pain he felt from the Shadow struggling within him.

As Ereshkigal turned Salmetu's head toward the sound of his laughter, she recognized the sound as not Nagutan, but that of Nergal.

The expression on Nagutan's face changed from one of humor to that of determination. The blade came down and entered his chest in a single stroke that the Shadow had no time to prevent. The Mi-Ib Karshi held no stone in the hilt to trap the Shadow as it began to pour from Nagutan's body. It was not the only foreign entity being released from him.

Nergal's shi burst forth, pushing the last of the Shadow from his son's slumping form.

As Nagutan fell to the floor, the blade in his chest fell free and dissolved into dust. He looked down at his open chest as the lifeblood streamed forth and spread out and the linen shirt he wore soaked up the fluid until it could hold no more. The pool of blood slowed and spread below him as he worked with what was left of his strength to close the wound.

Nergal gathered his shi before the Gizzu'Su as they reentered the bodies they had left lying on the floor where they entered the chamber. "You should understand that I know you better than you know yourselves," his spirit said to them. "I knew that should you ever escape the prison I placed you in so long ago, that you would seek to regain corporeal form. Since your own bodies would no longer be of use after, breaching the stone would be the only escape, you would require other Sumerian skin."

Ereshkigal twisted Salmetu's face with hatred fed anger. "Those stones around their necks will not stop us," she spat. "We will have your pathetic followers as our own vessels, and those stars will again disappear in the night as they did when this war began."

Nergal's ghostly head tilted to one side as he glanced over Salmetu's shoulder at the surging lights emanating from the gems. "Those wards are not to simply prevent you taking the bodies, they will continue to increase in intensity until you have been consumed… or you leave."

The Gizzu'Su immediately disappeared in swirls of Shadow, leaving Ereshkigal in her host Salmetu to brood over the loss of her victory in taking Durangug. "You may have stopped our plans here, but we have taken something you value more than these Sumerian lapdogs of yours." She looked toward Nagutan's dying body before returning Nergal's laugh and disappearing into the Shadow.

Nergal floated toward Nagutan and pushed his hands into his chest. He used what strength he had left to heal his son and then transform him to gugtu. His spirit form began to fade as he finished his task of preserving Nagutan's body in hope that it was not too late. He looked up and called out for the presence he sensed, to appear. "You can show yourselves now," he said looking at the red scale lying next to Nagutan's statue.

The imp and Tianna's ghost, both appeared before him. "This is what I hoped would not ever happen," the imp said. "But I am prepared for what must be done."

"No," Nergal said as his weariness spread. "It is not that time yet, imp. You must hide yourself until this ends the way we have planned. Only then will you fulfill your duty." Nergal turned to Tianna as the imp disappeared. "You must listen to me carefully for there is little time. I must return to the Emmuku'Gu and you must bring your brother here and repeat to him what I tell you."

Chapter Twenty-One

Shuran Appeared with the enormous green gemstone tribute that was Jade both past and eternally captured within the precious stone bearing her name. The Zidu'Si anticipated his return, having experienced everything that transpired through their bond of service to the Shin'Ar. They greeted Aglia and Thyrin with mixed emotions. They had just lost a member of their family and were accepting a new one, a replacement as some of them felt.

Aglia was a part of the Zidu'Si now so she could sense the emotions and feelings directed toward her. "I do not wish to be taken as a replacement for Gregoran nor Thyrin as that of Jade. We are filling a need among the Zidu'Si that was left by the loss of your comrades." Her tone was even and emotionless as she turned to Shuran. "I will leave you to your memorial. Thyrin and I will see the caretakers about accommodations."

"Rubbish," Moona croaked through her own tears over their loss. "You'll be comin' with me young woman." Moona took Aglia by the arm. When Aglia resisted, Moona glared at her. "Don' keep we waitin' fire starter," Moona said as she let go of Aglia and headed toward the buildings behind them.

Codger sidled up to Aglia and cleared his throat. "One thing ya best learn quick child, is that ya don' go against ol' Moony."

The other Zidu'Si agreed as Shuran nodded for Aglia to go along after

Moona.

Zak arrived to show Shuran a place where Jade's tribute would be both available for all those who wished to visit, as well as a peaceful and serene garden for her to eternally rest. He remained to speak with Shuran after Jade was moved and the many mourners began to enter the gardens to visit her and leave tokens to memorialize her and Gregoran.

"We shall soon be at the end of our service here Shin'Ar," Zak started as they sat below his favored tree.

Shuran turned to his old dwarf friend. "What do you mean Zak? We need the Entar'Lu now more than ever."

Zak smiled and drank from the wineskin Shuran offered. "Our task was only to prepare this place for the time when you would come to reclaim it Shin'Ar. Even now we can feel the millennia settling in our old bones."

"Why would the Sumer stop providing for you now when all these people have come for shelter? This is not a permanent solution; we only fled here to buy time."

"You have brought these people precisely where they need to be, for this city will rise again and be the center of everything on Ersetu." Zak stood and handed the wineskin back to Shuran. "Come with me, there is much to discuss and show you. They have decided it time you should claim this place, so you must learn its secrets."

Shuran and Zak disappeared into the depths of the city and were gone for several hours before they resurfaced. Shuran did not share the experiences with the Zidu'Si since he still actively focused on blocking the spread of Moltar's affliction to himself. The effort of doing so allowed him to block the accidental flow of information. He was not certain yet what to think of what he just learned, since part of him already knew what Zak was showing. The memories of Nergal in Badgaldingir confirmed what Zak told him was true.

"How much time have you before you must leave?" Shuran asked Zak.

"We shall be leaving in a day's time. We would ask that you take us back to Duranekur so we may meet the end of our days among our descendants." Zak left Shuran with the salute of the caretakers and disappeared down the halls of the central building.

Shuran stared at the alcove where he first communed with the voices of the Emmuku'Gu, what he thought until now to be only the Sumer within speaking to him. His thoughts were interrupted by a gentle touch of a tender hand upon his arm. He jumped in surprise.

Coralil smiled at him. "I am sorry to have startled you Shuran," she said. "I thought you might like to talk or perhaps just sit quietly with a friend?"

Shuran returned the smile and took her hand. "That would be nice, Cora. Perhaps you would accompany me as I walk to the medical ward to check on Andra… or should I start calling him adda?"

They took their time walking the halls and chatting about everything that had recently happened. Shuran was confused and hurt that he was not told of Andra's true identity. He understood that knowing certain things would possible effect decisions and Nagutan took a great deal of care in making certain events played out precisely to bring them all to this place and time. He only hoped there were no more surprises in store for him.

"I cannot pretend to understand all that you have gone through Shuran," Cora said, squeezing his hand. "Perhaps knowing these things in the order they have been revealed has been the proper way, perhaps not. Since there is no traveling against the natural passage of time, you will not have the opportunity to find out. I suggest you focus on the present and plan for the future."

Shuran glanced at her and spared her a quick smile as they arrived at the ward to find Sulura sitting beside Andra or rather Dalgon, his father. He thanked Coralil for walking with him and sharing in his overwhelming concerns.

Dara and Vala were in the ward as well, attending to healing wounds with Moona. When they saw Coralil arrive with Shuran, they noticed them holding hands and smiled. When Shuran and Coralil parted, the other Zidu'Si women called her over to help them, and to gossip.

Shuran approached his mother, seeing her holding Dalgon's hand and holding back her own tears. "How is his recovery, mother?" Shuran asked.

Sulura looked up at Shuran before reaching out for him to come closer. She stroked his hair as he knelt before her and laid his head in the fold of her arm. "I am without words to express the feelings that race through me my son. I never even knew Dalgon had this ability to shift, never mind that he was engaging with you since your birth, but it explains a great many mysteries."

Shuran looked up at her. "What do you mean mother?"

"For one thing, I never told 'Andra' what your name was to be, as Moona has shared. Only Dalgon knew the name we chose for our son." Sulura continued to tell Shuran of what she knew and did over the years to bring about the prophecy.

She was born in the Foresworn Territories nearly three hundred years ago, the only child born in those lands that was not Arakharat. "I was conceived in Aurderia," she told him. "My mother was not among those who first settled those harsh lands beyond the Great Sea. Whatever happened to cause the defects in the mix-bloods and poison the land, did not effect my gestation."

Sulura went on to explain that she did not know the history of what transpired in the Foresworn Territories before she was born, only that it was something none who lived there spoke about openly. The land was damaged and barren. This also caused most of the women to become barren or have difficulty carrying children to term. Those children to survive were the shifters known as Arakharat.

Sulura's own mother died during her birth and she was raised by the leader known as Nabusa, who considered herself grandmother to all the Foresworn. She was a difficult woman and eventually drove Sulura to rebel and return to Aurderia to seek out any family she may still have, including her father. "I never found him or any who knew my mother. It was, after all, nearly one hundred years since my mother left, and human mixed-bloods do not have the longevity of the other races mixes."

After a time, Sulura gave up her search and settled in Rivenwood. There in the northern town, she settled into a life as a healer and mystic. Living in the Northern settlements, people tended to overlook the fact that someone may have mixed blood. "Survival for those living so far from major cities means relying on one another. Having folks around that could wield, was more favored than frowned upon. I would not say that there was none who had prejudices, but they were not openly hostile."

One night before settling in for the night, a young man came to her with a need for healing his ailing adda. They were traveling from the western forests and his father had taken ill. Sulura took them in and nursed the old man back to health over the course of several weeks. During this time, she grew close to the young man and they began to court. His name was Shinar

150

Dalgonson and his father was Nagutan. She did not care for his first name so she called him Dalgon.

Once they were ready to move on, Dalgon promised to return after seeing his father home to New Draven. He returned as promised and they began their life together. He was a trader and hunter, so he would often leave and be gone for weeks or months at a time. "I only now understand why. He was a Guardian, or at least pretending to be," she said looking at the man she married. "In time, when he wakes, he will have to fill in what is missing."

They moved several times, since they did not age as the humans did. It was one thing for folks to tolerate the presence of those with mixed blood. When those people remain young as others age and die around them, that brings out the ugly. "If you ask me, that is the true reason behind the Sikil'Mah. We did not frighten people, they were jealous. The fear they held was of passing from this life and we were reminders of something they could not achieve, immortality." The mixed-bloods were not immortal, but to humans who lived an average of eighty to one hundred years, those who measured age in centuries or millennia, were as close to immortal as they could imagine.

In time, Sulura began to become informed of plans that were in motion to bring about balance to the Essence. One day, Nagutan appeared in a small village that Sulura and Dalgon were living in. He discussed something with Dalgon, whom then left the next day to follow the path laid out by his father.

For her part, Nagutan told Sulura that she would give birth to twins who would bring balance to the Essence. She knew that Nagutan was powerful and had visions, so she did not doubt his words, and followed what he planned to keep her safe. She was told to return to Rivenwood and seek out the moon mother named Evalria. Sulura stayed with Moona during her pregnancy.

Things changed the night she was taken from Rivenwood. "Nagutan only said I would be giving birth at the Altar of Chaos. There was never a mention of three children. Dalgon and I always said when we first conceived that if we had a son we would name him Shuran. He will need to explain the change in the prophecy if he even knows how it changed."

Shuran sat back and looked at Dalgon. "And Nagutan, he performed the ceremony of your joining in love and life." Shuran told her rather than asked the question. When she looked at him in surprise, he smiled. "In a way I was there, I saw the memory of a man who was present during your ceremony."

"Who was this man?" she asked.

"I knew him as Kettanu, but I do not think he was a guest. He was Arakharat and was most likely spying." Shuran said without knowing why he came to this conclusion. He then looked back at Dalgon. "So is this the face he always wore?"

Surprised by the question, Sulura stifled a nervous laugh. "Yes, why do you ask that?"

"Because it is the one face he consistently chose when playing the part of friend and guide throughout my growing of age. I think he cheated in Nagutan's game by letting me see him for who he really was." Shuran smiled at this thought. He figured Nagutan would not be happy when he finds this out.

Tianna then appeared in the ward looking for Shuran. "You must come, Shuran," she said. "There has been a breach in Durangug, I wonder at why you could not sense it?"

Shuran stood and ran to her. "I have been blocking my bonds to prevent succumbing to a spell cast upon Moltar. What has happened?"

"Follow me and I will explain." Tianna faded from sight.

Shuran had disappeared without a word to anyone before he departed.

"What is all this noise in my medical ward?" Moona asked. "Where did Shuran just pop off ta?"

Sulura shrugged and turned back to her husband.

Moona watched Sulura, stroking her husband's hair and wiping his brow with a damp cloth. She remembered a time when she had felt the same for Old Codger. The feeling faded as she saw Dara and Vala talking to Coralil. "Oye! You three find the torch girl Aglia and bring her ta me. Time we ladies all had a bit o' talking 'bout these men and their takin' off half minded!"

Not wishing to anger Moona, Dara and Vala went to find Aglia while Coralil and Penelle found a table where they could set out food and drink for a ladies gossip circle. When Dara and Vala returned with Aglia, they joined the rest of the women, including Sulura, for tea and light food.

Moona, being her tactful self, decided to be the first to welcome the newest members of the Zidu'Si. "Coralil and Aglia, you two come sit next ta old Moony here," she said padding the bench where she settled her sizable fanny.

"Thas'it," she said as the two girls sat down. "There we go, earth, wind, and fire all in a row. Has a nice ring to it, three of the more powerful elementals I should say." Moona took a long draw from her pipe and smiled at the girls.

Coralil smiled at Moona graciously while Aglia bowed her head and remained seated stiff and emotionless.

Moona's toothy smile reversed at Aglia's lack of cheer. "Out with it fire starter, what's with the face? Ya look like ya ain' had a good girl talk in a while."

"I have never had a 'girl talk' as you call it, there is little time or need of talk among the women of the Ag'Lu," Aglia said.

Moona would not give up easily. "Yak scat, you ain' in the Highlands now child an' we girls need ta stick close if we wanna keep the boys in line." Moona turned to find Codger walking past. "Codge! Go get us some wine from that lazy pirate Aknard." Turning back to the table containing tea, she pushed her cup away. "This stuff 'ill keep ya up all night without a fine memory to go with it."

Codger soon returned with a few bottles of Aknard's best wine and set it on the table. He began to sit himself among the ladies when a grumble from across the table stopped him.

"You see any other fella's sittin' 'round this table Codge?" Moona asked. "Be off with ya." Moona grabbed the first bottle of wine and set about dumping the tea from everyone's cups and filling them with a deep red fruity drink. "Now then," she started as she sat back down with her own cup. "This is gonna be a girls' chat right proper!"

For well into the next few hours, the ladies of the Zidu'Si and Shuran's extended family spoke openly and candidly about all things girlish. Aglia eventually loosened up some and was seen with the smallest hint of a smile forming from time to time. Moona dominated the conversation most naturally, with tales of the exploits of a young Shuran, Mallick, and Bastien. She even told happy stories of her own son Vardoran. She spoke openly to them of the trouble the boys got up to, as well as the wonders in Essence Shuran performed while growing of age.

"Seems to me he had the perfect one looking out for him," Sulura said. "I only wish I could have recovered in a timely manner and been there for him. He seems so serious all the time."

"Biddley-diddles Sulura, you was healin', and seems to me that old fool Nagutan planned him ta be with me an' Old Codger anyhow," Moona said. "As for bein' serious, aye he has a set mind, but seems the young lady of the wind here has brought him to ground some." Moona smiled at Coralil who blushed at the attention.

"I am not the only one with a distraction of late," Coralil said looking at Vala. "How has Bastien's wand work been going?"

Vala's eyes widened as she smiled in mock horror. "What are you insinuating? Bastien can hardly be distracted from his spelling, let alone notice my attention."

"Men are durs," Moona said. "No, I take that back, even a jackass has more brains than a man." She took another bottle of the wine and poured more for those who wished, including Aglia.

"Bastien is preoccupied, maybe I could light his britches aflame so you could douse them with water," Aglia hiccuped. She was not used to distilled or fermented spirits and it was affecting her. Flames flared upon her head, accompanying each hiccup.

"That'll be 'nough drink for you or yer like to burn the city to ash," Moona said, taking away Aglia's cup. "Best be takin' an empty cot and sleepin' it off dear."

Vala and Dara helped Aglia to a cot and left her there to sleep off her drink.

Chapter Twenty-Two

The Vault was in complete disarray. Shuran walked through the circular structure, observing the damage. Tables were turned on end. Shelves were displaced or knocked over, spilling all their contents on the floor. Scrolls were scorched and books burnt. His first thought was that Moona's padiri'bur that were stored in the Vault had gone off in response to the breach, but then he saw they were intact since the primary activation spell was not triggered, they did not automatically explode when the Shadow entered the Vault.

He began levitating things back to their proper place and as he did so, the preservation spells began to restore the items to their pristine condition. A quick check on the hidden chamber, verified that it had not been tampered with, though someone attempted to gain the central chamber without success.

"Shuran, over here," Tianna called. "I will explain what happened," she said as Shuran looked from her and then to Nagutan's gugtu covered body.

Tianna told Shuran all that had occurred when Nagutan entered the Vault, infested with the Shadow. She watched as he struggled with, then destroyed the first dagger and displayed resistance with the second as the Gizzu'Su arrived. As she replayed the events that transpired in his Vault, she drifted around in circles at a frantic pace. She then told him about Nergal and that he returned to the Emmuku'Gu but not before sharing things with Tianna that she needed to relay to Shuran.

Shuran stared at what remained of the Mi'Ib dagger next to Nagutan. "What are we to do now Tianna, we needed those blades?"

"That is what I am attempting to tell you if you would listen. Nergal said that you would not need the blades. He said that all you need is already within you." She lifted her arms up in surrender. "I have no idea what the man meant Shuran. All I know is we are running out of time. Each time Ereshkigal has slipped out of Salmetu I have regained some strength, but she is not leaving again anytime soon."

Tianna told Shuran the remainder of what Nergal said. The Gizzu'Su attempted to take over the bodies of the Sumer held within the stasis statues. The gems around their necks were a ward placed to protect them and the vault from the Shadow, but their power is now weakened. He told her that Shuran would need to prevent the central chamber of the Vault from being taken and protect the stasis statues of the Sumer and Nagutan. The Vault must return to its proper place. "What does that mean Shuran?"

Shuran was only partially listening. He was now without the use of the daggers and Nagutan, the only one with all the answers, was beyond his reach. After hearing that Nagutan was consumed by the Shadow, he closed off his mind and tried to work out what he should do. He was on his own now. Nagutan was gone. His father Dalgon was not yet conscious. Nergal was weakened and drifting in the Emmuku'Gu, unable to communicate further. Shuran was near breaking when he fell to his knees and dipped his head to notice the red scale lying next to him.

"Where did this come from?" Shuran demanded as he lifted the large scale. "Moltar has been far too large to have been in the chamber for some time, and he does not shed scales."

"Were you not listening? Nergal said that Nagutan took it from Nabusa." Tianna repeated what she said when Shuran stopped listening to her repeating Nergal's words. While Nergal sought refuge within Nagutan after the Gizzu'Su escaped, he helped shield Nagutan's mind and learned what transpired in the Foresworn Territories. The fight, Nabusa's death, who she was, and what she gave the kashshaptu.

Nabusa was the Telukukal, who helped create the kashshaptu. When the war between the ancients was ending, she hid among the witches and was responsible for the breaking apart into covens. She tried many times to become the leader of several covens but was far too hungry for power. Her last attempt and failure to lead was with Penelle's coven and being vindictive, she altered the spell that ultimately led to the creation of the trolls. This was another catalyst that started the Sikil'Mah.

She finally found her way to become a leader when the Foresworn looked for a safe place to live. Nabusa, having been the Telukukal apprentice to Ereshkigal, already knew of the lands beyond the Great Sea and was able to gather the mixed-bloods for the first exodus. They began to settle in the new land, but this was not enough for her.

She wanted more followers, so she began sending out seekers, who later became the Guardians, to find more of those who were shunned and bring them to her. Eventually, something happened during some experiment or spell that spoiled their lands and brought about the problems with procreation. This was when the Arakharat were born. "Nergal did not share what this disaster was, but said one day you would find those answers. For now, you have what you need to complete your true purpose."

Shuran placed the scale in his pocket. "The scales that Moltar lost in the swamps. It was the kashshaptu who refused my healing her appearance that must have gathered them. Nabusa used blood magic to create the talisman." Shuran stood with renewed purpose. "Nagutan and Nabusa were not the only ones who practiced blood magic."

"What are you saying, Shuran?" Tianna asked.

"There is another who could help me break Moltar's spelled condition. Penelle and her coven were cursed and sent to the swamps for what they did to the dwarves that served them. It was blood magic that created the trolls."

He ran to the central chamber and opened it. He once used the chamber to send Dalgon, who at the time he thought was Andra, back to the Foresworn Territories. Around his worktable, he collected seven shards of crystal and returned to the chamber. As he placed each of the colored shards in their elemental pedestals, he activated them. "Tianna, I need you to go back to Badgaldingir and tell them to prepare for… I am not sure what will happen. Just tell them I will be returning and I am bringing the Vault."

Tianna hovered for a moment, confused. "What are you planning, brother?"

"I am joining the first two rings!"

Chapter Twenty-Three

The Vault began to shake as the chamber charged and began to power after millennia of not being used in such a manner. Shuran watched as the various shelves, tables and other objects around the Vault began to glow with a field of force that held them in place. He knew what was about to happen as the knowledge was there in his mind, just waiting for the proper time to be accessed.

He needed no spell weaving or Essence wielding to accomplish what he was about to do. The Vault knew what needed to be done; it wanted nothing more than to return to its proper place within the belly of Badgaldingir. This was the technology of the ancients, not magic.

Shuran reached out to grab something to hold on to when a field of force wrapped around him as it did everything else. As the central chamber powered enough, the inner alcove filled with swirling light of all the elemental Essence hues associated with the crystal shards. He walked up to the light and stared into it as he thought of the empty circular room that Zak had shown him earlier that same day. The control room, he had called it. Shuran now saw it as the first ring. Shuran reached into the flow of energy, and Durangug disappeared from below the earth of the northern forests.

The entire Vault slipped into the fabric between the Emmuku'Gu and

Shadow, then traveled the way Shuran had when Moltar pulled him. Shuran only now realized that this was the same way he accessed the Vault instantly without using the lines of power already present in Ersetu.

He was somehow yet able to move around the Vault, but the shaking he felt no longer affected him as the field around him was dampening the effects. He walked around the power core and marveled at what he saw. The knowledge of what it truly was filled his mind as the pulsing of the lights suddenly slowed to a sluggish swirl. He had arrived at his destination.

Tianna had only just begun to warn the people in the city when the ground beneath them began to vibrate. The effect was short and ended with a sudden jolt, which knock a few off their feet and sent various objects to the floor.

"What in the seven hells?" Moona croaked as she gripped Dara for support. "The Shadow, is it attacking?"

Dara smiled down to Moona. "No, it is Shuran he is back. Shall we go see what he has brought with him?"

The Zidu'Si along with Moona, Codger, and several others raced through the halls following Tianna's ghost. They traveled areas none had visited or knew existed, and downstairs to a place where Shuran awaited them. When they reached a familiar wall, they stopped and gasped in unison.

"Isn' that the doorway-" Codger started.

His words were cut short as the door opened to reveal Shuran standing on the opposite side wearing a smug grin and holding a red scale. "I will explain in a moment but right now we have to figure out how to use this," he said as he held the scale out to Penelle. "Blood magic, it is what Nabusa used to create the talisman for your former sisters."

Penelle stared at him shocked. "Who is this Nabusa?"

Shuran knew Penelle was aware who Nabusa was, but did not say anything. "Was," Shuran said. "She was the kashshaptu to blame for your failed spell that created the trolls, and she was a Telukukal."

"What do you mean was?" Sulura asked.

"She was killed when she fought Nagutan, but not before telling him what she did with Moltar's scales that he shed in the Mist Swamps." Shuran explained what he learned about Nagutan's actions when he last left Britengate. When he retold the part about Nagutan's battle with the Shadow inside him and use of the Mi-Ib Karshi, Penelle ran through the chamber in search of his statue. "Can he be revived?" she cried.

Shuran stood behind her and only now realized the depth of the relationship once shared between them. "I cannot say. He was being consumed by Shadow and Nergal said there was too much of his shi lost." He placed a hand on her shoulder to both comfort and remind her of a pressing need. "If there is hope he will be preserved for the future. I have need of your talents at present."

Penelle wiped away her tears as she took to her feet. She wrapped her emotions in a face of determination and looked at Shuran. "I need a place to work and several tools and ingredients."

"I think you will find all the tools you need here." Shuran said and took her to Moona's work area. "What ingredients are required?"

Penelle explained what she needed, but the complexity of the original spell would make breaking the casting difficult. "This is different from what we used to enhance the strength of the dwarves who became trolls."

"But not dissimilar from that which was used to create the rotting curse on the kashshaptu," Shuran suggested.

Penelle then had an idea. "Perhaps what is needed is to alter the object of the first talisman." Penelle explained how the spell used by the kashshaptu should have had a greater effect on Moltar than it had. What caused the lessor effect was likely the fact that Moltar had been altered by his visits to the Gula'Lu valley in combination with a change in his bond with Shuran. "We can use this scale to temporarily block the first spell, but Moltar will need to be changed to a degree that will render the original spell ineffective."

With Moona's aid, Penelle worked through morning to create the new talisman. Once it was ready, she waited for Shuran to return from escorting the Entar'Lu back to Duranekur.

Shuran was unable to use the Emmuku'Gu to travel direct to the dwarven capital. Since the base of the mountains was sealed and the rock and minerals transmuted to gugtu in order to block the Shadow, the Emmuku'Gu was also cut off from the direct route up. He traveled with the former caretakers along a detour that took them to the base of the mountains. There he met with Avrank where they boarded a magurmu and flew to the top of the mountain.

The Royal family met them at the great entrance to their city within the mountain. A grand procession brought the ancient dwarves to the awaiting celebration of their return from the millennia caring for the ancient city of the Gods.

Shuran said his good-byes and regrets that he could not stay for the festivities. "I must get back to Moltar and prepare for the coming battle."

Zak and Dravard both saluted Shuran and nodded in understanding. "You have much to prepare for Shuran the Shin'Ar," Zak said. "Perhaps you will visit when this is over. Though we age now and have numbered days, they are not so few that we will not have time to meet again."

Shuran returned the salute and turned to leave.

Aknard stopped him. "I can have you back at the base of the Orenthal quickly Shuran," he said.

"No need my friend. I will call when we prepare for the final battle." Shuran stepped away and then with a short run, leapt from the mountain and gathered the winds beneath him. He drifted on the breezes like a bird gliding on updrafts. When he was far enough from the side of the mountains, he tucked his arms to his sides and angled himself down. He reveled in the rush of adrenaline. He allowed himself the exhilarating thrill that allowed him to momentarily leave his troubles behind.

He let go of the winds and plummeted toward the earth, increasing in speed exponentially. When he was nearing the ground, he began reaching out for the Emmuku'Gu and grabbed hold. Just before he would have hit the ground, he disappeared.

Shuran was not properly prepared for the accelerated exit from the lines of power. When he exited the Emmuku'Gu, he propelled into the courtyard and nearly knocked over a couple elves that were standing near his exit point. He rolled to his feet laughing while the elves stared at him as though he were out of his mind.

He raced along the halls and stairs to the Vault that he now knew to be the control room for the starship. He found Penelle and Moona both napping, leaned over the table. Moona's snoring echoed throughout the chamber bringing a smile to Shuran's face. As he approached them, Penelle awoke.

"It is ready," she said through the foggy mindedness of waking.

"Thank you," he said and smiled. Shuran took the talisman and headed directly to his bonded drakkon. When he arrived, he found Thyrin lying next to Moltar, dwarfed by the larger drakkon's massive red and gleaming body.

He walked up to Moltar, watching the slow movement of his sides expanding as he took in depth slow breaths. The sleep spell and compulsion used to subdue him had kept him in a deep slumber for days. "It is time to wake my beloved," Shuran whispered, then woke Thyrin to give him space to work.

"Will this work, Shin'Ar?" Thyrin asked. "I only now understand Moltar since I have become bonded. When first we met in Drakkon Port, I was less than cordial. We drakkon of the Highlands always looked down on those who chose to become servants to a master."

"And what has changed your opinion?" Shuran asked.

Thyrin stood and lumbered around to move from Shuran's way toward Moltar's side. "The bond, I have now come to feel, is not one of servitudes but of partnership. I feel things I never thought possible, emotions beside those of anger and fury of the fires."

Shuran smiled in understanding. "Aglia will be finding these emotions difficult I imagine?"

Thyrin returned Shuran's smile with a toothy grin. "Indeed she is."

"You have become far too loose with your tongue Thyrin," Aglia said as she appeared in the gardens. She attempted to sound scolding, but her half grin gave away her growing love for the beast. "We thought you may wish support," she said to Shuran as the other Zidu'Si approached.

Shuran accepted their presence and turned back to Moltar. "Let us wake the little monster." Shuran gripped the talisman and spoke the words to activate it. He felt the result immediately. The blood magic that was twisting within his bonded stopped and began to reduce but not entirely disappear. Shuran stepped closer and placed his hands on Moltar's side. He reached in with his shi much in the way he did with Penelle and the kashshaptu; however this malignancy was different. It was created from Moltar's own scales, so Shuran decided that he needed to alter the object of the spell.

As Shuran worked his alteration, Moltar began to glow. His already gleaming red scales shimmered as they grew more intense. Shuran was unsure how first to change Moltar's scales until a moment of inspiration hit him. He focused on the one thing in his own make-up that combined with the others made him different from any other on Ersetu. The marker in his blood that was not man, Telukukal, or Sumer. He pushed on that genetic block and passed a piece of that to Moltar. When it met with the drakkon's own blood, the resulting change was subtle to the eye, but inside his body, the changes dissolved the spell and woke the drakkon.

Shuran was thrown back as Moltar raised up on his legs and stretched out his wings. A fiery yawn escaped his mighty mouth. As he blinked the sleep away from his eyes, he looked around in confusion. "Lugaldur, am I dreaming? Why is everything so bright?" The questions rolled off his tongue between licks to Shuran's face.

Shuran could not hold back his joyful laughter. "Easy Moltar, we are in Badgaldingir. I will release the wall around our bond so that you may know all." Shuran dismantled the shield he had placed around the secondary bond they shared. He and Moltar both, immediately stiffened at the reconnection and a flood of information and images transferred from Shuran to Moltar.

The great red drakkon fell to the ground in grief and despair. "What have I done? And my mother... I have missed much, but through you have experienced everything." Moltar stood back up and snatched Shuran up with his tail to place him upon his back. "I wish to go to Jade's garden." He took to the air and flew a short distance to where Jade's tribute rested. When they arrived, they found someone was there waiting for them.

Dalgon was sitting next to Jade on a stone bench that had been placed in the garden. Someone, likely Dalgon, had thought to clear a spot large enough so that Moltar would comfortably fit in the garden without tromping down the plants and flowers.

Moltar sat behind Jade and rested his head on her hardened stone body. He let go of a deep sigh that sent rings of smoke from his nostrils. While he lay there, he raised one eye and watched the interaction between Shuran and Dalgon.

Dalgon looked at Shuran with a father's love. "Where would you like me to begin?" he asked.

Shuran ran to him and took him into an embrace. "How about you start by telling me how you got mixed up with Nagutan's plan?"

Chapter Twenty-Four

Dalgon started his tale from the beginning. He was born nearly three thousand years earlier, the son of Nagutan. His mother did not survive the birth of a Telukukal child. Nagutan did not speak about her. When he came of age, Nagutan shared the knowledge of what his plans were and why he created a son. "He loved me, but I hold no illusion that my primary purpose was to be a tool in his and Nergal's master plan to restore balance."

His part was to first become involved with the Guardians by assuming the guise of an Arakharat. He made his way to the Foresworn Territories where he was welcomed into the Guardians five hundred years earlier. He worked to find those who were fleeing from persecution, but he did not take them all back to the Nabusa. "They were settled in lands farther west, on the opposite side of the world. We did not want the poisoned lands of the Territories to effect them the way they had the others."

"Did the Nabusa not suspect something when you did not return with many refugees?" Shuran asked.

"Certainly she did," Dalgon replied. "That was expected, though I did return with the older mixed-bloods who were beyond the ages of fertility." The Guardians and Arakharat always suspected Dalgon of some duplicity, but they did not act on their doubts until the last few years. He played both sides for so long that he sometimes lost whom he was until he met Sulura.

He knew that Nagutan had played a part in getting him and Sulura to meet. "I could have healed him had he truly been ill, so I knew there was something amiss. I had not seen him for many years, and when he finally tracked me down and pretended sickness, I knew there was meddling involved. But when I set eyes on your mother, I felt myself fall for her in that instant."

Shuran enjoyed hearing how his father felt about his mother. He missed out on this familial bonding, but realized he did have a family, and his father was always around watching over him in the guise of Andra. "So is this your real face?" Shuran asked.

Dalgon laughed and smiled. "Yes, my son this is my true face. I only took the role of a 'shifter', it is a gift some of the Telukukal inherited from the Sumer."

"So not all Telukukal can change their appearance?" Shuran asked.

"Not in the same way, some such as Nagutan used spells. Their spells, strong as they were, could not withstand the scrutiny of another Telukukal. I believe this is the reason I was chosen to take the position of infiltrating the Arakharat."

Moltar finally dropped his head down and sniffed at Dalgon. "You do not stink anymore?"

"That was part of my guise, I had to smell the part or they would have known I was not one of them immediately," Dalgon admitted.

"What do you know of the activities of the Arakharat? There was one I met, Kettanu, who I discovered was at your bonding of marriage with mother." Shuran asked. "He was not a pleasant man." Shuran explained to Dalgon what occurred in Aluanu and the part Kettanu played in those events.

"That is a name I have not heard in many decades. He was the one who gave me Barurbe to leave in Drakk. I believe she was his daughter."

"The Arakharat can have children?" Shuran was not surprised by this fact. "Why would not the poison of the land in the Territories have made them barren?"

The problems with the lands in the Foresworn Territories that led to the birth of their race did not have the same result on the Arakharat strong enough to survive birth. It was a guarded secret among their kind. "Not even the Nabusa knows that they can procreate." Dalgon admitted.

"What the Nabusa knew or did not know is no longer an issue. She is dead."

Shuran told him all he knew of what happened between Nabusa and Nagutan before he was consumed by Shadow. He did not have all the details and only Nagutan would be able to fill in more of what happened, but he was encased in gugtu with very little shi left to survive.

"I would not worry overmuch about your grandfather's current state. Nergal would not have placed him in stasis if there were not the chance of him recovering." Dalgon smiled and let Shuran help him to his feet. "If and when he recovers, we can find out what Nabusa's fascination was with Durangug and the central chamber."

Shuran was not sure what Dalgon meant. "What do you mean? I know the Gizzu'Su wanted access to it as well, but I do not think they had the same plans as Nabusa." Shuran and Dalgon began the walk out of the gardens, leaving Moltar to mourn his mother alone. He was not alone, however, Shuran felt everything Moltar felt. He thought of blocking the emotions but decided to share the burden.

"Nabusa was constantly asking me if I had seen the chamber and to describe it in full detail. I, of course, left out important details since I assumed that whatever the reason, her interest would interfere with my father's plans." Dalgon's strength was returning quicker than he expected. He stretched and worked out his kinks. "I assume you know what the chamber's true purpose is?"

Shuran nodded. "Would you like to see it?" he asked wearing a devious grin.

"I am not quite up for a trip to Durangug, son. Perhaps-"

"Come along, it is no longer in Durangug. I have brought it home." Shuran took Dalgon through the lower levels and to the very center of the massive structure that was Badgaldingir.

As they approached, Dalgon was feeling better the closer they came to the chamber. When they arrived, Dalgon felt and understood why he recovered so quickly. "What is it?"

"The power core and control center for Badgaldingir," Shuran started. "It is also one of the three rings of the prophecy. Two down one left to discover."

Dalgon looked at Shuran with pride and wonder. His boy was indeed powerful to have brought this entire structure here from the other end of the continent. "I am surprised you are able to walk or speak after transporting this here."

A laugh escaped Shuran's mouth as he walked his father around the fully active chamber. "I did not use my own strength. The Chamber provides the power and I channeled it to transport the Vault. When I created a link to Durangug to use as a keep-safe, I inadvertently connected myself to the power of the core, which is how I was able to channel power from Durangug. I pulled on the power through the space between, the same way that I was able to move things in and out of Durangug as though reaching into my pocket."

"What do you mean, the space between?" Dalgon asked.

"You traveled by way of that space when I sent you back to the Foresworn Territories. Did you not notice a difference? I assume you know how to travel the Emmuku'Gu."

"I had wondered at how seamless and without resistance the trip was. It was as though I moved through nothingness, a void," he realized.

Shuran nodded at the comparison. "Yes, it is a void between the Emmuku'Gu and the Shadow. A place where neither exists and their energies repel one another."

"But it is not an empty space is it?" Dalgon asked.

"Currently, no it is not empty. It will return to a true void soon enough I believe, but I will explain that later." Shuran decided he would wait to explain further since he was still trying to understand himself.

They completed their tour of the control room and headed back up to the top levels where they found the rest of the Zidu'Si preparing a feast of celebration.

Aglia was more amiable with the other women, and though she was not as relaxed and open as Coralil, Dara, or Vala, she did not back away when someone touched her while leaning past to add a platter of food to the table.

Moona rushed around barking orders and smacking Codger.

Sulura sat down with Penelle and glanced at Dalgon and Shuran and smiled.

Moltar was busy teaching Thyrin his bad habit of snatching food from the table with a flick of his tongue. Shuran smiled but was reminded of the impending troubles ahead.

The Zidu'Si men were well into their cups and telling bad jokes.

The meal was enjoyable and Shuran welcomed the release of troubles, but he looked at his parents and felt the missing piece of their family circle. Tianna needed saving and he had to figure out how to do it without the Mi'Ib daggers. The evening was cut short though, when word came by communication stone that the Gizzu'Su had attempted to enter the forests of Entensiama.

"Burn off your spirits my friends, we need to see what the Gizzu'Su have been up to," Shuran said as he stood up and kissed his mother. He put a hand on Dalgon's shoulder as he moved to get up from the table. "Stay with mother, it has been too long since you have been together. The Zidu'Si will simply be checking on the movement of the Shadow, we will not intentionally engage unless necessary."

Coralil caught Shuran's eye and smiled at his words causing him to blush. He turned to his bonded drakkon and laughed at the sight of him and Thyrin playing. "Come along children, we have work to do."

Moltar and Thyrin grunted at Shuran, hiding their embarrassment over being caught playing.

Shuran took the Zidu'Si to the outskirts of the forest where the Gizzu'Su attempted to travel to the elfin city located within. They traveled through the void now that Shuran knew it was there. The others were not able to travel this space between the lines without his or Moltar's assistance, but they could travel the Emmuku'Gu on their own.

"That is much preferred over the bump and drag of the Emmuku'Gu, Shuran," Avrank said. "I can keep my dinner traveling this way, though I think my ears might have exploded when they popped." His continued rambling was cut off by a low whistle from Mallick.

"Look at this shield," Mallick said pointing out the green glowing wall of force that protected the forest. "What is that energy, I have not felt that before?"

"It is the power of Coosco," a Dryad said from the opposite side. It lumbered forward on its trunks to stand directly before them, walking directly through the shield unaffected. "Greetings Zidu'Si and Shin'Ar, you have come through the void to follow the darkness?"

"We are only now finding out of the visit the Shadow and Gizzu'Su paid recently," Shuran said. "How did you know how we arrived here?" Shuran asked suspecting the answer.

"It is the way our kind moves about the world." The Dryad told them about the Shadow attempting to gain access to the forests and how they protected them. The wicked one wearing his sister's skin was not pleased when they were not allowed to pass. "She thinks we do not remember her part in the destruction of our forest in what you call Drakk."

"Ereshkigal did that?" Bastien asked.

"She did not destroy the forest in person, but her kind was responsible for the damage to Ersetu that causes Coosco to react in pain and destroy the surface of Ersetu." The Dryad told them that the dark ones left and headed in the direction of Drakk.

Shuran took them back into the void and first to the center of what was once Britengate. They all stood in silence at the emptiness of the land. A layer of black soot and ash lay flat across an area many times larger than what was once the confines of the city. The only sound that penetrated the stillness of the scene was a deep rumble that came from Moltar.

When the Zidu'Si turned to look at him, Moltar tilted his head and glanced at Thyrin. "Wasn' me!" he lied.

Shuran used his communication stone bracer to try to reach Fallon. After many unsuccessful attempts, Shuran gave up and rounded up the Zidu'Si for another trip through the void.

They arrived outside the castle of Baron de Drakk in Drakkfoth to find the area deserted. Few had stayed behind in the city but for those who did, Fallon refused to leave them without his leadership. While Britengate was being evacuated, Fallon insisted on being returned to Drakk so he might look after those who remained in the tunnels and caves below the surface.

Shuran reached out with his shi to locate any signs of life and was upset to find none. He sent the drakkon to scout the area and locate some trace of any living thing. Shuran knew Fallon would not have left unless absolutely necessary and it would have been no small task without the aid of the Zidu'Si, Ag'Lu, or Lil'Du. He sent out messages to the races of the Highlands to find that they had not lent help to the Baron.

The Lil'Du and Ag'Lu decided to return from their homes to begin patrolling the realms after hearing of the Shadow's latest actions.

Moltar and Thyrin returned with more bad news. The drakkon were gone and there were signs of struggle. "There is also a horrid smell of taint in the air. I fear for what has become of them," Thyrin said. "The scent leads off to the West."

Shuran stood for a few moments, thinking about what next to do. "We need to track them. I suspect they headed back to the Academy where they waited for Nagutan to breach Durangug. We will head first to Middleton and see if they made any other stops on the way."

"There is something else we discovered," Moltar said. "There are no bodies from the battle at the Highlands border."

"Then Ereshkigal is using Salmetu's gift for necromancy and filling them with Shadow to build her forces. I only hope that it was only dead that they found when they were here." Shuran said.

Coralil wrinkled her nose in disgust. "Why would you say such a thing?"

"Because if they found any of the kashshaptu still alive, they would have millennia of strength and knowledge adding to their own for a start," Shuran explained. "Worse, however, is what those poor misguided weavers will go through as their shi is eaten away."

<h1 style="text-align:center"><u>Chapter Twenty-Five</u></h1>

The scent of the tainted drakkon was everywhere in Middleton. The buildings in the city were demolished and burnt out shells. The city was void of all life as well.

"Bastien and Mallick, can you two devise a spell to show us what happened here?" Orian asked. "I can fuel it with the residual energy that was left behind."

The three of them huddled together to come up with something that would show them what happened when the Shadow was there. They wanted to know what their enemy was doing and how many victims the Shadow was claiming.

While they worked, Shuran walked around the decimated town taking in the scene and hoping that it was empty when the Gizzu'Su arrived. Deep down he knew this was not the case. He could see the clues around him that there was a struggle. Staggered footprints led in every direction, indicating people running from something.

It was not long before the spell was ready and the Zidu'Si moved to the center of town to have the best view of the result. Once the blended weaving and wielding started, the energy build-up around them sent sparks across their skin as the air charged. Ghostly images began to appear and move around them. The scene that played out was horrifying.

Grotesque winged beasts of black surrounded the town and began ripping off roofs and tearing down walls. They reached inside and pulled away screaming and panicked townsfolk, woken in the night to the things of nightmares. Anyone who ran from them was chased down and batted around with clubbed tails or cut in twain only to become rejoined and twisted into a monstrous creature that now served the Shadow and its Queen.

Coralil grabbed hold of Shuran as she watched a child warped into what appeared a small ogre but with ears like a bat and covered in quills. She buried her face in his shoulder and sobbed for the lives that were lost.

The spell not only allowed them to replay the events in crystal clarity, but as the residual energy that was used to power the spell grew, it also allowed them to feel the fear and terror. They were so transfixed on watching the scenes play out, they did not notice that the energy was having another effect. It was attracting something from the darkness.

The Shadow fed on the fear, anger, hatred, and other darker emotions. When it sensed the beacon of energy buildup, it tracked them to Middleton and began to stir.

The flash of light that occurred when the Shadow touched Moltar was enough to break them from the macabre show. "Shadow," he cried out.

Shuran immediately pulled Coralil tight against him and called the Zidu'Si into the void, returning them all to Badgaldingir. They left as Ereshkigal appeared in the town from the Shadow.

"Shuran," she hissed. "So you come out of hiding to witness my work." She stood where only moments before, Shuran and his Zidu'Si stood watching her handy work. The spell continued even after they left as it was fed by the energy left behind. Ereshkigal spread Shadow throughout the town and feasted on the energy, dispersing the images. "What a lovely trick your Zidu'Si have performed. I do enjoy leftovers, and now you have left me a trail to follow."

When the Zidu'Si reappeared in Badgaldingir, Tianna was there to greet them. "Shuran, she knows where you are. I do not know how, but she gathers the Shadow on the borders outside the dome of Emmuku'Gu," she said. "With that much power collected in one spot, they will breach the barrier."

"Let them come, we will not be here for long," Shuran announced. "Dara, I need you to go see if those collars are ready. Please take Coralil with you. I think she could benefit from the sight of something as beautiful as she is after what we witnessed in Middleton. Travel back to Britengate on your return." He gave Coralil a brief kiss on the forehead before the two women disappeared in the Emmuku'Gu.

Dalgon walked over to protest Shuran's decision. He was not alone. All of Shuran's extended family joined in the argument.

Shuran had allowed the protests for a minute before he silenced all arguments with a word. "Prophecy," he said in a booming voice. Once all voices silenced, he continued to explain. "This place will not resist an attack in this confined space with that much Shadow at the barrier. We stand a better chance in the open and what was once Britengate is now more than enough space for Badgaldingir."

"What are you talking about Shuran, how can you move an entire city?" Vardoran asked.

"Vardy not now," Moona said. "What are ya talkin' 'bout Shuran, how can you move the whole city?"

Shuran gave Vardoran a sympathetic look of shared frustration at Moona. "This is not simply a city as you will all soon find out. Moltar, please take Thyrin to Britengate and render all the ash and dust to a sheet of crystal and then wait clear from the ring of glass. The rest of you follow me." Shuran raced off to the control room with a sizable following.

Moltar and Thyrin flew around the remains of Britengate blasting the ground with fire and energy, melting the ground to a layer of molten earth and stone. They each reached within the collective of power and gathered the elements to transmute the molten sheet to silicate materials suitable to create the crystal Shuran requested. They then called upon the winds to put pressure on the cooling mass to make it as smooth as ice while they pulled the heat from the ground. When they were finished, the once blackened area reflected a perfect image of a clear starry night above them.

"I am not in the least bit tired from this working," Thyrin said with a grin.

"It is the power of the Chamber, I am able to draw from it now the way Shuran has. When he changed my scales, he altered more of me than just the outside," Moltar realized. "Come we should move up into the sky and out of the way. The city will be coming soon."

Shuran arrived in the control room that had once been Durangug.

Vardoran stood next to him. "So you really did move your Vault here. I knew you were strong, but this is beyond anything I could have imagined."

"Vardoran, you should not confuse strength with ability, and it was not my ability with Essence alone that allowed me to bring this place here. This is where it belongs and it brought me here as much as I lifted it from the earth in Durangug. Now everyone, prepare yourself for a slight shake. The ship needs to break free of the earth packed around it over the many millennia." Shuran reached his hand into the multicolored flow of energy within the central chamber and pushed his will into the machine.

"What does he mean ship?" Codger asked as the city began to shake.

Shells of energy enveloped every last thing within the confines of the ship as is lifted from the ground. The barrier of Emmuku'Gu that surrounded and protected the city for longer than recorded time disappeared taking with it the perpetual daylight that it provided. The glow of the power coursing through the city provided for more than enough light to see for the few moments the city hovered.

The Shadow was already waiting but was not quick enough to respond when the barrier dropped. The city disappeared with a pop that echoed through the now empty chamber. The echoes continued and grew louder, causing the domed ceiling to shatter and collapse. When the dust settled, any who ever ventured into the remains of the former location of the City of the Gods would find the richest deposit of pure gold that ever existed.

Once the city was free of the earth, the shaking stopped and the city slipped smoothly from below the mountain and out into the fresh air of the outside world. As the city appeared, it hovered just above the surface of the crystal sheet. The crystal began to glow as the power of what once filled the void, flowed up into it from the depths. The power was not directed by the shi within the lines, the ship was pulling it back into the core. The control room, at Shuran's direction, was pulling back its power from the lines within the planet.

"Something is changing in the energy of the lines Shin'Ar," Orian said. "I can still feel them but it is weaker than before.

Shuran pulled his hand free of the flow of energy that began swirling faster as the colors within blurred to become a blue-white intense glow. "That is

176

because I am removing that which was never meant to be a part of the Emmuku'Gu. The power core of this starship was merged with the lines nearly twenty thousand years ago. It was the start of the imbalance."

"Are you restoring the balance now?" Avrank asked as he jumped around.

"It has begun, but the difficult part is yet to come," Shuran said.

"Ha," Moona beamed. "The difficult part he says. Ya just moved the entire city, or ship, out from under a mountain Shuran."

"I only fed the ship instructions, it did the moving."

Vardoran reached out his hand to Shuran. "I am humbled by all you have done Shuran and am grateful for the honor you afforded me to witness this."

Shuran took his hand without hesitation. "I am honored that you have seen past your desires, to find the man inside the monster and returned to your family."

Shuran's communication crystal to the Queen of the Elves began to glow. "Yes, Queen Florisia, I suppose you have felt the change in the energy of Ersetu?"

"Yes, but that is not why I have contacted you," she replied. "The Dryads have left. Their trees remain but the shield is gone and they asked me to pass you a message. They said that you have fulfilled your obligation and they will return the gift when the time is right. They say when you have a need, all you must do is reach out to Coosco and she will listen. What is that supposed to mean?"

"I will explain another time," he said. "Now that their barrier is down you must adjust to the frequency change in the Emmuku'Gu and prepare troops for battle. I will have Moltar bring them here to Badgal-Shin'Ar, the City of the Watchers."

Shuran sent Moltar a message to go bring the elfin warriors and rangers to the new floating city of the Shin'Ar through the void. It would take them time to adjust to the change in the power of Essence of Ersetu and any who once traveled the lines would have to learn how to do so again. Shuran sent his own Zidu'Si the way with a thought, since he already instinctively knew what the changes were that began to spread through the lines. And it was not just the Emmuku'Gu that was affected. The Shadow was causing difficulty for Chaos to move the dark lines as well.

Ereshkigal, the Gizzu'Su, and the Shadow Army were all thrown from the

Shadow lines far to the southwest of Tarangale. She howled into the night with rage because she knew what was happening. "That little abomination has moved the controls back to the ship," she told the Gizzu'Su. "I need that engine disabled. Find me the elf."

Chapter Twenty-Six

Shuran left the control room to go back to what was the open deck of the ship once thought as the surface of the city. It was, in fact, the gardens designed to produce breathable air and recycle carbon dioxide while traveling among the stars. He walked to the edge of the vast ship and placed his hand on the barely visible shield that covered the exposed area in a dome. At his touch, the shield lowered and let in the cool evening air.

Moltar then arrived with the elves, and Queen Florisia upon his back dressed in full battle armor.

She jumped down from his back and walked directly to Shuran with sparks dancing across her hands. "What in the name of the seven hells is going on here, and what is this place," she said before here voice trailed off when she looked out over the edge. She gasped, and the sparks died out.

"I see you have adjusted to the change in the power of the Emmuku'Gu," Shuran said.

"What? Oh yes that, easily enough done... what am I standing on, this is not a city is it?" she asked.

"Welcome to the ancient Sumerian ship that brought our makers to this world," Shuran said matter-of-factly. "Would you like the tour?" he jested.

Florisia looked at him sharply then smiled. "Fresh... where is that Moona of yours, I assume she is here?"

Shuran pointed her to Moona and cringed at the thought of the two women conspiring together. The only thing that would make matters worse would be Levdrianda. He must have been developing a talent for seeing the future because as he turned back to the open sky, he saw a magurmu sailing quickly toward them, and he could sense who was aboard the flying vessel. The dwarf royal family was arriving with an army of dwarves on the magurmu that followed behind them.

Shuran met Aknard and his regal passengers when they landed in an open area behind him. He watched as Levdrianda attempted to construct steps from the ship deck up to the side of the magurmu. "I am afraid you will not be able to create a stairway down my Queen," Shuran said.

"I have been having difficulties today, but this is a complete disconnection," she admitted.

"That is because this ship you have landed upon is not earth or of this world, you will not be able to manipulate the surface." Shuran smiled at her confusion. "Please allow me to bring you aboard." Shuran raised his hands and lifted the dwarven royals off the ship and down to the outer deck of the ancient starship. "Welcome to the new city of the Shin'Ar, better known as Badgaldingir. I will explain later as I believe we have more guests to welcome and a council of the races to convene."

"Where can a dwarf get a drink around here?" Aknard asked, to the agreement of Vraduun. "My nephew sends his regrets but someone had to stay in Duranekur."

"I understand. Brakvar is safer than the rest of us I am afraid, for tomorrow will see the final battle against the Shadow." Shuran was not going to sugar coat the situation.

"And you are certain of this Shin'Ar?" Levdrianda asked.

He nodded. "I have, as you dwarves say, thoroughly pissed up the wrong tree. The ancient dark Sumer, Ereshkigal, who possesses my sister's body, wanted this ship and the control room that was Durangug. Now that I have already joined two of the three rings, I have her full attention."

"Yak Scat, you know how to throw down the gauntlet my boy," Levdrianda said.

"As you say my Queen."

"Queen my fanny Shuran. You have just taken on the responsibility for the entire planet; we should be bowing to you as Supreme Chancellor or some such yak scat title. Where can I get that drink?" Levdrianda walked off toward the closest group of people gathered atop the new home of the Shin'Ar.

Shuran just thumbed for the King to follow his wife as he shook his head. "She has a way with words, Vraduun."

"That's my Levi," he answered.

"I heard that!" she said.

Aknard stayed behind with Shuran. "What can we expect Shin'Ar? My ships stand ready, but I want to know what we can expect."

"There are many more padiri'bur that are ready to be loaded aboard your ships and those of the Lil'Du that will arrive soon, but I fear they will not be enough. The Shadow has taken drakkon and twisted them into unspeakable beasts. Your ships have shields but the Lil'Du have none. I would ask that when the time comes. You disperse among their ranks to help deflect attacks."

"As you say, Shin'Ar."

"Please Aknard we are alone, call me Shuran."

Aknard stepped back and saluted Shuran. "We are at war my friend, and I will address you according to the title you have earned. But I will still drink with you, so hurry up with the receiving line and find me wherever there is ale flowing freely." Aknard winked and ran off to follow his brother and sister-in-law.

Shuran watched the ranks of dwarven soldiers exit gangplanks from the many magurmu that landed upon his ship. Aknard must have shared the plans for the flying vessels, because there were at least twice the number he once had, and the newer ones flew the sigil of the King, a war-hammer smashing a mountain.

Shuran stood with Moltar, scratching his lowered chin when he felt a shift in the energy around him. He felt Dara struggling to return from Hakkisuru, the power being pulled from the Emmuku'Gu troubled her. He reached into the flow of energy and pulled her and her company free. Standing before and above him was Dara along with Awilzag and Coralil. Shuran dipped his head in respect and lifted it to find the King on his knee before him.

Coralil headed off to meet the Lil'Du as they arrived.

"Shuran Shin'Ar, it is time I present my kingdom to your wise rule," the majestic and giant Gula'Lu King said. "We have felt the changes and stand ready to do what we must to end this strife."

Shuran climbed on top of Moltar's head so that he could look the Gula'Lu King in the eyes. "Please stand sir, the Gula'Lu do not owe me a kingdom, only their kinship."

The Gula'Lu king stood and smiled at Shuran. "You have become everything that my daughter has described and more. Will we have a council?"

"Yes, but we await the Badur'Lu. The Lil'Du and Ag'Lu have just arrived on the opposite side of the ship and make their way to the central hall. Please join them and freshen yourself. I will join you all when the Badur'Lu arrive."

"And will Coralil be here with you?" Awilzag asked. "Dara tells me you and this wind woman have become close?"

Shuran blushed.

"I see. We will await your council." Awilzag turned and left, leaving Dara to shrug apologetically for gossiping.

"I will never understand the need your manling women have for spitting out every word that bounces about their heads Lugaldur," Moltar said.

"Women like to share, my beloved. What you find silly, they cherish as bonding among each other." Shuran felt Moltar's disagreeable notion. "It is silly I agree, but never say that in their presence."

"Say what in our presence," Vala said as she arrived with the Chancellor of the Badur'Lu. "Were you talking about Cora?"

"I was… Welcome Chancellor Gilean," Shuran managed. "We have all gathered so if you will join me we shall begin this council of the races."

Shuran followed behind the Badur'Lu to the hall where they found everyone already beginning to sit. He failed to notice the last passenger to depart one of the magurmu after all the other dwarfs and elves had disembarked.

A cloaked figure slinked down the gangplank and disappeared into the crowd of gathering city dwellers.

There was no mystery behind the reason to why they were all present and what was going to transpire. The significance of the first time in millennia that all seven races of man would meet and in response to the balance of Essence, was causing a stir in the city. Many of the citizens congregated along the walkway to the central hall. They shouted greetings and well wishes to the representatives from the races as they passed.

The Hall was filled to standing room only. While Shuran was greeting the representatives of the other races, the Zidu'Si found benches and chairs to fill the space. All the seats were filled, and the walls lined with standing observers. Two long tables were lined in opposite orientation one crossing the top of the other so that Shuran sat in the center of a table lined with the Zidu'Si. The other table spread long-way from Shuran's spot so that he might look upon all the representatives. All eyes in the hall were locked upon Shuran as he walked up to the head of Zidu'Si table.

Shuran raised a hand to quiet the room. He did not require the use of Essence; all in attendance were present to hear what he had to say. "Friends, we are at the precipice of righting a wrong within Ersetu that has been mounting for twenty millennia. This floating city we meet in was the vessel that brought the ancient Sumerian scientists from the heavens. When they discovered the power of Ersetu, they created a bridge between their own technology and the Essence.

"The core of this ship is an energy source that I do not yet fully understand, but it has been flowing within the Emmuku'Gu since the control room was depleted of power and fed into the Essence. This joining of two different powers is what caused the balance to break within Ersetu. Coosco, the great mother of Ersetu, has suffered all this time because the Sumerians did not understand what they did to the planet. When their leader, Nergal, discovered their error he attempted to correct the mistake, but some of the Sumer did not wish to loose the gain in abilities they achieved when their powers combined with the Essence."

Shuran explained what Nergal and Nagutan did as they nurtured and manipulated the races of man in an effort to create two children able to grow in power to one day bring balance to the Essence. The first effort failed and what followed was not entirely unexpected. The Sikil'Mah provided Nagutan the opportunity to progress the races in ability and strength as separate pure races. He then guided the mixing of various families across the races to finally bring about the birth of Shuran and his sister.

Moona was the first to correct his speech. "There been three sprats born that day, I was there remember."

Shuran smiled and looked at her. "It was made to appear that there were three children born, but it was an illusion, a powerful spell performed so that you might make off with the boy child. Nagutan created and spread the prophecy. He also used blood magic to separate Tianna's shi and make her look whole at birth. This is why the blade of the Mi-Ib Karshi burst the illusion, and she dispersed."

"What are you saying Shin'Ar," Florisia asked, reverting to his formal title in open court.

"Salmetu is a title given the body of Tianna when the Order of Chaos claimed her as their Priestess. The Sumerian Ereshkigal is possessing Tianna and her disembodied shi presents as a ghost because she is linked to me as her anchor." Shuran paused while the murmurs and shocked voices came to understand his words. "Tianna and I are the only two children born and have been linked since the day we were brought into this world."

Tianna appeared in the hall, behind and to the right of Shuran. She hovered and looked around at the overfilled room of people. "We shall join the third ring to the others and restore balance," she said, her voice weakening. "We must move quickly Shuran, I have not much time," she said only for his ears.

Shuran acknowledged her with understanding and moved the council along at a quickened pace. "We must move this along. Time is wasting, and Ereshkigal and the Gizzu'Su will be making for this ship overland and at great speed. They will have been expelled from the Shadow as they took corporeal forms and need time to adjust to the lessening of Sumer energy from the power of Essence. This ship is pulling that energy back into its core, and the Gizzu'Su will want it back."

The council discussed how best to deploy their troops and vessels. Knowing the Shadow and Gizzu'Su would be unable to enter the city easily, they would need to move the magurmu and Lil'Du airships outside the force shield of Badgaldingir. The hope was that they could separate the Gizzu'Su and capture them separately. As the council broke, and the hall emptied to move their plans into action, Shuran and the Zidu'Si headed to the control room.

"Why are we going to the chamber Shuran," Cora asked.

Shuran took her hand and pointed at the collar she held. "These four collars that the Gula'Lu created, but could not power, require the energy of the Sumer. These collars represent the third ring, to be joined with the others." Shuran explained how the first ring was the circular chamber deep inside

Badgaldingir. Shuran joined this ring to the chamber of Durangug, the control room. Once these two were joined, he could use the power of the Sumer to charge the four collars. Five collars will then have the ability to shackle the Gizzu'Su and trap them while they remained within the bodies they possessed.

"How do you know all these things Shuran?" Dara asked, looking at the collar she carried. "Have you been in contact with the Gods... I mean Sumerians…that live within the Emmuku'Gu?"

"Nergal left this information within my mind. It has all been surfacing slowly as events unfolded. Once I moved Durangug to its proper place, all that I need has become moved to the front of my thoughts except one," he said.

Mallick looked at Shuran. "Sheesh, you will figure out how to save Tianna without the blades. I am sorry I have found nothing in the library that could help. No information of what the blades were made of exists. The only thing mentioned is that they were forged from the bond of life."

Shuran took the information as though he expected little more help. He stopped before the entrance to the control room, opened the door and led the Zidu'Si to the central control chamber. One after the next, Shuran took the rings and placed them within the central flow of energy. He stacked them to charge within the pulsing lights.

"I have one last thing to do for you all," he said as he led them back outside the room, leaving the collars to charge. "Each of you must place a bled hand upon the door where I have carved the symbol of your names."

As they each placed their hands upon the door, Shuran said the words to bond them to the control room and all its contents. As each Zidu'Si wavered from the flood of power and connection to the chamber, Shuran smiled and helped them steady. Since the Zidu'Si was complete, none passed out of consciousness as Shuran did when first he connected himself.

"During the battle, when any are close enough to collar a Gizzu'Su, call a ring from the chamber and lock it around their neck. The first obstacle will be to figure out what bodies the other Gizzu'Su have taken," Shuran said. "My best guess is that they will be standing apart from the engagement, not wanting to get themselves too close to risking their bodies."

The Zidu'Si went back into the chamber to place their weapons inside so they could practice calling them out to their aid. Once they were satisfied they could call an object from the room, they prepared to leave when the call of alarm was raised. The Shadow was approaching.

Shuran ran ahead, raising the ship's shield once he felt all the airships and magurmu were clear. He and the Zidu'Si left the chamber, leaving the door open.

Chapter Twenty-Seven

The first volley of gug hit the shields of Badgaldingir, sending a ripple of energy through the dome. Twisted loadstone of all sizes bombarded the shield but did not penetrate. The ogres and trolls that launched the projectiles grunted, swore, and shouted as they continued their futile displays of aggression. The Gizzu'Su led army of Shadow spread out along the western side of the city but kept a cautious distance from the white glowing disk of crystal that pulsed on the ground below the floating vessel.

The front lines of the dark army met with the force of human weavers, elves, dwarfs, Lil'Du, and Badur'Lu. The Gula'Lu, though they wished to fight, were not allowed to leave the valley for fear of one or more falling victim to the Shadow. Their age and strength would bolster the darkness' power and their king was only allowed to view the battle from behind the shields of Badgaldingir. Dara was the only Gula'Lu to fight; being Zidu'Si she would have the protection of that bond.

The Zidu'Si all exited the city and joined in the fight, all the while seeking out who the Gizzu'Su might be possessing. As soon as they passed through the shields, Moltar and Thyrin took to the air with Shuran and Aglia upon their backs. Dara took to the wind with Vala to board each a magurmu and La'Bun Masua. Bastien and Mallick used spells and air weaving to fly toward the enemy while Orian and Avrank leaped to the ground to forge ahead with the ground troops. Coralil flew with Shuran atop Moltar until he delivered her to a La'Bun Masua. She could have traveled on her own, but Shuran insisted on escorting her.

Shuran had no difficulty locating Ereshkigal. She flew aboard the largest and most menacing of the great twisted beasts that were once drakkon. As Moltar turned his body toward her at Shuran's instruction, she sent a blast of red plasma in his direction, but it was a high shot meant to get his attention. Shuran acknowledged her greeting with a blast of white-hot electric fire that hit her beast and sent it spiraling to its death as Ereshkigal lifted from its back and retreated to the West. The rest of her army and Gizzu'Su followed suit.

Shuran and the other Zidu'Si took after them while he sent Vala a message to rally the Badur'Lu. He wanted them to be ready in the lake around the Academy castle. Shuran with the aid of the fully powered Zidu'Si began pulling half of the armies and flying vessels into the void so they could surprise the Gizzu'Su. They would be waiting for them at the Academy where Shuran knew his sister's possessor would retreat.

The Academy was not unprepared when the forces of Light arrived. They were, however, not expecting the tremendous pop that followed as they exited from the void. While the dark forces cleared the ringing in their ears, Shuran and his army had a moment to prepare for the unexpected presence of Shadow aligned Essence wielders, weavers, and walking dead that awaited them. It was a trap.

Dozens of twisted drakkon circled the ramparts of the castle, ready to engage the Ag'Lu and their own steeds. The grotesque creatures were not the only airborne threat; the Gizzu'Su had been busy guiding their forces to build magurmu or their own. The enemy had a fleet of not less than two dozen smaller and more maneuverable vessels that had no wings or sails. These flying ships were constructed of gugtu and nearly flat. They had no steam engine, only a pedestal containing a crystal for power and a weaver to pilot while four dark Essence users stood ready to attack. The moment to prepare was ended, and the attack began in earnest.

The vulgar creations of twisted drakkon broke from circling around the turrets of the Academy castle and headed directly for the Ag'Lu riders. Streams of red plasma mixed with dark smoke jetted toward the drakkon as

188

they engaged in an aerial battle. The Ag'Lu separated from the flying vessels of Shuran's army to meet the dark drakkon out near the castle. They collided in midair raking claws and hammering tails at one another while their riders loosed elemental fire and energies at one another. Many of the drakkon of the Ag'Lu received major cuts and slashes from the razor sharp pointed scales and barbed tails of their enemy.

While the Ag'Lu were able to heal their drakkon well enough to continue, the energy required to maintain a defense and prevent fatal injuries was taking a toll. Soon the Ag'Lu had to break off and regroup behind a defensive barrier that the Zidu'Si erected for tending to the wounded.

Shuran and Moltar spared little time on the ground to help setup the barrier. They took to the air with Aglia and Thyrin to begin dispatching the drakkon beasts before Ereshkigal arrived with the forces she had in what used to be Britengate. One by one the two of them forced the enemy beasts out of the air with injuries that would kill them under normal circumstances. These beasts were anything but normal. If they were not destroyed instantly, the Shadow would regenerate them, and they would soon regain the air.

While Coralil and Dara looked after the final setup of the domed shield of protection, Coralil noticed a kashshaptu sitting back from the battle. She saw the witch moving around the saddle of a small twisted drakkon, as though orchestrating the movements of a group of death walkers. Coralil immediately knew this was one of the Gizzu'Su. She took to the winds and lifted herself out of the barrier and around the battle to come at the witch from the side. As she approached, the kashshaptu caught sight of her and lifted higher into the air. Coralil followed and increased her speed to catch up to the Gizzu'Su.

As she closed the gap, Coralil called to the chamber in the Vault and pulled a collar from the energy column. Before she could open the collar, a tendril of dark energy sent by the kashshaptu host, hit her. The collar was knocked from her hand and plummeted toward the earth. Coralil dove after the collar and grabbed hold of it with the winds to pull it back into her grasp. As another blast of energy came at her, she disappeared from view.

The Gizzu'Su watched as Coralil reached for the collar and sent a bolt of darkness at her. When the smoke dissipated, the kashshaptu's face broadened into a wide grin at the elimination of the Zidu'Si air wielder. The grin led to a wicked cackle that silenced abruptly with the clank of the collar that closed around her neck from behind.

Coralil reappeared directly behind the witch and opened the collar. While the Gizzu'Su was distracted, she closed the collar and watched as the host body went limp and fell from the saddle of its beast. Coralil used the wind to ease the fall of the kashshaptu and followed her to the ground.

Watching the scene of the first Gizzu'Su being shackled, Aglia destroyed the abandoned beast with fire. She turned to go after another drakkon when she noticed a shrill scream of agony mixed with rage come from another rider nearby. It was another kashshaptu and was obviously that of a dead or near death body, reanimated for the use of playing host to a Gizzu'Su. Aglia turned to the witch and rode hard to shackle another dark Sumer.

The Gizzu'Su saw Aglia coming and knew what it would mean to get caught. She swirled her hands around her host's body, thrusting murky black smoke in all directions to mask her escape.

Aglia transformed herself and Thyrin into living fire as they connected with the billowing darkness. They burned the gloom away as they flew through the inky cloud. With a thought from Shuran, who was sensing the chase, Aglia reached with her shi to sense the dark Sumer within the clouds. The moment she found the kashshaptu host, she called another collar from the Vault and made ready for engagement. To prevent the witch's escape, Aglia surrounded her within a fiery sphere. She reached out as the kashshaptu screamed with the Gizzu'Su's voice and snapped the collar closed around her neck. Aglia did not help the witch to the ground easily. The Gizzu'Su's host hit the ground with a tremendous cracking sound and went still.

The small magurmu were fast and turned on a razor's edge as they flew through the airships of Lil'Du and Aknard's fleet. They each had four dark weavers aboard that threw spells as they zigged and zagged between the larger and less maneuverable crafts. The shields on Aknard's ships held but they needed to disengage them occasionally to throw padiri'bur at the enemy ships. The Lil'Du were able to use air Essence to deflect the assaults easily enough, but their luck ran out for one ship that was distracted with two attacks, they did not see the third.

The La'Bun Masua was taken down with a well-placed fireball to the bladder of the ship. The rubber melted and burst open on the side. Though the escaping air blew the fire out, the vessel began plummeting to the ground. The Lil'Du Gardu'Lil leapt from the carriage and carried themselves clear of the falling ship. They took themselves to the ground where they carried on the fight, calling winds to knock weavers from their own vessels.

The ground forces had little combat to face since most of the foot soldiers of the Shadow seemed to have been with Ereshkigal, who would be arriving at any time. They prepared themselves for the carnage that was to come when Tianna's body carried Ereshkigal back to the Academy on Shadow driven winds.

A third Gizzu'Su was spotted by Mallick and Bastien. He was running for cover along the bridge to the Academy main hall. The Gizzu'Su was within a human male weaver and he saw Mallick and Bastien running after him.

Mallick called to the library for a spell, and once he had it, he signaled Bastien to get around to the other side of the Gizzu'Su. Mallick produced a collar in his hand as he continued to run after the Gizzu'Su while Bastien doubled back and disappeared over the side of the bridge.

The Gizzu'Su gathered dark energy and sent it flying toward the collar in Mallick's hand. The resulting recoil of force knocked the weaver off-balance. The man stumbled and turned over to push himself upright. As he sat up on his knees, the last image he saw was Bastien appearing before him, collar in hand.

Bastien locked the genuine collar around the weaver's neck, both trapping the Gizzu'Su within and rendering his host unconscious. As the body fell over limp, Bastien could not help but feel a tinge of guilt at watching the unwilling host of the dark and ancient Sumerian, wilt under the shackles of Sumer power that now coursed through his body trapping the Gizzu'Su. Mallick assisted him in lifting the Gizzu'Su and taking him back behind the shield to lie beside the other two.

As they placed the body down, Mallick looked up at Moona, who stood above them tittering. "Not so all mighty, these Gizzards eh?"

"GIZ-ZU-SU Moona," Bastien snickered.

"Not if I had my way with 'em," she snapped and walked off.

Bastien glanced at Mallick who just shrugged and pointed to Codger. "Codge, could you make sure Moona does not get too close to these prisoners."

Codger looked from Bastien to Moona and back again. "If I have to drug her

to do it I won' have any blame placed on me."
Before anyone could say more, the alarm was raised, sounding the arrival of Ereshkigal and her ground forces.

Chapter Twenty-Eight

Moona returned with several sacks and set them gently on the ground before the Zidu'Si. "Take these out to the ground forces," she said. "These are my latest weapons against the Shadow, non-lethal. I think we have lost enough life to unwillin' tools of the Shadow. When these go off, they will chase the Shadow from the host and leave them knocked out senseless. If they was unwillin' vessels, then they can be saved." She further explained that these were created in a similar manner as the padiri'bur except they were already spelled and ready to go. This meant they could be used by anyone with or without the ability to wield Essence. They also did not have the same destructive result as the padiri'bur since they were designed to be non-lethal.

"What are these new weapons?" Bastien asked.

Moona explained the new weapons she and the ladies of the Zidu'Si helped her create. They were small fragments of gugtu, the size of small rocks and pebbles one might find on a riverbed. With the help of the Zidu'Si women, Moona created the spell that stored Essence drawn from the Emmuku'Gu into the stones that would trigger at the direct touch of Shadow. The use was simple, throw or launch the stones at the enemy who were infested with the Shadow and it would render the host unconscious and cause the Shadow to retreat from their body. "They ain' been properly tested but now 's good a time as any," Moona winked.

While the sacks of gugtu were passed out among the ranks of foot soldiers, they were transferred to smaller sacks and pockets among the fighters.

The Zidu'Si left to join the battle once they finished helping to distribute the new gugtu 'Shadow Busters' as Avrank called them.

Shuran stood upon Moltar's neck just behind his head sending out the whispers on the wind to his Zidu'Si and army. He watched as Ereshkigal and her own dark army floated in from the East and settled around the castle lake. He watched her call one of the twisted drakkon down from the turret and lifted herself atop the hideous creature before rising into the skies to meet him.

The rage rolled across her face as she came within view. "What have you done to my Gizzu'Su?" she screamed. "How dare you employ the Gub'ba Dur Gu'gal, they are the tools of the ME and Sumer people, not some bastard third generation Telukukal mutt!"

Shuran remained still upon Moltar's back. His bonded drakkon stopped beating his wings to hover and remained fixed in the air, motionless as he gathered the air Essence below himself for support. "And still they work so well, would you not like for me to fit you with one as well, Queen of the Netherworld."

Tianna's possessed face went blank in response to Shuran's offer. "I should like to see you attempt such a feat with no head," she said before lashing out with a force of blue pulsing light.

Shuran raised his hand and blocked the attack without effort or exertion. "You will have to do much better than that I am afraid. Give up now and the Zidu'Si will show mercy."

Ereshkigal laughed before riding her beast directly for him.

Shuran jumped down to his saddle upon Moltar's back and pushed his bonded on toward the oncoming threat. Shuran conjured a ball of light to thrust at the darkness infused beast that his sister's possessed body rode upon. As the ball of light reached closer, an opposing force of Shadow dissipated it.

Ereshkigal was weakened by the loss of three Gizzu'Su and still adjusting to the drain of Sumer energy from the Emmuku'Gu.

The power that was infused into the power lines of Ersetu filled the void between the Light and the Dark side of the Balance. That energy had given power to both sides of the Essence for millennia. When power shifted from one side to the other, Ersetu felt the shift in the void and reacted to that unbalance of energy with the many upheavals, quakes, and forces of nature that wreaked havoc across the world.

Shuran had shared access to the power now filling the central chamber of the Vault. He and his Zidu'Si alone now stood above all others in power, so they might vanquish the darkness and restore peace. As Shuran dueled with Ereshkigal, he held this power back for fear of hurting his sister's body. He sent only that which he was certain the Gizzu'Su Queen of Shadow could withstand.

Ereshkigal began to sense Shuran's ploy and played along. She was buying time. She still had one Gizzu'Su remaining un-collared, the one wearing Fallon's body. She scanned the grounds for his whereabouts, when she found him surrounded by her forces, holding back the Zidu'Si that threatened to collar him.

Fallon stood on the banks of the castle lake, his back to the Academy walls and surrounded by dark warriors. Several Zidu'Si fought to gain the lines and draw near enough to call a collar from the Vault and trap the Gizzu'Su. Others in Shuran's army were engaged in battle along the remaining shores surrounding the castle. The forces around Fallon's possessed vessel were falling to the effects of the small gugtu stones being thrown at them from the advancing forces of Light.

The forces of Light had the upper hand when it came to strength and numbers, but the Shadow warriors were powered by darkness that refused to die. Even when they fell to the effects of Moona's new weapon, the effect did not last long and for those whose body was already dead the weapons did not work. Too much Shadow was coursing through the dead bodies to be forced from their host at the hit of a single stone; it took many hits to slow them down. Most of the ground forces were the vilest of creatures that did not have the Shadow infesting their body, so the stones were of no use on them. Ogres, trolls, death walkers, and townsfolk turned into beasts of the Netherworld, marched against the dwarves, elves, Lil'Du, humans, and Dara. Only the 'Shadow Busters' could take down the death walkers and the supply was already dwindling.

Dara was an army of one. She stood before a host of dark enemies and with lightening from one hand and stretching out the other with the gauntlet upon it, struck down scores of the enemy in each turn. Her determination began to waver as she watched her previous fell of enemy, regenerate and stand to face her again.

Lil'Du airships that had not yet been taken from the skies continued to sail around the perimeter of the Academy, forcing gusts of wind at twisted drakkon and the small magurmu of the enemy, sending riders and weavers to their temporary deaths. Her only comfort was the mighty heart of the warrior who would not leave her side, Avrank.

"You leave the cleanup to me my dear, I shall move the earth to clear your path." Avrank opened the ground beneath the reviving death walkers and swallowed them up in the ground and transmuted the packed earth to gugtu for good measure. "Lead the way my love."

Orian released electric bolt after another into the array of darkness from his mighty bow. "TURD, pay attention to your task and stop flirting. This is not the time for love-play."

"This is precisely the time my shoe-making friend. For if we should fall, there will be no time at all," he replied with a flourishing bow. His gesture was stopped by the sharp zing of a bolt from Mallick.

"Pay attention Turd!"

The Zidu'Si and army were fighting a battle that would not relent. As long as the Gizzu'Su inside Fallon could still bolster the Queen and channel Shadow to the army, they would continue to revive and return to the conflict. They resorted to fire and electric Essence when possible to render their enemy to ash, but this was not always possible in closed quarters of battle for fear of friendly fire. They also wondered if the Shadow was defeated, would these people return to their previous selves? There was no telling how the mind would remain after the taint of the Shadow was gone. If there were enough shi remaining in their bodies, would the bodies even recover? This was a constant question on each Zidu'Si mind as they attempted to take care with those who were possessed, not to inflict mortal wounds. As they passed felled victims of Shadow, they placed the gugtu stones upon the body to keep the Shadow from retaking the host.

As the fighting continued, and Shuran chased Ereshkigal around the castle, no one noticed the ripple that formed across the surface of the waters of Academy Lake. With all the weaving of spells and wielding of elemental Essence, the movement of the lake was not the concern it should have been for the Gizzu'Su infesting Fallon.

The water rose up before his protectors and slammed down on them, drawing them into the lake to drown. Fallon raised his hands to pull them back up from the depths while others came around to protect him, leaving his backside exposed. While the Gizzu'Su was distracted by the foe in front of his defensive line, he failed to notice the one thrusting from the waters behind him.

Vala lifted from the lake with added force of a waterspout and the wind to push her toward her target. She focused on the Vault and pulled hard on the object within the flow of power in the central chamber. Collar in hand she grabbed it with the other and opened it as she flew through the air toward Fallon's body.

Ereshkigal watched in horror as the scene played out. She swerved in the direction of the threat to her last remaining follower but was too far away. In a moment of desperation, she let out a scream of warning but was cut off by the envelope of air the surrounded her.

Shuran took advantage of Ereshkigal's distraction and created a bubble of air around her that cut off the sound from her warning. He saw Vala thrust from the waters and retrieve a collar to shackle the last Gizzu'Su comrade of the Queen of Shadow. When her sounds of warning became trapped in his construct, he turned to watch the last of her boost in power fall.

Vala clamped the collar around Fallon's neck with a force that knocked him to the ground before the power of the Sumer could enter his body and affect the dark Sumer within. She followed his fall, unable to react in time from the momentum of her Essence assisted leap from the water. As she rolled over him and tried to gain her feet, an ogre wielding a gugtu club struck her from behind.

Seeing Vala fall, Dara fought with new purpose. She had to reach Vala and pull her free of the threat posed by the ogre that loomed over her still body. With a thrust of her gauntleted arm, Dara began clearing a path to the lakeshore. When she arrived she thrust out her arms and wrapped them around the legs of the ogre, pulling him clear of Vala and into the water. She planted her arms firm around Vala and carried her from the opposite shore and continued back toward the barrier erected around the triage tents of Shuran's forces.

While the borders of Badgaldingir remained quiet after the departure of the Shadow forces, the cloaked stranger that arrived upon a magurmu wandered the lower halls of the city ship seeking his instructed destination. When at last he approached the large doorway, he was relieved to find the passage open and drew back his hood.

Voreen grinned as he passed through the open doorway and headed directly to the central chamber as ordered. He did not have a drop of Shadow within him; otherwise the statues' wards would have protested his presence. His willingness to enter the city and do the bidding of Ereshkigal was in no way out of obedience or loyalty to the Shadow. He wanted revenge for his ancestor who was dismissed from service to the Shin'Ar.

It mattered not that Shuran had exposed the truth of his great grand sire's failure. The hatred festered in his blood and that of his father for so long, all reason left them, and now he was insane with fury and the taste for retribution. Voreen moved toward the pedestal that held the white crystal, the shard that represented the power of his people, and the only one he could touch.

Ereshkigal explained that he only needed to remove the one stone from the machine to stop the process of draining the power from the void. Once the siphoning stopped without being complete, the power would begin to flow back into the emptying void and give the Shadow back and Voreen would be able to jump into the Emmuku'Gu to escape.

Voreen grabbed hold of the crystal and immediately felt a strange power within the chamber flow through the stone and into his hands. He fought the urge to release the shard. When he gained enough strength of will, he pulled with all his might and the stone came free of its slot in the stone pedestal.

The swirl of energy in the central chamber stopped and dulled in brilliance. It reversed and the power began to drain from the chamber and flow back into the void.

The Shadow roiled with renewed power that in-turn fed Ereshkigal and her warriors. The tide of the battle turned. The Shadow renewed its attack.

Shuran felt the power leave his body in a convulsion that threw him from

198

Moltar's back.

Having lost his Lugaldur before, Moltar kept a close watch on where his bonded master was at all times, but with a secondary link and the changes that Shuran made in his physiology, Moltar was equally effected by the shift of Sumer energy flowing back into the void. His massive body fell from the sky behind his master and they both hurtled toward the surface of the lake below them. Moltar's body was the only of the two that met with the surface of the water.

Shuran spun in the air, attempting to gather his will to wield Essence of any kind to help himself. He was unable to react in time when the tendril of Shadow reached up from the breaking earth and grabbed him. He was pulled into the darkness and surrounded by pure Chaos.

Chapter Twenty-Nine

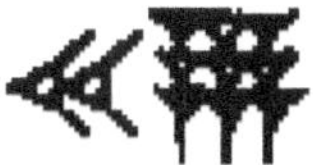

Voreen was knocked clear of the central chamber by the recoil of energy that flowed out from the crystal he dropped as he landed. He convulsed and foamed from the mouth as the seizure took his life force.

The crystal hit the floor of the chamber and shattered into countless fragments.

The deed was done and the Shadow now had the power while the Zidu'Si adjusted to the loss of advantage and the dizzying effect of the shift in Essence.

Ersetu reacted with violent tremors that split the earth.

Dark warriors gained an influx of power that overwhelmed the advancing armies of the Light. They wielded dark energy at their foe with renewed vigor. Blasts of woven Essence accompanied thrusts of gugtu clubs from ogres and slings of stone from trolls. Twisted little evil gnomes that were once children pounced upon the weakened forces of dwarves and elves that were supplemented by downed Lil'Du warriors.

The only remaining trusted weapons were the padiri'bur aboard the magurmu, and the gugtu stone Moona only that day revealed, but they were running short. Several ships had already run empty on supply of padiri'bur.

While the airships of the Lil'Du fell under attack, the warriors aboard managed to lift themselves to the magurmu nearby. Aknard commanded his ships to rescue as many as possible before cloaking and slipping away until they could adjust to the change in the Essence.

The Badur'Lu in the lake fared no better as they struggled to wield walls of water and ice to deflect oncoming assaults. The twisted drakkon that remained fired a supercooled plasma into the water in an attempt to freeze the Badur'Lu in place.

Ag'Lu drakkon, remaining fueled by the fight and un-bonded, were not affected by the change in flow of energies. They renewed their assault on the few remaining twisted beast of their kind. They held no sentimentality toward a possible recovery if they won this battle. The animal instinct was to survive and they ripped at the beasts without concern for the razor sharp scales or destructive tails on these evil creatures that threatened all life upon Ersetu.

While they fought, Moltar struggled beneath the waves of the turbulent lake, trying to both gain his composure and reconnect to the Emmuku'Gu. He felt the power returning and radiated out a heat that saturated the waters and evaporated the sheen of ice forming above him. He felt his Lugaldur trapped within the Shadow and he tried to pull him free. He failed at each attempt; unable to break the hold Chaos had surrounded his master's shi.

Shuran struggled to right himself in the empty blackness of the depths of the Shadow. He was surrounded by darkness that was so deep it pulled the breath from his lungs. He attempted to reach out to the power of Essence but was severed from it. He could not reach his bonded or the Zidu'Si. He was alone when he saw the swirling of deeper darkness before him.

Ereshkigal appeared before Shuran, Smug grin upon Tianna's face. "You thought to take on the very forces that are responsible for your very existence," she spat. "The arrogance you possess makes me want to rip you apart now, but the link you have with this inferior host troubles me. She has an unsavory attachment to you that I cannot seem to dispense with, so as a compromise, I shall leave you here, in the Shadow for eternity." She left him without another word.

Shuran was alone, without his power, without his Zidu'Si's voices in his head, without his bonded. He was not, however, without his former links to past

Zidu'Si, for some reason they remained linked. As he neared true death and loss of his shi, a strange tingle began to spread throughout his body.

Gimagala sensed the pain that Shuran was feeling. She had been catching glimpses of the events as they transpired and understood this to be the time she had been awaiting. When she finally concentrated only on Shuran, she felt as he did, the disconnection of all his strength, his family, his friends, and his love.

She stood before the great flowing mercurial river of the Gula'Lu and poured herself into the flow. Her fellow Gula'Lu and first among the races of man, protested her presence for the first time, for they knew what was to transpire. She fought against their disapproval and resistance, to push herself deeper toward the bottom of the river of mercury until she found the riverbed. She focused her strength on pushing into the earth to find the flow of energy that could reach the Shin'Ar of her present time. She refused to allow the disagreeable among her race to keep her from the promise she made to the Shin'Ar of her past.

Gimagala pushed through hard-packed ground and rock to reach the Emmuku'Gu, and when she touched it, she turned her form from mercury to the one mineral that would forge a connection between all the ancient age and strength of the Gula'Lu, to the one power that only the Shin'Ar could access. She transformed herself to gold as she bridged the Gula'Lu river of ancient shi, to the Emmuku'Gu. A new power and strength, the one the ancients warned should never be given to the dark Sumer, was now at Shuran's command.

Shuran felt the power fill him as though he stood upon the spot where lightning from the sky had stuck. The pain he felt turned in an instant to pure power and invigorated his shi. Where he was feeling debilitating sadness, he now felt a surge that filled his heart with such joy, he cried out against the Shadow that enveloped him. Though he knew what Gimagala had done the instant she transformed, he knew it was what her promise had been to Nergal.

The Shadow evaporated from around Shuran as he glowed with light that rivaled Utu. He pushed himself from the darkness and into the Emmuku'Gu to appear above the Academy Castle. "Ereshkigal," he said in a low steady voice that penetrated every fiber of those who battled below.

Every weapon dropped. Every spell fizzled. Every wielder paused. All eyes were transfixed on the heavenly image of Shuran Shin'Ar hovering in the night sky flanked on each side by a bright star in the heavens.

"This is the time for the balance to become restored, and you are not balanced," he said as light poured from his eyes and landed upon Tianna's possessed body. "You will plague this earth no longer." As her body floated up toward him, Shuran pulled the last collar from the Vault.

"You can do nothing with that device. Shin'Ar," Ereshkigal moaned. "It is not fully powered and the chamber is emptying into the void. We will return."

Shuran looked from Ereshkigal's worried eyes to the collar and fed power into the device. "I can fill the collar with your Sumer energy without the chamber. Now that I know the taste of each power I can separate them." He charged the collar and wrapped it around Tianna's neck, cradling her now limp body.

With the final Gizzu'Su shackled, the Shadow lost its hold on those who fought in its name. Ogres ran for safety while trolls fell to a knee for mercy. The death walkers lost their false lives and rotted away in seconds. While some of the weavers regained their wits, the kashshaptu who lost their Shadow powered abilities and possession fled through the fires that burned around the battlefield.

Shuran lowered himself to the ground and laid Tianna's body next to those of the other's possessed by the Gizzu'Su. He turned to his Zidu'Si as they gather around.

Dara laid Vala at his feet. She was alive but barely after the attack she endured following the collaring of Fallon's Gizzu'Su oppressor.

Shuran laid a hand upon her body and poured the last of the extended strength the Gula'Lu lent him into Vala's weakening body.

She began to glow a radiant blue that shimmered like the shallow seas of a tidal reef. As her eyes began to flutter, the wounds on her body healed and she was restored.

Shuran slumped over from the loss of the connection to the power of the Gula'Lu. The strength of their connection became lost, as Gimagala was lost to her golden state of being. "Take these bodies aboard a magurmu, and I will follow upon Moltar to the Altar of Chaos," Shuran said as he looked upon his mighty drakkon shaking the water from his body, much to the dislike of Moona.

"Mind your pet Shuran!" she shouted with a half smile and wink. She walked past the huge drakkon and scratched him below the chin as she past. "Tell anyone about this and I'll deny it!"

Shuran sat back and took a deep breath as his Zidu'Si gathered around. "We must find out what happened in the chamber to send Sumer energy back into the void. I feel I have broken my oath to Coosco."

Bastien stepped forward and placed his hand upon Shuran's shoulder. "You have broken no oath Shin'Ar, only require more time. I have already found out from Dalgon what has happened. Voreen of the elves somehow gained access to the city and the control room. He removed the white crystal from the device."

Shuran fought back the anger at hearing of Voreen's presence in Badgaldingir. He looked at his bracer to find the communication crystals destroyed. "How did you hear of this?"

"He sent the message by way of a Lil'Du who whispered on the wind," Coralil said as she kissed his lips.

Shuran delighted in the moment briefly before forcing himself to reality but not letting go of her. "Can you send him a message to replace the crystal?"

Coralil shook her head. "He has said that the crystal shattered upon removal and there are no other of its kind in the Vault pure enough to take its place."

Bastien stood straight and winked at Shuran. He grabbed Avrank's arm. "Leave that to us!" Then the two were gone into the Emmuku'Gu. Bastien and Avrank exited the Emmuku'Gu at the entrance of a small cave in the woods of Birchshire. "This was where I first witnessed the use of Essence," Bastien said. He and Avrank entered the small cavern and began searching through the various crystal shards protruding from the walls and floor. When they finally had several to choose from, they returned to the Vault where Shuran was waiting.

Shuran took the crystals and sensed where they came from, and smiled at Bastien. "I had forgotten about that place. It seems ages ago when we first found that cave with all the crystals." Shuran examined the shards and found the best sample to use in the chamber. He walked over to the controls and placed the white crystal into the slot on its pedestal representing the Essence of electricity.

Sumer energy began to once again flow from the void and into the chamber.

The sudden influx of energy again, caused the Zidu'Si to shudder as a chill ran the length of their bodies.

"Time to join the others in Drakk," Shuran said. He reached out and felt the void now stable enough to travel. He took hold of Bastien and Avrank then reached for Moltar. He pulled his friends along with him to Moltar's back and then into the void. The light blurred around them and the landscape stretched past as they entered. The pressure in their ears released with the pop that accompanied their exit into the air over the ruined Altar of Chaos.

Moltar flew down to land and let Shuran, Bastien, and Avrank join the others who stood watch over the Gizzu'Su. His passengers walked over to the group of Zidu'Si, who sat talking and keeping watch over the six bodies.

Each of the dark Sumer was trapped within the body of a host human. The collars had a different effect on Sumer possessed humans. Where Dalgon was sent into a slow paralysis and his body shook, the bodies lying before them now were still as death.

Orian stepped forward from the others. "Shuran, what will become of the hosts?"

"I hope that the Shadow will be extracted from them and perhaps their own shi will heal," he answered and sighed. "I do not know what will happen in all honesty. The vessels that prepare to enter our skies were designed as recovery ships." Shuran looked up at the twin stars that reflected the landscape as they approached the altar from the star-filled night sky.

Chapter Thirty

The Zidu'Si looked up in the direction Shuran gestured. The Stars, that grew brighter in the night sky since the twins grew in power were not stars but reflective orbs. Crafted to operate as emergency rescue and destroy probes that only Nergal knew how to call forth from their deep orbit in the far reaches of the solar system.

The day Nagutan confirmed Sulura's pregnancy with twins; he activated the device in Durangug that called the probes back to Ersetu. One probe was built to destroy the Sumerian devices and technology left behind as the other was created to transport the Sumerians away from the planet and back to their home world. When Tianna's illusion was broken at birth and her shi separated from her body, the probe to transport the Sumer away began to fall back and slowed its approach as it began sending signals out to detect Sumerian life forms. When Shuran was joined to Nergal by taking the emuq abnu from the Mellamu Nanna, the probe detected Sumer life again and proceeded in its approach for rescue.

"What will happen to Badgaldingir if the destruction occurs?" Coralil asked.

Shuran shrugged and turned to the Gizzu'Su. "One problem at a turn, Cora, first I need to figure out how to return Tianna to her body." Shuran approached the Gizzu'Su and noticed one too many. "Who is this sixth person? There are only five Gizzu'Su including Ereshkigal." He leaned over the mysterious human body and looked first at the un-collared neck before recognizing the partially healed face of the kashshaptu. "I know this-"

The witch leapt up from her lain out position in a single unnatural stiff movement. The crone reached her hands toward Shuran and stopped a hair away from his throat. She cast her red glowing eyes down at her chest to find a blade in her chest that formed from Shuran's forearm.

Shuran reacted on instinct as the kashshaptu's eyes opened and shone bright red. His arm thrust forward and began transforming into gugtu and stretched out into a sword with a razor's edge. The kashshaptu was possessed by a demon; Shuran felt it and reacted without thought.

The dark mist began oozing from every pore and orifice of the witch. The disembodied presence used the witch's mouth as it left her body. "You will die for taking my master's from me before they could give me back my body," Telalsu said before dissipating into the ground.

Shuran did not address the presence of the demon warrior; he looked down at his arm and realized what he needed for returning Tianna's shi to her body. "TIANNA," he called out. "Come now, it is time."

Shuran knelt over Tianna's still form and positioned his hand over her chest. When her shi appeared before him, he held up his other hand, transforming it to gold. He nodded to her, knowing she understood what he was going to do. Shuran turned to the Zidu'Si. "Heal the witch and make sure there is enough life left in her body then bring her to my side."

Shuran shifted his hand into a sharp gugtu blade and pushed it carefully into Tianna's chest. He looked up at her shi and nodded. "Now," he whispered.

Tianna swirled before Shuran's hand and slipped into his body. As her ghostly form funneled into his hand, Shuran shivered and fought the convulsions that overtook his body. A glow rippled across his skin from his golden hand, across his chest and down the other arm. Her shi traveled along the blade and into her own body.

Shuran regained his composure and withdrew his hand from his sister's chest, replacing the blade for fingers. He waved the Zidu'Si over with the crone's body. "Lay her next to Tianna and back away," he instructed. He reached down to Tianna's neck and took hold of the collar. "Su'bar Tu," he said, lifting away the shackling device. In a flash of movement, he stepped back

208

and watched as Tianna buckled and twitched. She was fighting for her body, and trying to push the Shadow and darkness free.

The Shadow flowed out and into the ground, but a darker shape rose up from the body shifting frantically. It began reaching its billowing arms around in blind fury, seeking a body. Ereshkigal was being evicted from her host. Unwilling to give up a corporeal form after millennia in the Shadow, she latched on to the nearest vessel, the kashshaptu.

Once the dark shi of Ereshkigal was completely within the witch, Shuran jumped forward and locked the Gub'ba Dur Gu'gal around the kashshaptu's neck, sealing the Gizzu'Su leader within her new prison. "We need to place a shield over their bodies and leave a guard keeping constant watch until we find how to create a permanent prison." Shuran encased them in a sphere of energy to take them back to Badgaldingir. He turned back to Tianna who was settling into her healing body.

"How do you feel?" Shuran asked Tianna as he helped her to sit upright and looked at her grey streaked hair.

Words were difficult for her to form at first and she croaked.

Vala stepped up and called water into her hand to wet Tianna's throat. "Drink this it will help," she said looking at her hair. "And do not fret over your hair, I have some dyes from creatures of the deep water that will give you any color you wish."

Tianna sipped the water and allowed it to moisten her mouth and tongue before attempting to speak again. "I… I feel alive," she said. She reached out and took Shuran in an embrace. "Thank you." Her features were beginning to soften and the menacing appearance that the Shadow and Ereshkigal caused upon Salmetu's appearance, began to fade into Tianna's true face.

Shuran helped his sister to her feet and after several false starts, he loosened his grip and held her steady as she became used to having her body back since before her birth. "It think it best we return to the city now, mother and father will be waiting to meet you properly and placed in your body." With a smile to his sister and Zidu'Si, Shuran pulled them all into the void and back to Badgaldingir.

Sulura and Dalgon were outside in the large courtyard when Shuran and the others returned. Sulura ran to Tianna and pulled her close. Tears streamed down her face as she pulled back to look into Tianna's own eyes for the first time. "You have your adda's eyes." She pulled her back into her arms.

"Do not be selfish with her Sulura, she is my daughter as well," Dalgon said as he approached. Once he understood that his wife would not be letting loose of her daughter, he wrapped his arms around them both and waved his hand for Shuran to join them.

Shuran left the Zidu'Si in charge of finding an appropriate place to temporarily hold the Gizzu'Su prisoners. He joined his family in a well-needed familial hug. He felt the tinge on the edge of his mind from Moltar. His bonded lost his mother, but she would forever be near, living on through the memorialized jade stone statue in the gardens.

"You have rejoined another ring, Lugaldur," Moltar said in their shared consciousness.

"And you are as much a part of this ring as I, my beloved." Shuran called for Moltar to join them, but he declined, deciding to stay with his own mother.

Dalgon noticed Shuran's distraction. "He will heal in time my son. He is a different sort of drakkon I think, most do not hold such relationships important beyond their bond. I wonder that you have not spoiled the beast."

When the four reunited family members broke free of their shared embrace, Shuran left Tianna in Sulura's care, while he and Dalgon called the council to reconvene.

The hall this time was not filled to capacity as only the representatives of the seven races, the Zidu'Si, Shuran, and several others were only invited to discuss what were the next actions to be taken toward peace and rebuilding of Aurderia.

"The threat still exists so long as the Gizzu'Su remain," Dalgon said. "What you have said about the two stars being probes or vessels, how does that factor into ridding our world of the dark Sumer?" Dalgon looked to Shuran for an answer.

Shuran looked out across the table to find all eyes upon him. "For all the knowledge and experience Nergal left within my mind, he did not leave me the means of using these vessels to extract the Gizzu'Su. It is my hope that whatever he set in motion will work itself out."

Moona grunted from her seat at the table. "Sooner before later I hope."

Shuran shook his head. "I cannot be certain, but I do not think it will happen before this city has fully charged the control core in the Vault. I feel that once all the Sumer energy has been removed from the void, things will sort themselves."

"Did the Sumerian wraith that squatted in your head tell you that?" Moona asked drawing from her pipe.

"No, Nergal did not say anything, but there is a feeling I have that perhaps was left residually upon his departure." Shuran smiled back at Moona as she glared but did not rebut.

Shuran continued the discussions on what was to begin immediately. The troops of the Ag'Lu and Lil'Du would fly throughout Aurderia and report on all activity. Shuran wanted to know most importantly where those who survived the Shadow might be hiding, they needed informing of what has happened. Any settlements, refugees, or small groups of people were to be helped in any way required.

Next enemies to find in the searches were any of those who survived among the dark forces. Many who were conscripted into the Shadow armies, were forced unwillingly. If any still retained a shred of their own shi after the Shadow was forced back into the depths of the Netherworld, they would need attention. Most would be confused or perhaps oblivious to anything that occurred since the time they were taken by darkness.

The ogres, trolls, dark weavers, and kashshaptu needed rounding up and taken prisoner. "Any who resist and threaten the safety or life of another should be dealt with immediately." Shuran was not willing to show mercy to those who willingly served the Shadow and Ereshkigal. Once any activity was located, the flying scouts would report back and Aknard's magurmu would fly out to lend assistance, or the Zidu'Si would arrive to dispense justice.

During the next several days, bands of humans were found hiding in small woods, villages that went unnoticed, and the many farms that were far from most settlements. The people were frightened and fled from the Ag'Lu or Lil'Du ships, but were more willing to listen once a flying vessel full of dwarves bearing food and supplies appeared soon after. The people were told the news of what happened and the downfall of the possessed Queen of Shadow.

Finding the ogres was an easy task. They left a trail of trampled fields and trees, marking their march back to their mountain homes. The trolls were not found nor were there any traces of the kashshaptu that may have survived.

The Ag'Lu found the scene at the Academy the hardest to witness.

The bodies of both forces that met in battle lie rotting among the grounds surrounding the Essence Academy. While some survivors wandered aimlessly around the remains of former friend or foe, others looted the bodies of anything deemed of value. At the site of approaching drakkon, those with enough wits ran for cover while several attempted to play dead among the fallen bodies.

Ag'Lu warriors warned those who wished to live should leave the bodies at once or prepare to meet the fires intended to burn the dead to ash. Once the last of the survivors were escorted to safety or ran from fear, the Ag'Lu and drakkon reduced the dead bodies to dust. The Lil'Du then called the winds to lift the dust into the sky where they carried it out to the sea and let it settle to the depths.

There was no sign of the twisted drakkon that were not destroyed during the battle. If they survived after the Shadow was forced back to the Netherworld, finding them would be a priority to the Ag'Lu. They were unnatural and would require a merciful death if they did not return to their prior forms.

Of all the cities, villages, and towns that were not destroyed over the course of the war, only one human settlement faired well and ready to return to normal. Elmwood was nearly rebuilt to serve as a functional river town. Though the people received the news of what happened to the Queen of Shadow and her followers, they appeared cavalier and uninterested in help or further involvement with the rest of Aurderia. They would trade openly and welcome business, but they wanted no part in taking on refugees or assisting in the rebuilding of neighboring towns.

Shuran would make a special visit to this settlement when he had the first opportunity.

Chapter Thirty-One

Shuran sat before Nagutan looking at the pendant his grandsire wore when he was flesh. He flipped the circular pendant over in his palm mesmerized by the play of light dancing off every gem imbedded in the greenish metal. His attention was caught by the sound of the door to the Vault opening.

Coralil walked in followed by Dara, Vala, and Tianna. She walked up to Shuran and gave him a light kiss on the cheek. "When you can break away Shin'Ar, I would very much like the pleasure of your company for dinner," she whispered.

Shuran was struck dumb silent. He blinked and smiled as Tianna skipped over.

"Sheesh! Look what Vala and Coralil did to my hair," she said turning in circles to display the deep red locks braided into the shape of a butterfly on the back of her head. She giggled and kissed him on the opposite cheek that Coralil did and gave her a wink. "The girls and I wanted to have a look at the hidden chamber. Mallick said tha-"

"Mallick said what exactly? And where are the men of the Zidu'Si?" Shuran asked as he regained the use of his tongue.

"Seems that Aknard has decided, since his tavern in Britengate was destroyed, he should rebuild here in a large outer building," Dara said.

"It is nice really. It has outdoor tables and a view of Jade's memorial. Moltar was a bit disagreeable at first but eventually gave his approval. I think Thyrin had a word in convincing him," Aglia said as she walked into the room. "I think your drakkon has been making mine a bit more civilized." Aglia smirked as she looked at Shuran with a wink.

"It is the bond to both you and the Zidu'Si. It would seem he is not the only one becoming adjusted to emotional displays." Shuran had noticed on numerous occasions, the meetings between Aglia and Mallick. "I image, Aglia, that it was you Mallick spoke to about the hidden room?"

"He said that there was a room that only the Shin'Ar could enter and it contained a cryptic book of gold, and so on." She leaned close to Shuran and whispered in his ear. "Really it was only an excuse for Cora to come see you."

Shuran understood and his facial expression gave Aglia the thanks it required. He stood and joined the ladies as they strolled toward the center chamber of flowing energy. "The room for now is of no use until we understand its purpose."

"Perhaps I can be of assistance in that matter," said the imp as he popped into existence sitting upon Nagutan's stasis statue.

"What is going on imp?" Shuran asked as he ran over to the small black creature sitting upon Nagutan's chest. "Where have you been?"

The imp lifted the medallion from Nagutan's chest where Shuran left it. "I have been traveling Ersetu as I always do when my master does not call." The imp placed the pendant back down on Nagutan's chest and looked up at Shuran. "My master calls and I return."

Shuran looked down at the statue of Nagutan seeing it still motionless and no signs of returning to flesh. "My grandsire is not in a place to call to you imp."

The imp giggled and grinned showing his sharp teeth. "I did not say that Nagutan called. I was created by blood magic and that blood calls to me, no matter whose body it flows within."

Shuran did not understand. "I am blood of his blood, are you saying that makes me your master?"

"In a manner of speaking, but I am not here for you alone. My time is done and I must return my Essence to my true master. When I have gone, what remains will give you the answers you seek." The imp grinned and bowed its head and then dissolved into the statue in a wisp of glowing red smoke. What remained was a small metallic disc and Nagutan's pendant.

Shuran approached Nagutan's statue, feeling the shi that now radiated within. "Blood magic," he said with distaste. Shuran felt his grandsire growing in strength within the statue. He grabbed the pendant and disc as the statue began to crack and melt into flesh. He stood back and watched as his grandsire reformed from gugtu.

Nagutan stretched and bent the kinks out of his neck. "Oh, I thought I would never get free of that shell," he said as he turned and stood. "Ah grandson, how have things progressed without my interference?"

Shuran looked at Nagutan with happiness that he returned, but also with confusion as to the timing. "How have you recovered?"

Nagutan looked blank at Shuran for a moment before accepting a cup of water from Vala. "Thank you dear." He turned back to Shuran and took a sizable drink. "Simple really, my imp and I traded places."

Nagutan explained how he created the imp centuries ago from the use of blood magic and stored a portion of himself within the creature. When last he saw the imp, he performed a spell that stored the larger piece of himself within the imp and sent it away to hide within the Emmuku'Gu until called. When Shuran, being of the same bloodline, called for answers to the hidden room, that called the imp from the river of power. "Of course you see the imp served as guardian to that disc as well."

Shuran looked at the disc he was holding cavalierly and grasped hold tighter. "You mean this is the compendium?" Shuran realized.

"Oh dear, boy you are catching on. Yes, in part it is, but you will need to take it back to the hidden room." Nagutan pointed to the section of wall that hid the chamber containing the book of gold.

Shuran hugged his grandsire and headed toward the chamber, but Nagutan stopped him.

"Shuran," he said pointing to his grandson's other hand. "You will need the pendant as well, and be careful the questions you ask for you may not like the answers." He turned to Tianna. "Go with him child, he will need your help. I will be taking a nap in that empty alcove, I believe my energy is less than I thought." Nagutan passed out and slumped over.

Shuran and Tianna levitated Nagutan over to the empty alcove and gathered animal skins to lay him upon. With Tianna in hand, Shuran stepped up to the wall where the hidden doorway opened at his request. The two of them stepped within the small room. The door closed behind them.

"Shuran, what is this room?" Tianna asked. "Where have the lights gone?"

Shuran led her over to where he remembered the panel and pulled it free to remove the golden book. As he pulled the book free, the pedestal raised and the globe of light appeared from above. "This is the room of knowledge I think," he said. He took hold of the pendant and noticed that it was the same shape as the indentation atop the book cover. He placed the pendant on top of the book and waited. Nothing happened.

"The disc," Tianna suggested. "What is its purpose?"

Shuran looked at the small metal object and wondered at its use. He also noticed that it was made of metal he never before encountered and there were microscopic marks throughout both sides. He looked down at the pendant and again at the disc and began to have an idea. He retrieved the pendant and looked for a slot or clasp along its edge. While looking, he held the pendant up to the light and observed it as it spun slowly on the chain. As the light sparkled off the gemstones, he caught a glimpse of the thin slot along the side.

He lowered the pendant and held it while Tianna placed the disc inside. The pendant began to radiate light from each gem set upon the top. Shuran returned the pendant to the book's cover and waited.

The walls sparkled with light and began to expand. As the scenes in the pictures stretched, Shuran and Tianna grasped hands and stepped through the wall. The pictures closed in around them and grew brighter in white light until it was only Shuran and Tianna standing in a space of pure white, no walls, no pictures, no book.

"What is this place?" Tianna asked.

"It is the compendium of the Sumer people," an echoing voice sounded.

"Show yourself," Shuran shouted to the voice as he and Tianna spun in circles.

A shimmer formed before them and an apparition appeared in the form of a tall and thin Sumerian. "What knowledge have you come to seek masters?" it asked.

"Who are you?" Shuran asked.

"I am the compendium."

"You hold all the knowledge of the Sumerian people?" Tianna asked.

"Yes, I am the storage unit for the Sumerian history and knowledge of the last twenty thousand years of events on this world."

"How do we remove the darkness from the Shadow and send the Gizzu'Su away?" Shuran asked.

The apparition told them of the controls for working the ship they now occupied. While transferring this knowledge to them directly, the room began to change and the light gathered into sections behind the walls. The pedestal where the book rested, expanded and changed into a large console of controls and buttons with lights and moving pictures of the outside of the ship and the heavens surrounding the planet.

While Shuran and Tianna were in the room with the compendium, the Zidu'Si men arrived in the Vault sensing something change in the energy of the chamber.

Bastien walked up to the central energy flow and looked into the swirl of light. "Something is different, I can feel a change in the energy."

"The draw of Sumer power has completed," Shuran said as he and Tianna emerged from the hidden room.

As they exited, the door remained open and expanded to become an alcove. The pedestal and book shifted to the center of the alcove and continued to expand into the console to control the ship as the book dissolved leaving behind the pendant glowing in the center. The pictures on the walls opened to reveal racks of crystals on which each stored information. It was the history and documentation of the compendium, recorded within the crystals.

The Zidu'Si turned away from the central power core to gather at the new control alcove that replaced the hidden chamber.

Chapter Thirty-Two

Mallick was the first to test the boundary to find if it was protected by a barrier of energy as the room had been. When he moved his hand toward the expected boundary, Avrank made a buzzing sound, causing Mallick to retract his hand. "Turd," he shouted.

"Just a joke," Avrank said. "There is no longer a protective shield Shuran?"

"No longer required," Tianna said. "The control panel only transformed into the room under a concealment working of Sumer technology. There is currently no reason for the compendium to remain hidden."

Shuran explained how the room was created when the control chamber was separated from the city ship. As the war began, Nergal knew that the dark Sumer would seek to gain control of the vessel and the records of all their people's knowledge of technology and magic. He decided to eject all the Sumer energy into the void and remove the control room from the city. This was when he buried the core room in Durangug and the vessel of Badgaldingir beneath the lands that became the Orenthal Mountains.

When Nergal performed this task, he did not understand the impact it would have upon the Emmuku'Gu of Ersetu. To the Sumer, the void was a space that existed outside of the corporeal realm. His mistake was soon realized when the Emmuku'Gu became unstable and when it swallowed the city ship, causing the Orenthal Mountains to rise up over the vessel. Nergal then received a visit from the Tal'Ba-ad.

The void existed between the dark and light of the Emmuku'Gu. When Nergal released the energy from the Sumer vessel, it polluted the flow of natural Essence within Ersetu and created an imbalance. Nergal did not have the power to undo what he started. He needed time to find a way to correct his mistake, but he first had to stop the dark dealings of the Gizzu'Su.

During the wars that escalated over centuries, Nergal began to understand the impact the Sumer energy was having upon Ersetu. He ultimately trapped the Gizzu'Su in stasis within the gugtu shells. He attempted to move the control chamber back to Badgaldingir, but was unable without the combined power of all the Sumer. Since he could not release the Gizzu'Su Nergal decided to form a new collective of power and knowledge, thus the Zidu'Si was created.

The first Zidu'Si was a bonded group of both the remaining Sumerians and the Telukukal, who fought alongside them in the War of the Gods. The first Zidu'Si began working toward their plan to extract the Sumer power and return the control room back into Badgaldingir. The release of the Gizzu'Su from their stasis derailed their plans.

"How did the Gizzu'Su get released in the first place?" Bastien interrupted.

Before Shuran could answer, a weak voice answered from a nearby alcove. "Perhaps I can elaborate on the events of the Gizzu'Su release," Nagutan said as he stepped from the alcove. He appeared tired, but otherwise restored.

"Nagutan, you have awoken," Shuran said taking his grandsire in an embrace. "I suspected you would revive quickly but not this soon."

Patting Shuran on the back, Nagutan pointed at the central energy chamber. "You can thank the Sumer energy for my quick return. It has a healing effect upon the part of me that is Sumerian. That is part of the reason the Gizzu'Su have been focused on gaining the chamber."

Nagutan told them how the Gizzu'Su were freed by the attempts of Nabusa to trap their shi within crystals at the end of the Mi-Ib Karshi. She had been the mistreated apprentice of Ereshkigal and when the war came, she abandoned her master to follow Nergal. After the Gizzu'Su were trapped, her hunger for power overrode her reason and she created the blades to take the power of the Gizzu'Su in order to create her own collective.

"If she created the Mi-Ib daggers, how did the Gizzu'Su end up in the Shadow?" Shuran asked.

"Nabusa was always one to take the short route rather than do her work thoroughly," Nagutan continued. "She misinterpreted the spells and used the wrong dagger. Once Ereshkigal's shi burst free of the stasis chamber, she used Nabusa to free the others. When Nabusa was freed from Ereshkigal's possession, she cast the Gizzu'Su to the Netherworld with a spell and blast of energy."

"And that is what poisoned the Shadow," Tianna said.

Nagutan took a seat that Shuran offered and continued his telling of Nabusa's tale. "When Nabusa cast the Gizzu'Su to the Shadow, she unintentionally linked them to the source of new power, the shi of those damned to eternal torment. Within the Shadow, there was disorganized emotions of the worst kind and Ereshkigal manipulated that energy into Chaos. It was many centuries later when Nabusa finally understood her folly. Nabusa decided to work out a new plan to create a strong following of Essence users. She tried to recreate the Telukukal."

As Nagutan ate a light meal and drank the offered wine, he continued to explain what Nabusa attempted when she hid herself in the Foresworn Territories. Those lands were not always poisoned and barren. Before the War of the Gods and when Nabusa first returned to them, there was an outpost of the dark Sumer where they performed their own experiments upon the people and creatures of Ersetu. Once Nabusa returned, she continued the work she began under Ereshkigal's tutelage before the wars. This time she would expand upon it and attempt to alter any with mixed blood to forcibly create the bloodline of the Telukukal.

She needed subjects for her experiments, but she needed them to be willing, so she devised a plan to allow herself to become their savior. Nabusa began the seeding of hatred among the races for mixed bloods. That hatred grew in time to lead up to the Sikil'Mah. Nabusa began gathering the mixed-bloods in secret, telling them of a land far from Aurderia and the persecution of 'purists'. She offered sanctuary and community.

"Eventually she persuaded enough of them to follower her and allow her to make them more powerful. Her experiments failed of course, as with much, she did not fully understand the method that the Sumerians used when creating the Telukukal. The result was the poisoning of the reproduction in the poor souls who volunteered, but worse, the power she attempted to siphon from the void, came from Coosco and she spread through the area, purposefully tainting the lands that they lived off of as punishment."

"Nagutan, is this how the Arakharat were created?" Coralil asked.

He nodded. "Nabusa was misguided, in fact for a short time we were rather close before the wars. She did succeed in creating a new race, but that backfired on her as well."

"The Arakharat began to turn on her I assume," Shuran said. "While she mothered them they secretly resented her and created their own plans I suspect."

"Yes, my boy you do plan the game well," Dalgon said. He decided it was his cue to speak on his knowledge of the Arakharat. "Many of the shifters you now know as Arakharat became Guardians charged with the duties of finding, protecting, and relocating any mixed-bloods they could find in Aurderia. Not all were taken back to Nabusa willingly. For my part I only took back those who wished to go, others I guided to alternate places where they might live peacefully. Knowing that Nabusa wished to create a family and civilization of mixed-bloods to follower her, I was tasked with keeping and ear to the ground and eyes on her activities."

"But she discovered you were a spy?" Shuran asked.

Nagutan interrupted before Dalgon could respond. "The mother of witches already knew who he was when he first arrived." Nagutan raised his hand to stop Dalgon's questions. "I only discovered the truth when I faced her in the Territories before my unfortunate encounter with the Shadow and Ereshkigal." Nagutan repeated what he learned while in her lair and what then led up to his freeing Sulura and becoming a tool for the Shadow. "I must say that having both the Shadow and Nergal in my head at the same time made it quite crowded."

Penelle listened to all of what was said and remained silent but could not any longer. "You are saying that this Nabusa is the same kashshaptu that created the covens and worked to take leadership before I was made Grand Kashshaptu? This same woman was actually a Telukukal and took part in the creation of my sister kind? I never… we never suspected her of anything more than a power hungry witch."

Nagutan took Penelle's hand and patted it. "Power hungry is an apt term dear. She was always overreaching, that was always her problem. Nabusa could not grasp the principles of equality and sharing power. She always wanted all the power but did not understand the responsibilities that accompany such a position.

"What do we do about the Arakharat?" Orian asked.

"We need first to determine what their plans are and what they have been working at. Now that Nabusa is gone, they are free to carry their work forward. If Kettanu was party to their schemes, then we may yet have another conflict to resolve." Shuran was worried he had not yet heard from Barurbe since she arrived in Elmwood. "Once the Gizzu'Su problem has been resolved, we shall have a visit to Elmwood and check on what the Arakharat are preparing."

"And how do we rid our world of the Gizzu'Su?" Nagutan asked. "Nergal did not share that with me. All my years seeking that knowledge and I never found any indication as to how."

"The stars," Tianna said. "They are escape and rescue ships from this large vessel the Sumerians arrived within. Nergal dispatched them to the outer edges our system, to wait until they could pick-up a signal from Ersetu. The creation of two new Telukukal lives made with Sumerian roots," she said. "It is all recorded in the central storage control." She pointed at the new alcove that was previously the hidden room. "The moment Shuran and I were conceived, the Telukukal energy of our Sumerian lineage signaled the ships return. One would be for evacuation, the other for a prison ship."

Moona pushed her way forward and poked her pipe at Shuran. "Then why was it one o' them there stars started to wink out?"

"When Tianna's life force wavered, the rescue turned into a task to destroy the planet taking the Sumerians and all they created with it. As Tianna grew in strength and remained near her body as well as mine, the signal returned and the second vessel resumed its approach." Shuran explained. "As we exited the alcove, we completed the necessary tasks of activating the probes and will soon be able to return the Sumerians and Gizzu'Su to their own world."

"An' what o' them statues," Moona asked.

"Now that the chamber has extracted all the Sumer energy, including the shi of each Sumerian, we can release them," Shuran said. Shuran stepped over to the central power core and placed his hand within the flow of undulating energy. As he moved his hand in a deliberate motion, streamers of energy began to float from the source and reach out to the stasis statues of the Sumerians safely held within their alcoves. Five flows of energy pulsed from the core and into the awaiting bodies within the gugtu encasing and preserving the elements to reform their corporeal forms.

"What of Nergal?" Tianna asked. "There are only the five stasis held bodies here, where will Nergal find his body?"

"I do not know," Nagutan said. "Nergal may be lost after the energy he exerted saving me from the Shadow. His stasis chamber was hidden away to protect it, not even I was told where he sent it once we separated his shi."

"There is something I do not yet understand," Sulura said. "Shuran has mentioned the difference in his blood, part of him that is not Telukukal, Sumerian, or of any other race of man. What precisely is different in him that is not part of his father or myself?"

Nagutan shifted uncomfortably in his seat. "That is a bit of my meddling I am afraid." Nagutan explained how when he joined Andra and Sulura in marriage, he tampered with the bridal wine that Sulura drank that evening. He added something to several of her glasses that would both ensure a successful conception of mixed blood, and would set the stage for her twins and their connection to one another, strengthened by a link to Coosco.

"You added Essence Extract to her drink?" Shuran asked. "Did that not go against the demands of Coosco not to meddle with the Essence in such a manner?"

"Grey area," Nagutan started. "The sample used was of the original collection taken when we created the first races of man. It was saved in the Vault and I put it to use. I did not violate the terms specifically."

Shuran glared at his grandsire. "Are you finished manipulating events?"

Nagutan lifted his arms in mock surrender. "You needed a stronger bond to have the strength to succeed, just as Tianna needed that strength to hold her shi together."

Shuran decided that since they had time until the Sumerians revived, they would spend that time being productive. He gathered scraps of gugtu from the remains of what was collected back in the woods where they first encountered trolls. He gave the metal to Dara to form into collars much like those used to shackle the Gizzu'Su.

Mallick accessed the compendium to locate the knowledge of how the original collars were created and with Bastien's help they made the alterations to the cuneiform runes Shuran requested. The new collars would serve a new purpose for a different possible threat.

All the Zidu'Si busied themselves with cleaning the space and preparing for the Sumerians awakening. Tables were moved together and linens set for a banquet with the finest plates and cups that could be found in Badgaldingir. Tracking things down was more a task than previously since the Sumerians were no longer working from within the Emmuku'Gu. The city provided but now the inhabitants had to look for what they required.

It was late into the evening when the first signs of life began to appear upon the stasis statues.

Chapter Thirty-Three

The chamber Vault began to darken as all the light was drawn to the center chamber as it completed siphoning all Sumer shi from the void between the light and dark power of Ersetu. The crystals on each of the pedestals hummed in a symphonic harmony of tones as they vibrated and began to glow in their individual colors. Red of fire, blue of water, green of earth, clear of air, white of electricity, deep purple of metal, and smoky-grey of human spell work, all these colors pulled energy from the central flow and grew brighter and louder until they burst.

Dust scattered around the entire space and glistened as it floated to the floor. The Zidu'Si and others stood in the room wondering what was happening to the light. The flow of power in the central chamber glowed bright enough to fill the space, but something seemed to be absorbing the rays as they escaped the center of the room. The lights from the pendants on the Sumerian stasis statues went dark as the gems shattered.

"The last of the Sumer energy is in the core now, and the Sumerians have been separated from that power," Shuran said as he stood and shook the dust from his clothes and hair. "They will begin to awaken soon and will need food to nourish their reformed bodies."

Moona took the lady Zidu'Si and exited the chamber to collect the food and drink for the Sumerians that were started in the kitchens earlier in the evening. By the time they returned, Shuran and the other Zidu'Si were helping the reawakened ancient beings to seats at one of the tables. As the women set out the food and drink, they averted their eyes, not wanting to look directly at whom they still saw as Gods.

"We are not Gods," Damkianna said as she touched Moona's hand. "Only older, sometimes wiser and more powerful than our children we are."

"It would seem our wisdom failed us during our time upon this world Damkianna," Enki, Lord of Earth said as he took a healthy plate of fruits and meat. "But under Nergal and his son's guidance, a champion prevailed." Enki saluted Shuran.

"We did not work alone, Enki. Nergal had as much to do with the work in planning and guiding my grandson, but it was Shuran, his family, and his friends that truly deserve the credit for your return." Nagutan joined the elders in eating. He motioned for the others to join in as well. "Do not offend the Gods by refusing to sup with them," he laughed.

Damkianna snorted at his jest. "Come now children, eat and drink. Today is a glorious day. I only wish Nergal was able to join us."

Shuran took a seat across from Damkianna and Enki. He sat between Hebat and Nina. "And what of Nergal, will he be forever trapped in the core? Will you be able to find him a new body?"

Ninti, the Lady of Life, answered the question. "Nergal would not accept another's body. We could grow him a new one with our technologies, but he would refuse. This is why he will stay within the core until you find and return his stasis pod here."

"Then tell us where it is and we shall fetch it immediately," Bastien said.

Ninti shook her head. "He is too weakened to tell us where his body was sent, therefore, the galactic vessel you call Badgaldingir, will remain in your care until you find and return him to his body. We shall return to one of our closest worlds using the approaching escape modules."

"You said worlds," Coralil said. "Just how many are there?"

Hebat, Lady of the Sky, smiled at Coralil. "Far too many to know, we believe. Our people have traveled far and wide and seen many worlds both wondrous and frightening. Some have natural magic such as the Essence of Ersetu others have none whatsoever. There are some worlds that have advanced in

228

technology and science to create their own magic of a sort, if you did not understand the science of their workings. For as many stars as you see in the night sky, there are billions and more that you do not see and each of them has the potential of supporting life on orbiting planets.

"Life is abundant in this universe and varies in oddness from the life of the children of Coosco to the Sumerian people to those more advanced than ourselves and everywhere in between. Unfortunately, we had to learn our lesson on Ersetu, not to meddle in things we did not understand fully. On another world, one with limited magic, where our kind was called the Anunnaki, there were others who failed in nurturing the man-like races they found. We thought those like the Gizzu'Su learned a lesson there when the humans they created and then enslaved revolted against that group of Sumerians. Some experiences seem to be destine to repeat themselves."

"What is it you are saying my lady, I thought you were on the side of Nergal and fought for good?" Coralil asked.

Hebat smiled at her and leaned over to Shuran. "You have a smart young woman in this one Shin'Ar." She looked back to Coralil, who was blushing near as much as Shuran. "When we created the Telukukal from our own genetics, we should have left well enough alone. But when we discovered the life force of the tiny creatures throughout Ersetu, we did not understand they were part of a collective being, part of Coosco. We collected them and used them to create the seven races of man."

"Essence Extract," Shuran whispered.

Hebat and the other Sumer in turn explained how the seven races were created and why they made a mistake in using the life Essence of Coosco. The creation of the races with that life force combined with that of Telukukal created the Gula'Lu. They were the strongest and would be longest lived of the races. They then weakened the dose of Telukukal genetics and created the other races, making slight adjustments and tuning them to specific traits. The races in the beginning were well blended, but as they began to procreate, the changes began to mutate their abilities and they became only able to wield a specific element or weave spells as the humans. Coosco had affected the races and then the warning came from the Dryads.

The dryads made their first appearance among the races and warned that the abuse of Coosco's Essence meant that she now claimed the races of man and would take them as her children. We were warned to never again meddle with the Essence lest Ersetu swallow us up. The Gizzu'Su failed to heed the warning and continued their own experiments, the worst of which transforming their Telukukal followers into demon warriors without the tether of corporeal mass.

"Telalsu," Shuran said.

"Precisely, young Shin'Ar," Hebat said. "That destroyed the pact. Nergal made a promise and the Gizzu'Su broke it. As a result, Coosco prevented access to Badgaldingir and all of us were to be imprisoned in the Emmuku'Gu until Nergal could make amends."

Enki pushed away from the table and stood, slapping his belly. "That certainly filled the void of my hunger. Now shall we see to removing the villainous Gizzu'Su from your friends?"

"They are but one of them, enemies before the Shadow influenced them. Fallon we hope can be saved; the others will be imprisoned at best." Shuran included no doubt in his tone as he spoke as to how he would deal with the enemy. "Will Fallon recover?"

"Time will tell, Shin'Ar." Enki said. "But as for the others you would call enemy, their actions before the Shadow influenced them may have come from fear. Perhaps if you show them mercy and understanding, then you may gain more allies."

Shuran was not convinced, but he would keep an open heart and mind. While he and the Zidu'Si went to the room where the Gizzu'Su were held, the Sumerians headed to the surface level of the ship that contained the gardens.

Moltar greeted them with a curious look but did not leave his mother's memorial as they kept a respectful distance and extended their regrets.

They gathered in the large central courtyard and the Zidu'Si lowered the shackled and unconscious Gizzu'Su hosts down on the ground. The Sumerians all lifted their arms to the sky and sent a series of pulsing energy into the air in a deliberate pattern. When they finished, the clouds above the floating city ship began to part as a sphere began to descend toward their location.

While the sphere lowered, a glow began to form upon the bottom of the probe that grew whiter and cast daylight upon the area. A beam of that light fell down upon the possessed bodies laying on the ground. As the beam began to pulsate, the undulating caused the cuneiform markings to glow and the collars fell open to each side of the bodies.

As each of the bodies began to spasm and attempt to gain their feet, the dark misty form of the Gizzu'Su started being pulled from their hosts. The Gizzu'Su fought to remain within their vessels, but the pulsing light grew more rapid until the tainted shi of the Gizzu'Su was ripped away and pulled up into a vessel they did not wish to reside.

"What will happen to them, the Gizzu'Su?" Tianna asked. She watched as the other Zidu'Si collected the waking former hosts of dark Sumer. Four of them were taken directly to prison cells created from empty storage rooms in the lower levels. Fallon was taken to the medical ward.

"They will be placed within new bodies, and stand trial. It will be swift and just for they have many crimes that mean immediate dispersion," Damkianna said. "We are not able to die in the same sense as the human form or that of the Telukukal, who closely match us genetically. Our only true death or as close as we come is to have our spirit dispersed throughout the vastness of the Universes."

"You speak as though there is more than one universe my lady," Mallick said. He was already searching the library in the Vault for information.

"There are my boy, perhaps one day if you are ready, I might come back and show them to you." Damkianna then looked to the heavens and was gone in a ball of light, heading for the other probe as it replaced the one leaving with the Gizzu'Su.

"Good-life our children, you have done well. Now you must rebuild this world and establish a peaceful existence. Strive for greatness but do not place yourself above another," Enki said. "This ship shall be your platform for establishing a new world, but in order to survive, you must blend the bloodlines to strengthen the races of man and become one people. There is no place for prejudice on a big world that is so small compared to the vastness of life in the universe. One day you will understand that you are all children of one race and humanity must survive."

As Enki and the remaining Sumerians left in individual balls of light, the Zidu'Si watched in wonder as the probes ascended to the heavens and became the likeness of stars once again. Twin flashes scattered across their vision as those celestial lights winked out of the sky and disappeared into the heavens.

As the on-lookers left the outer gardens of the ship, Moltar came forward to nuzzle Shuran. "What comes next Lugaldur," Moltar said.

Shuran caressed his bonded below the chin. "As with everything else my beloved, time will tell. For now, I simply wish to feel the winds on my face and ride the winds." Shuran leapt into the air and landed in the saddle as Moltar pushed his massive neck forward to catch his master. "Fly my friend, as high as you can take us."

"What direction Lugaldur?" Moltar asked.

"We head to Elmwood."

Chapter Thirty-Four

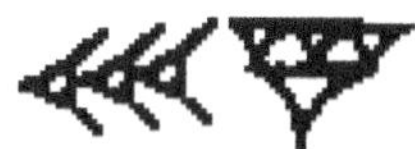

Shuran and Moltar flew for only a few hours in near weightlessness of the boundary between the atmosphere of Ersetu and the vacuum of space. As he pulled the air they needed from the planet below, Shuran marveled at the vastness of space and the possibilities of life that the Sumerians imparted upon him and the Zidu'Si. "It is hard to believe that there could be more like us out there," Shuran thought to Moltar.

"And why not my Lugaldur? As unique as we may believe ourselves, that makes us not the most special in the vast expanse of what exists beyond our own existence," Moltar thought back.

Shuran patted his friend and bonded on the neck. "When did you become so philosophical?"

Moltar only returned a low grumbling purr as a response.

Shuran and Moltar descended as they approached the area where Elmwood soon would spread out before them. "Circle the village a few times then take us down in the center of town if you can fit."

"Are you calling me fat, Lugaldur?" Moltar jested. Moltar circled the fully rebuilt village of Elmwood before admitting he would not easily land in the center of the town. He hovered above the area as people gathered and watched while Shuran glided on the wind and slowly descended to the ground.

The villagers looked on from their storefronts and shops as Shuran made his way down the center of the town square. He admired the craftsmanship of the rebuilt village. If he had not seen for himself, the devastation brought down upon Elmwood by the Death Walkers, he would not have thought the town recently remade. Nearly every building was a newer, cleaner version of what once stood.

Though most ignored or simply nodded a forced greeting his direction, the Arakharat inhabitants seemed little bothered by Shuran's presence. Shuran watched the reactions on their false faces, seeing the recognition in their eyes. They knew who he was and were expecting him to come. "Moltar, keep an eye on these people, I am heading to the inn to see if I can find out who is leading these people," Shuran thought to his drakkon. Shuran continued walking, taking in the faces around him, noticing that the one thing missing from the town was any sign of children. He now knew that the Arakharat were able to procreate and it was early yet in the evening that running children would be a normal sight in any other town. If there were no children in this village, the Arakharat kept them elsewhere.

Shuran found an inn that looked busy enough and appeared the most popular if not the only establishment of its kind in town. He made his way to the bar and ordered a tankard of ale from the barmaid standing behind the counter with her back to him. When she turned around, Shuran held his expression blank.

Barurbe handed Shuran the tankard without batting an eye or raising a brow. She knew he was coming like the others. She made only the simplest expression of acknowledgment when she briefly masked her shifter scent and then released.

Shuran thanked her and asked where he might find the local magistrate or leader of the village.

Barurbe turned back to Shuran. "We have only a town council, no magistrate to speak of. We are a peaceful town and have no need for law enforcement."

Shuran took this to mean that he had no need to become concerned over an ambush or conflict of any kind. "Is there someone from the council I might speak to? I have news of the balance and extraction of the dark Sumer from Ersetu."

Barurbe put her towel on the bar and indicated Shuran should wait where he was. "I will bring someone here to greet you, Sir."

Shuran had a short wait. The innkeeper greeted him.

"Greetings Shuran Shin'Ar, I am Dabnik, proprietor of this fine establishment and member of the town council." Dabnik held his hand out to shake Shuran's. "I understand you have news of the so-called Queen of Shadow and her followers?"

Shuran pulled his hand from Dabnik's firm yet friendly grip. "I have arrived to inform your people personally of the extraction of the Gizzu'Su from the Shadow and the departure of the Sumerian ancients once thought to be gods." Shuran waited for any sign of surprise on the man's face but received only a smile and a slight nod. "You are not surprised by this news?"

"No, we are not, just as you do not seem surprised that we know who you are," Dabnik said as he led Shuran to a table and sat. "Are you hungry? We have excellent river bass on the menu tonight."

Shuran was uncertain the motives of the innkeeper but would play along. "That would be favorable, thank you."

Shuran and Dabnik ate and spoke about the changes that would come to pass now that the Shadow was under control and the Gizzu'Su and Sumerians were no longer present upon Ersetu. Dabnik listened to all that Shuran had to say without interrupting or appearing surprised by any of the news. Shuran wondered whether the Arakharat possessed a seer or used scrying spells to keep apprised of the situation in Aurderia. If they had, neither that would mean they still kept spies working within the realms.

Dabnik sent a tavern girl off to fetch more ale and food while he raised his tankard and drank with Shuran. "That is quite a specimen of drakkon you have there, no doubt a result of the bond with the Shin'Ar."

"Yes, our bond is unique and you can see the result." Shuran was deciding that the small talk was some stalling tactic on Dabnik's part. The confirmation came when Moltar sent him the thought of a familiar scent leaving the town in the form of a fox. "Since my news does not come to you as a surprise, I will not trouble you with anything that might already have met your ears. So let me get to the point of my visit to Elmwood."

"We know why you are here Shin'Ar, and we do not wish to move or accept former villagers back to the town we have rebuilt," Dabnik warned.

"You misunderstand my visit, Dabnik. The Zidu'Si and I have no requirements of you other than to maintain the peace we wish to spread across the realms. Any former occupants of Elmwood are likely to settle in other villages or cities at any rate."

Dabnik raised his brow to Shuran and a half-smirk began to form. "And you expect us to believe that there will be no repercussions for any among us who may have been tangled up with plots of the Order of Chaos or other unnamed parties?"

Shuran returned the knowing grin. "There will be no blame held against any who no longer attempt to defy justice and peace in this world. The Foresworn and Arakharat are welcome to travel or settle within Aurderia as they wish so long as they follow the edicts of living among many races without prejudice."

"I believe we have no issues with that request, however I sense a stipulation in your words," Dabnik said. "I also did not reveal what we call ourselves so I can assume Andra has revived, he would not be welcome to return to us as one of our own."

"Andra was never an Arakharat, many Telukukal can shift form." Shuran showed his point by shifting his appearance to that of Dabnik's face and back to his own. "As for the stipulation you sensed, I will be taking the one known as Tharell for his part in the kidnapping of my mother and subsequent torture of Andra, who is known as Dalgon."

This information coupled with Shuran's ability to shift, surprised Dabnik and he wore that shock on his face. "Your adda? Had we known his true identity we would not have followed along with Nabusa's plans? Tharell is far too radical for settling down here in Elmwood, he will not be missed. As for the Nabusa's plans, we were never fully informed of her ultimate end game, so abandoning her is easily done."

Shuran eased into a more relaxed position as he drank from his tankard. "Nabusa no longer lives so I have no worry of her meddling in Aurderian affairs. Her plans, however, I know what her end game was and I extend my regrets that the Arakharat have so long suffered at her hand. Though you may owe your very existence as a race to her ill-conceived plans and likely followed her out of a false sense of loyalty, she will torment Ersetu no longer."

"And what of her ultimate plans for the Arakharat? Do you know they involved a means to fix what causes our shifting?" Dabnik asked.

Shuran gathered from Dabnik's tone that he was not in favor of Nabusa's plan. "Her plan, if she actually had the knowledge and necessary pieces to proceed, would have allowed you a stable form, but you would still be able to shift. That is not a concern any longer as she is not alive to continue. Her research and laboratory will be destroyed when the Zidu'Si reach the Territories."

Shuran stood to accept Dabnik's hand again in a friendly shake as he rose to depart the tavern. "Will your other settlements on Ersetu be as accommodating to the adjustment of no longer living in the shadows?" Shuran noticed the questioning look on Dabnik's face. "I have come to know that the Arakharat are not inflicted with infertility as the other Foresworn. That said, I noticed that there were no children among the streets of Elmwood as I entered which leads me to suspect you have them elsewhere in another settlement."

Dabnik nodded his head in understanding that Shuran was much more than he expected. "We have other settlements, but they are not in Aurderia, I doubt there will be any problems."

"Aurderia is not the only settled lands of Ersetu," Shuran said. "Races of man have migrated to the opposite side of the world and eventually there will be interaction. The Zidu'Si and I will be traveling the world in the city ship Badgaldingir, bringing assistance, hope, and order to the entire world."

Dabnik accepted Shuran's friendship with grace and motioned to follow him out the doors of the inn and tavern.

Shuran turned as he passed the bar and called to the barkeep behind the counter. "Miss, please accept this token as my appreciation of a delicious meal and buy the house a round or two on the Zidu'Si in celebration of our new understandings."

Barurbe took the sack and after Shuran and Dabnik had exited, she emptied its content in her hand. The gold was more than enough to buy drinks for the village for the entire night. The red gemstone pendant, she palmed and slid into her pocket after making certain no eyes were upon her.

Shuran walked back to the end of town, where Moltar was waiting for him with his clawed front foot raised and balancing a sphere of energy containing a fox. "Lower him to the ground if you would Moltar," Shuran said as Dabnik stepped up behind him.

"How did you know this one was Tharell?" Dabnik asked.

"I could smell him," Moltar explained and lowered his nostril that could fit three human heads within, and he took a deep intake of Dabnik's scent. "Now I can smell you," Moltar said.

Shuran waved his hand over the fox and with that motion, forced Tharell into his known human guise. "You will be taken to Badgaldingir and placed on trial for the kidnapping of Sulura and the torturing of the one you believed Arakharat and named Andra, my adda Dalgon."

Tharell spat in the direction of Shuran's face, but the spittle had evaporated before it reached him. "Fancy trick Shuran Shin'Ar, but you will not scare me or those who do no not wish the return of the Watchers of the Lands. You can kill me if you wish, but there are others of us out there and we will see your plans disrupted until we get what is ours. We will have what the Nabusa promised."

Shuran called a collar from the Vault and held it before Tharell's face. "You will not have what Nabusa promised, because it is not possible and she knew that."

"You think you can hold me with that collar, it only works on your kind." Tharell's voice stopped, as did his movement when the collar closed around his neck.

"This is not the same collar you used on Dalgon in the forest, Tharell. This is a new one and it is made especially for your kind." Shuran turned to Dabnik. "I do not wish to use this or any other restraint on the Arakharat, but like any other race of this world, the Zidu'SI will not allow tyranny or lawlessness to persist." Shuran levitated Tharell's shackled and stiff form into the air as he raised himself to Moltar's back. "Good luck Dabnik may the next time we meet see us remaining friends." Shuran and Moltar, along with their captive, disappeared into the void with a resounding pop.

Dabnik began to walk back to his inn when another man walked up to him from between two buildings. The man stood in Dabnik's path.

"This is a dangerous game you have started Dabnik," the man said.

"We all have our parts to play. Just remember that it is easier to know what your enemy is up to when you keep them close as a friend." Dabnik watched as Barurbe served two patrons sitting at tables outside the tavern. "Some are kept closer than others."

Chapter Thirty-Five

The former home and lair of Nabusa and her Guardians was ransacked when the Zidu'Si arrived. Every room of each building in the underground fortress was torn apart as though upturned looking for valuables. Everywhere they searched, not a person could be found, all they discovered were ruins and signs of recent evacuation. The condition that Nabusa's own chambers were found in was worst of all.

Soot and ash littered the chamber where fires had been set to burn away the entire contents of the dwelling. Glass bottles and stoneware were scattered throughout the space of her former laboratory in a deliberate manner that indicated an act of vandalism.

In her bedchambers, dressers and chests were toppled, burned, and emptied of all valuables and not a single garment was left behind. Nabusa's body was not found.

"It appears that the Arakharat and Foresworn took everything of value and destroyed the remains," Coralil said to Shuran as they investigated the scene. "What is the purpose? They could have taken these furnishings with them, they will need things to start settling elsewhere."

Shuran stepped up to her and squeezed Coralil's hand. "I do not think they would want the reminder of the woman who poisoned them and used them to enact her own plans. In many ways, these people were her servants and subjects."

"Shuran," Bastien called from the outer room. "Come out here and witness what happened in this chamber."

Shuran and Coralil left the shambled bedchamber to step back into the outer laboratory where Mallick, Bastien, and Orian cast their wielded spell to past view the activities.

The scene played out from the point where Nagutan encountered Nabusa. The Zidu'Si witnessed her death at his hands and watched as the Guardians entered moments following Nagutan's departure. As the scene unfolded before them, they saw more Guardians enter and begin taking what was of value to them and then leave without destroying anything. They paused over Nabusa's body for a moment before leaving the dwelling.

"Can you push forward, I would like to see who caused all this willful vandalism," Shuran asked.

The three Zidu'Si casting the spell had quite far to move the viewing forward when three kashshaptu entered the room and began gathering some belongings of Nabusa's and then set a fire in the hearth. While one witch placed clothes, books, and a few jars full of ingredients into a large sack, the other two took hold of Nabusa's body and carried it to the fire where they vanished in a cloud of billowing green smoke. The remaining kashshaptu cast a spell and then followed her sisters into the fire. The spell then traveled the room sending objects flying and fires burning.

"That explains what happened, but what could they want with a dead body?" Avrank said. "A bit morbid to say the least." His face puckered more than seemed possible.

"Perhaps they are expecting the Shadow to remain active and wish to bring her back?" Mallick suggested.

Shuran shook his head and grunted in disgust. "The Shadow no longer has the Gizzu'Su and Sumer energy to source it into a collective being, but we all know that things do not always stay dead. The Shadow is not necessary to make the dead walk. There are still dark things lurking in the Shadow, Telalsu being one of them."

"Will we go after them?" Orian asked.

"Eventually, but our priority now is to rebuild the realm. Once that is well under way, we shall move Badgaldingir throughout Ersetu and find other settlements of the races of man to unite this world under common purpose. While we do so, we shall seek out the kashshaptu, Guardians, ogres, trolls, and any other dark influences to bring them to heel." Shuran was beginning to understand what the true purpose of being a Watcher of the Lands meant. He would need to create a secondary force of Zidu'Si to deploy and be stationed throughout the realms of Ersetu. Trusted warriors of the realms who could be where Shuran could not.

***

Rebuilding the Academy was no easy task. The castle was not damaged much outside during the battle, but what happened with its walls while occupied by the Queen of Shadow, made Shuran want to destroy it and start over from a pile of stone and wood. The Dwarves convinced him that it was better to repair what remained, so he left them to their work.

While the devastated villages and towns such as Middleton and Two Bridges were rebuilt from the ground up, many other abandoned settlements were now beginning to return to busy hamlets as the humans began to come out of hiding and return to their old lives. With the threat of the Queen of Shadow gone and the Shadow put to rest, life in Aurderia settled into a peaceful and prosperous routine.

Fallon recovered well enough though he appeared older and weaker than his once vital self. The effect of the Gizzu'Su possession on his body caused much of his life force to become used up in a matter of the days that he was host to Uggae. Though he enjoyed the comforts of Badgaldingir, he wanted nothing more than to return to his Barony and start again.

Before the Zidu'Si were ready to begin their travels of Ersetu, Shuran took his uncle back to Drakk to witness the transformation that took place, as a result, of Bastien's spell many months prior. Fallon looked upon a green and lush landscape, full of trees, plants, flowers, and shrubbery. Where once only blackened earth and stone littered the landscape, flowing grasses and streams returned drawing back the wildlife that once roamed the lands.

"Shin'Ar," the Baron stuttered while wiping tears from his eyes. "How could I ever repay what you have done to restore my lands?"

Shuran embraced his uncle. "It was not I, but Bastien who cast this spell, by accident really. Though I think, Coosco has something to do with the way in which it has spread."

Shuran left Fallon to his duties as Baron of Drakk, where his people returned from the highlands along with many Ag'Lu and Lil'Du who wished to join them. Magnar still remained the leader of the Ag'Lu but willingly shared the role of co-leader to the fire Essence people.

While the Lil'Du opened their home to other races, as did every other race in return, the seven races of man began a new era of understanding and blurring of the racial lines that once separated them by prejudice.

The Badur'Lu spent more time upon the dirt and even established a coastal city upon the surface.

The Gula'Lu ventured from their Valley and created a cable system with their sky cages that traversed the Frozen North through to the Dwarven Capital City of Duranekur.

The elves opened Tarangale up to all and allowed scheduled visits to Entensiama.

The races began to mix and blend bloodlines as once they did only out of necessity. Now the races of man began to find love and companionship among the others without the prior hatred and distrust bred from ignorance.

Many generations would come to pass in the peace and prosperity found under the care of the Zidu'Si and the agents of the Shin'Ar.

Peace settled over the land like a warm blanket on a chilly night. New schools for the training and use of Essence were constructed in the major cities throughout the realms and were open to any showing promise. The former curriculum was adjusted from what was taught in the old Academy, to include lessons from the compendium's vast stores of information.

Though the Urentel and Tal'Baad were not seen again, the Dryads could still be found from time to time, tending trees and plants in the many new forests that regrew around the planet. They imparted wisdom and teachings of Coosco on occasion at the various Essence schools and met with Shuran and Tianna whenever they had need. Since the races of man came to understand that they were connected to Coosco and her magic through Essence, they needed to learn the ways of Ersetu that existed long before the Sumerians arrived.

Shuran and Tianna became Regents of the lands and took in turn the responsibility of moving Badgaldingir around the planet as the Zidu'Si visited

242

realms to remain present for both aiding where needed, and keeping the peace. Though most of their time was spent with family and training the new generations of Essence users, they acted as arbitrators to many of the skirmishes over land and rights as the human population flourished and spread throughout Ersetu.

The eighth race, Arakharat, spread throughout the world as well and bided their time before they would make their move to put their own plans into action.

But that is another story...

Map of Aurderia

***

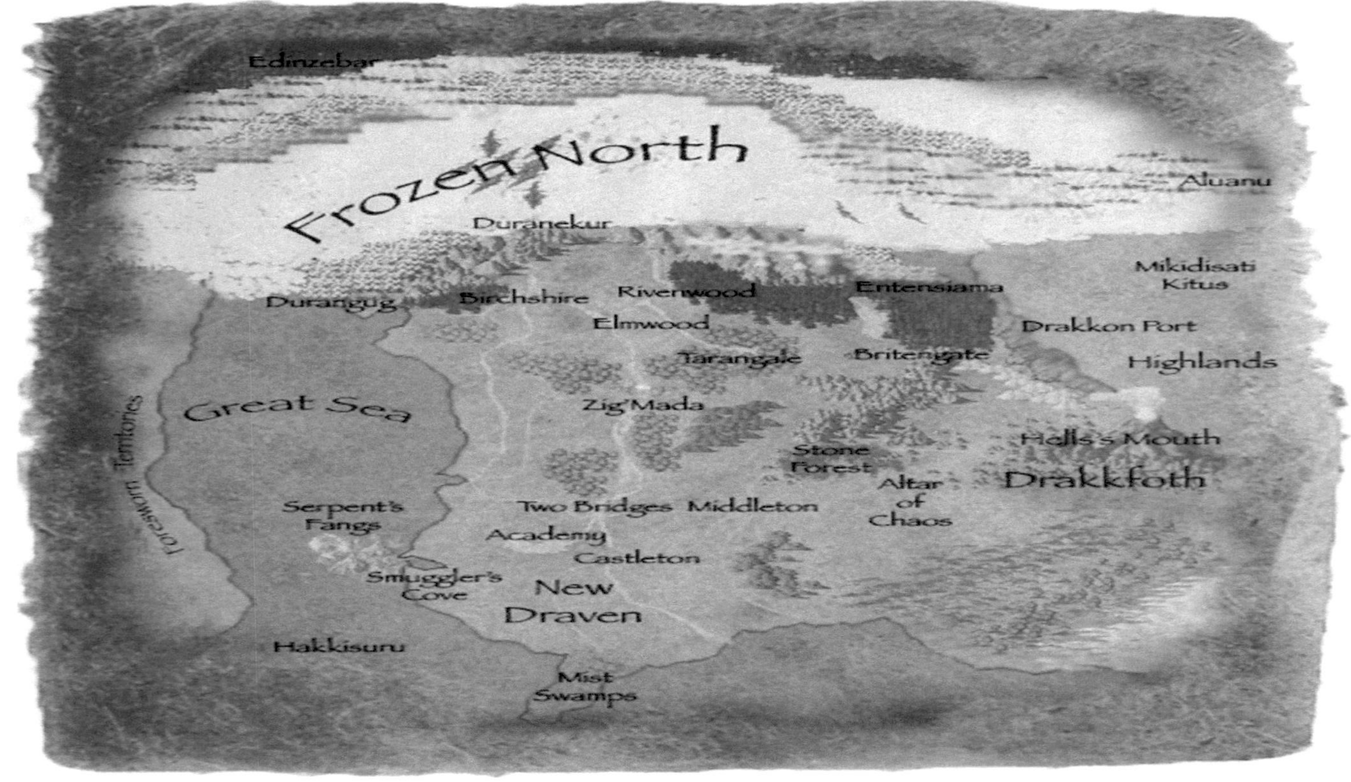
Frozen North
Edinzebar
Aluanu
Duranekur
Mikidisati
Kitus
Durangug
Birchshire
Riverwood
Entensiama
Elmwood
Drakkon Port
Tarangale
Britengate
Highlands
Great Sea
Zig'Mada
Foresworn Territories
Stone Forest
Hell's Mouth
Serpent's Fangs
Two Bridges
Middleton
Altar of Chaos
Drakkfoth
Academy
Castleton
Smuggler's Cove
New Draven
Hakkisuru
Mist Swamps

Glossary

A'Baddasu - Gauntlet of Strength (gug weapon of the Gula'Lu)

Abnu Emuq - Power Stone

Abzu Mu - deep source of water

Adda - Father

Agal Kastu - Mighty Bow /Weapon of gug held by the Zidu'Si elf

Alla - Evil God

Anse - Donkey / Ass

Anzillu - Abomination

Arakharat - The Eighth Race / Shifters

Asipu - Wizard / Mage / Magic Worker

Asakku - Earthy-watery/Dragon

Assinnu Isten - First of the Order / Cult Leader

Bad - Wall / Ground

Badgaldingir - Fortified City of the Gods

Baduruku (BA-DUR-UKU) - Water People

Bal - Transform

Bil - Burn (To)

Bitilu'Bir - Temple of Light, source of powering the force that keeps air over the city of Aluanu

Bitmu - Tree House

Coosco - Navel of the World

DAMKIANNA (DAM-KI-ANNA) - Mistress of Heaven and Earth

Diri - Huge

Dug - Heal

Dur - Jackass

Durani - Fortress

Ekur (E-KUR) - House that is like a Mountain

ELITUR (ELI-TUR) - Sacrilege

Emmuku'Gu (Emmuku-Gu) Ersetu - Power River (lei line) of Ersetu (World)

Emuku - Power

Entar'Lu - Caretakers

Ersetu (ER-SE-TU) - World

Gub'ba Dur Gu'gal - Bondage to stand claim to service/ restraint collar of the Telukukal

Gabara (Gaba-Ra-A) - Offering

Galla - Devil

Gardu'Lil - Air Warriors

Geshtu'Bad - Teacher / To give Wisdom

Gidri Zisura - Wand of Magical Power (Human Zidu'Si weapon)

Gisa'Ti - Tree of Life

Gub'ba Dur Gu'gal - Restraining collar / Energy Shackling device of the Telukukal

Gug - Lodestone

Gugtu (GUG-TU) \ Zisuragug (ZI-SU)RA-GUG) - Magic Stone

Hala'Sa - Sharing one Mind

Haza - Hold (used to immobilize something)

Il'Shi Ana Dah - To carry a part or a connection to another's shi for purpose of assistance

Iniminim Ma (Inim Inim Ma) - Book of Spells

Kalag-Ga - To Invigorate (Strength)

Kashshaptu (KASH-SHAP-TU) - Witch

Kes - Bind

Ki'Gal (Nether World)

248

Kigalba (KI-GAL-BA) - Great Fire Below / Hell

Ki'Ta (KI-TA) - Below

Kibur'Zisu - Trident of Power (gug weapon of the Badur'lu)

Kimmatu'Du (Kim-Ma-Tu'Du) - Son of the Clan/Family (adopted or honorary)

Kimmane (Kim-Ma-Ne) - Group of drakkon and riders.

Kin'Ge - Send message

Kin'Su - Accept Message

Kuliana - Mermaid

La'Bun Masua - Air-Bladder Ship (Zeppelin / blimp)

Lalli Mah (Lal-Li Mah) - Great Balance

Lam Mudutu - Abundant Knowledge

Lil - Air

Lugaldur - Bonded Master of a drakkon

Maaddir (Ma-Addir) - Ferry Boat

Magurmu (Ma-Gur-Mu) - Flying Boat

Masku (Mas-Ku) - Hide

Me - The grand council of Eleven Sumer elders that govern their Laws

Mellamu Nanna - Bright Moon (Steam powered Water ship that also flies under Crystal Shard power - Codgers Ship)

Menasutur (Me-Na-Su-Tur) - Sacred War Hammer of the Dwarves / Weapon of gug held by the Dwarven Zidu'Si

Mi-Ib Ag (Mi-Ib Ag) - Fire Sword / Weapon of gug wielded by the Drakkian Zidu'Si

Mi-Ib Karshi (Mi-Ib Kar-Shi) - Golden Dagger used to take souls

Mi-Ib Simshi (Mi-Ib Sim-Shi) - Golden Dagger used to place/restore a soul

Mu - Flying Machine

Mudutu'Har - Rings of Knowledge (Zidu'Si weapon of the Isten to Shin'Ar)

Nashi - River of Souls

Nashi'Zag - River of Metal Souls

Nime'Gar (Ni-Me-Gar) - Silence

Pad - Break into Pieces

Padiri - Explode / release restrained power

Padiri'bur - Vessel of explosion / Bomb

Peta - Open (for me)

Pilsug - Dirt Walker (slang of the Badur'Lu to refer to land dwellers)

Sa'nua - Mindless / Crazy

Sar A Nam'Mu - The Record of the Creator of Man (Nergal's Journal)

Sheesh (She-Esh) - Brother

Shi'Imbi - Staff of Life's Wind (gug weapon of the Lil'Du)

Shin'Ar - Watcher of the Lands / Lands of the Watchers

Sikil Mah - great purge of abominations

Sumeris - Ancient language of the Gods

Sutresi - Commanders

TAMU - To Swear Oath

Tartur Mamitu - Oath Breaker

Tel - Land

Telal - Warrior Demon

Tal'Ba-ad - Ice demons

Telukukal (Telu-Kuk-Al) - First Land People (First People)

Tul - Altar or Well

Tur - Small (to be) / Derogatory term used by dwarfs naming those smaller than themselves. *Also* - Sacred

Ukken ana su Geshtu-Bad - Meeting for the purpose of sharing great or ancient wisdom

Urentel - Frost Beasts demons

Usumaba - Sea Dragon (steed of the Badur'Lu)

Xul - Devil / Evil

Zag - The shine of metals

Zidu'Si - Faithful Companions

Zisuragug (ZI-SU-RA-GUG) \ Gugtu (GUG-TU) - Magic Stone

Zumru'Sa - Joining of Body and Mind; Gula'Lu ritual of blending and sharing knowledge and souls. See also **Hala'Sa**

<u>Spells and Sayings</u>

Ha Ina Gisnu'Zi, Dalla'E Anna'Te - May the Light of Life Shine upon you

Kima Parsi Labiruti - Deal with her in Accordance With the Ancient Rites

PAD TEGA NERU - Explode upon the touch of Evil.

GISNU SU SHI KES ANA AN-DUL A GIZZU - Join light to flesh binding your soul to protect it from Shadow

Bil-E Emmuku Te Gisnu - Burn by the Power of the Light

Si'Il Te Im Zi Gub - Part the winds to allow us passage